Old

Alex Walters has worked in the oil industry, broadcasting and banking and provided consultancy for the criminal justice sector. He is the author of thirteen previous novels including the DI Alec McKay series set around the Black Isle in the Scottish Highlands where Alex lives and runs the Solus Or Writing Retreat with his wife, occasional sons and frequent cats.

Also by Alex Walters

Detective Annie Delamere

Alex WALTERS
OLD EVILS

CANELO CRIME

First published in the United Kingdom in 2023 by

Canelo
Unit 9, 5th Floor
Cargo Works, 1-2 Hatfields
London SE1 9PG
United Kingdom

A CIP catalogue record for this book is available from the British Library.

Print ISBN 978 1 80436 468 0
Ebook ISBN 978 1 80436 469 7

This book is a work of fiction. Names, characters, businesses, organizations, places and events are either the product of the author's imagination or are used fictitiously. Any resemblance to actual persons, living or dead, events or locales is entirely coincidental.

Cover design by kid-ethic

Cover images © Shutterstock, Unsplash

Look for more great books at www.canelo.co

Printed and bound in Great Britain by Clays Ltd, Elcograf S.p.A.

I

CHAPTER ONE

'I reckon you'd better take a look out there.'

Robbie Crowther looked impatiently over his shoulder at Ellie, then continued pouring a measure of whisky. 'What is it? Can't you see I'm busy? There are people waiting here.' He handed over the whisky, accepting a crumpled fiver in return. Robbie grumbled all the time, but his bark was far worse than his bite.

'I'm just saying, you need to see what it's like out there. You might have a problem on your hands before long.'

'What do you mean?'

'Have a look. You'll see what I mean.' She knew that Robbie's curiosity would quickly overcome his inherent grumpiness. It wasn't as if they were that busy really, not for a Saturday night. The real rush would come when they started serving the festive menu. Then it would be manic up to Christmas Eve.

'You couldn't just tell me, I suppose?'

'You'll just think I'm exaggerating.'

He sighed exasperatedly. 'No peace for the bloody wicked. This better be worth it. Just hold the fort here in the meantime.'

She turned to serve the next customer, watching as Robbie made his way to the pub's main entrance. She'd have liked to see his reaction when he realised, but you can't have everything. A moment later, he reappeared, his expression a mix of worry and annoyance, as he strode back towards the bar. 'Why didn't you say earlier?'

'I've only just seen it myself. I popped out to check for any glasses. Then I came straight back in and told you.'

'Made me go and look for myself, more like.'

'Would you have believed me if I'd told you?'

'Probably not,' he conceded grudgingly. 'There was nothing at all half an hour ago. You'd have thought one of the bloody smokers would have thought to mention it.' He shook his head. 'Speaking of which, I'd better make sure all these buggers are aware.' He picked up the bell he used to signal last orders and rang it loudly.

The bar fell silent, faces turning towards him in surprise. From the back of the room, a voice shouted, 'You need to get a new watch, Robbie. It's not even nine thirty yet.'

'Ladies, gentlemen and mouthy Dave at the back there,' Robbie intoned, 'may I have your attention for a moment? For those of you who aren't aware, there seems to have been a very heavy snowfall in the last half hour. I've just been out to look. There's a good couple of inches already and it's still coming. Far be it from me to encourage the departure of paying customers – and I assure you we will keep serving till closing time – but given the steepness of the road out there, some of you may wish to leave before it gets much worse.'

Ellie could see customers peering through the windows, trying to determine whether the conditions were as bad as Robbie had implied. Anyone who knew Robbie would be aware he wouldn't drive away custom without very good reason.

She'd been shocked herself when she'd first stuck her head outside the front doors. There'd been a forecast of snow for the evening, but she'd been expecting no more than a sprinkling, even up here. Now it was coming down thick and fast, the flakes swirling in the spotlights that illuminated the car park.

The road down was probably still passable, with care, but she knew how quickly the snow could close the routes up here. The stretch immediately down from the pub could be particularly treacherous, with its steep inclines and tight bends. They'd had more than one car plough into the adjacent hedgerows.

Customers were already finishing up their meals and drinks, preparing to leave, some of them anxiously glancing through the window. Within twenty minutes, the pub was almost empty, except for a small knot of locals around the bar. Robbie looked around gloomily. 'That's ninety odd minutes of Saturday-night takings lost.' He looked along the cluster of locals. 'You'd better do your best to make up for it, lads.'

The nearest one in the group clattered his pint glass on to the bar. 'I'll do my bit. Fill her up.'

'Glad we can rely on you. Keep up the good work.' Robbie turned to pull a pint of a local ale. 'Must say, never expected this.'

Ellie had been looking at her phone. 'They've updated the forecast. Heavy snow for the next two to three hours at least. There's a weather warning now. Significant deposits on higher ground. May cause disruption to traffic. Blah, blah.'

'Good to know they've got the skills and technology to warn us about something that's already happened.' Robbie glanced towards the door leading to the domestic quarters at the rear of the pub, a look of anxiety crossing his face. 'You going to want to stay over, El?'

'If it's no trouble. Don't fancy driving in that.'

'I wouldn't let you even if you did, to be honest.' Ellie was still living with her parents in a neighbouring village, trying with her boyfriend to save up enough to get a place of their own. She normally drove home at the end of her shift, but the pub had some staff accommodation, which she'd used on a few occasions before, usually when they'd had a late licence extension. For all his grumbling, she knew Robbie and his wife wouldn't abandon her to the snow. 'Just need to check the room's fit for use. You'd better call your mum and dad.'

'Thanks, Robbie. Won't be a sec.'

'No rush, lass. The speed this bunch drink, I won't need to pull another pint before closing time.'

Robbie would have happily let her use the landline behind the bar, but she wanted to call her boyfriend, as well as her parents, and she thought it better to have that conversation in private. The signal up here was never strong, but it was usually okay out in the car park.

She stepped out into the shelter of the porch outside. The snow was coming down more heavily than before, the sky white with tumbling flakes. Her own little car, parked alone at the far side of the car park, was almost hidden under a coating of several inches. A chill wind was blowing in from the valley below, and substantial drifts were already accumulating against the pub walls and the surrounding hedgerows.

It took her parents a few minutes to answer the phone. She could envisage them going through the usual routine of searching for the remote control to turn down the TV. Eventually, her dad answered.

'Dad. It's Ellie. Just wanted to let you know I've got caught by the snow up at the Fox.'

'Snow?'

It was possible the snow hadn't reached their village, which was a couple of miles down the hill. More likely, her mum and dad had been glued to the TV and hadn't looked out of the window. 'The road down's likely too impassable by now. I'm not going to risk it, anyway. Robbie and Steph are happy for me to stay over.'

'You don't want me to try to fetch you?' It was the kind of offer her dad always felt obliged to make, even though they both knew she'd never accept it.

'Don't want you getting stuck too.'

'You're sure you'll be all right?'

'I'll be fine, Dad. You know Steph. She loves fussing round me.'

'See you tomorrow, then, I guess.'

'I'll let you know how it's looking in the morning. Night, then.'

She scrolled through her address book for her boyfriend's number. He hadn't been expecting to see her tonight and he didn't normally call her when she was working. But if he'd seen the snow, he might be worrying.

She was on the point of dialling his number, when she heard voices from across the car park. The sound was muffled by the snow and she could make out nothing beyond the glare of the spotlights. Then she saw a group of figures emerging from the snow.

'You're still open?' a man's voice called.

She could see now that there were three of them. A man and two women. She vaguely recognised them from earlier in the evening. They'd been eating in the small restaurant area.

'Robbie won't close as long as there's the possibility of custom, even on a night like this. Are you okay?'

'Just about.' The trio were close enough now for her to see that they looked chilled and sodden, their coats clearly unsuited to this kind of weather. 'We've managed to block the road, I'm afraid,' the man continued. 'Half a mile or so down the hill. There were a few cars in front of us who'd lost control, but managed to stay on the road. One of ours managed to get half stuck in a ditch, and it's left the road blocked.'

'You'd better get inside,' Ellie intervened. 'The fire's still going. Tell Robbie what's happened. He'll sort you out.' And then grumble at me for having suggested it, she added to herself.

She stepped aside to allow the group to enter the pub. They were probably in their late thirties, Ellie thought. Moderately affluent-looking types. The man was looking deeply uncomfortable, and Ellie thought she could detect some animosity between the two women. That might be the result of whatever had just happened to their cars, but Ellie recalled sensing some tension between the three of them when she'd served them earlier.

Her boyfriend, like her parents, had no inkling of the extent of the snowfall. In his case, that was more understandable, as he lived some miles away. 'We've had a few flurries, but nothing serious,' he said. 'You're really literally snowed in?' There was a slightly envious note in his voice.

'Really, literally,' she echoed. 'I'm having to throw myself on Robbie and Steph's mercy.'

'There are worse places to be snowed in than a pub, I suppose.'

They said their goodbyes – Ellie was relieved that Robbie and the regulars hadn't been able to overhear their endearments – and she made her way back into the bar. She was unsurprised to see that the man and women she'd encountered outside were already gathered round the log fire, being tended to by Steph, who'd presumably now finished in the kitchen. Ellie joined Robbie back behind the bar. He was in the middle of pouring three glasses of whisky. 'Thanks a bunch, lass. Looks like we're stuck with them for the night now.'

'What was I supposed to do? Send them away?'

'Steph's already offered them drinks on the house. Three bloody whiskies for nowt.'

'I bet that was you, not Steph. She'd have offered them hot chocolate.'

'She's done that and all. Three whiskies and two bloody hot chocolates. All for nowt. And we're somehow going to have to find them a bed for the night. Just hope no other buggers turn up.'

Robbie's way of dealing with any crisis was to grumble about it, but he'd do anything he could to help someone in trouble. 'Where are you going to put them? You can always use the staff bedroom, if you like. I can sleep on a couch or something.'

'Don't be daft, lass. We have to look after you to compensate for the pittance we pay you. This lot are just passing through.'

Ellie carried the tray of whiskies across to the group by the fire. The tensions she'd detected outside were still evident. The three were staring into the fire in silence, looking as if they'd rather be anywhere than in each other's company.

Ellie handed out the drinks. 'Let me know if there's anything else you need. Hope you're warming up a little.'

'Warming up and drying out,' the man said. 'It's good of you to look after us like this. We were afraid we'd get up here to find you'd shut for the night.'

'It takes a lot to make Robbie shut up shop. How're your cars?'

'I'm hoping they're all right. Alison here lost control on the bend and ended up sideways after half-ploughing into a ditch. It's blocking the road enough so anything else can't get past. We tried to get it back on the road, but couldn't manage to get enough traction.' He shook his head gloomily. 'Even if we had, I don't think we'd have got back up the hill, and I wouldn't have fancied having another shot at driving down it.'

'Robbie'll help you sort it in the morning,' Ellie said confidently. She had no idea how Robbie would do this, but he knew everyone in the vicinity. One way or another, he'd find a solution.

Steph reappeared from the kitchen, bearing two steaming mugs of hot chocolate, which she handed to the man and one of the women. She nodded to the second woman. 'You're sure you don't want one? It'll warm you up nicely.'

'I've said no once,' the woman said. She was staring at the flames and made no effort to turn towards Steph.

The fair-haired man coughed embarrassedly. 'I'm sorry. It's been a bit of a shock for all of us. It's kind of you to offer, but we don't want to put you to any more trouble.' He held up his whisky. 'And this is also warming me up very nicely, thank you.'

Steph gazed at him for a moment. She was the most generous of women, Ellie thought, but she gave the shortest of shrift to anyone who took her generosity for granted. The man's mollifying words had probably been just about sufficient to save the woman by the fire from a full dressing-down and, quite possibly, ejection back out into the snow. 'We'll need to sort out some sleeping arrangements for you,' Steph finally said.

'Don't go to any trouble,' the man said. 'I'm sure we can just make do in here till the morning.' Ellie noticed that he glanced over at the woman by the fire, as if half-expecting her to offer some unwanted opinion.

'We'll sort something out for you.'

Back at the bar, Steph exhaled suddenly, as if she'd been holding her breath since she'd last spoken. 'Rude bloody bitch.'

'There was something going on between them earlier,' Ellie said. 'A bit of an atmosphere.'

'It's no bloody excuse, though, is it? I mean, we take them in, give them drinks on the house, make bloody hot chocolate for them – and then that. "I've said no once." Stuck-up cow.'

Over the next half hour the pub gradually emptied, as even the hardiest and most alcoholic of the locals recognised that, with the snow still coming down heavily, they might struggle with the short walk back into the village. Steph had disappeared into the rear of the pub in search of camp beds. Ellie was polishing glasses, listening to Robbie chatting with the man, who'd approached the bar to buy another round of drinks. 'We were just saying we should pay you something for helping us out tonight.'

Robbie shook his head firmly. 'Don't be daft. It won't be exactly luxurious.'

'Still better than being out there. Look—'

'If you try to press money on me, I'll feel insulted. Tell you what, buy another round or two and I'll be more than happy.'

'Well, if you're sure.' The man glanced across at Ellie. 'I'm Brian, by the way. Brian Fairweather. You ought to at least know who's going to be sleeping under your roof. That's my wife, Carrie. And the other woman's Alison Evans.'

Robbie busied himself pouring a pint. 'Aye. I'm Robbie. Wife's Steph. You're not local?'

'Drove over from Chesterfield. Just for a pint and a bite to eat. Never expected all this.'

8

'None of us did,' Robbie said. 'Not even the bloody Met Office apparently.' He placed the newly pulled pint on the bar top. 'Can I just say something?'

'Of course.'

'My wife didn't take very kindly to the way your friend spoke to her. Not in the circumstances.'

Fairweather nodded. 'Alison? Yes, sorry about that. It was out of order. She's got a lot on her mind at the moment.'

'No excuse.'

'No, of course not. I was mortified.'

'Aye, well, no harm done. Trust me, though, Steph won't take it twice.'

'Understood.'

'I'm going to sort out some camp beds for you. We've had this happen before so we're quite well prepared. You'll have to rough it down here, but we'll sort out a decent breakfast for you in the morning.'

'You don't need—'

'We'll do whatever we can. No rush to drink up. I'll keep the bar open till the usual time so if you feel like another round, I'll be right here.'

Fairweather took the hint and carried the drinks back over to his companions. Ellie had been listening to his conversation with Robbie, and she saw Fairweather pause to say something to Alison Evans, who glared back at him without offering a response. 'She seems an odd one.' Ellie nodded her head in Evans's direction.

'She'll be a very stupid one if she gets on the wrong side of Steph again. Makes you wonder what goes through some people's minds. Speaking of which, I'd better go and see how Steph's doing. If she ends up carrying those camp beds through on her own, I'll be the one in trouble.'

Ellie remained behind the bar, watching the three gathered around the fire. They were still sitting largely in silence, though the Fairweathers exchanged a few words. Alison Evans, by contrast, was staring into the flames, a scowl fixed on her face.

9

Robbie emerged from the rear of the pub, bearing a couple of camp beds which he stacked beside the bar. He gestured to Brian Fairweather, who hurried over.

'Can we help you with that?' he said.

'I'll bring the other bed out. We've got some sleeping bags and some additional bedding. But you'll just have to make the best of it. I'll leave it to you where you want to set them up. We can move some of the tables back. You won't have a lot of privacy but I'm guessing you can cope with that for a night.'

'At least we'll be warm and dry. I'm not too fussed about anything else.'

Robbie and Fairweather spent the next ten minutes moving back tables and setting up the beds, while Steph and Ellie fetched the bedding. Ellie had expected that Fairweather would want to sleep close to his wife, but instead he set up the beds in different corners of the room.

Robbie looked at the clock over the bar. It was already nearly closing time. 'You people want a nightcap? I'll be locking up in a few minutes.'

'Why not?' Fairweather said. 'At least we can put a few pence in the till for you.'

Robbie served the final round of drinks and finished closing up the bar. 'We'll leave you to it. Want to be up bright and early in the morning to see how things are looking. Light switches are over there, when you're ready to sleep. You know where the facilities are. One other thing – the external doors are all alarmed overnight so I'd ask you not to try going outside for any reason.'

'We'll try not to disrupt things any more than necessary.'

Ellie followed Robbie and Steph through to the back of the pub. Their accommodation was upstairs, a decent-sized flat that occupied the first floor of the building. The staff bedroom was small, with an en-suite shower room, on the ground floor beside the kitchen. It was furnished only to a fairly basic level, but Ellie had found it comfortable enough on the occasions she'd used it.

She bade the others good night and closed the bedroom door behind her with some relief.

Steph had obviously tried to make the place welcoming for Ellie. She'd dug out an old dressing gown and a pair of pyjamas, and she'd turned on the heater to warm the room.

Ellie undressed, pulled on the pyjamas and climbed into bed, turning out the bedside light. She'd been expecting to find it difficult to sleep in an unfamiliar bed, but she'd been on duty since the early afternoon and the physical exhaustion hit her as soon as she lay down.

She fell asleep almost immediately. She was woken – what felt like only minutes later – by piercing and continuous screaming. It took her a terrified minute to realise the sound was not human or animal, but the shriek of the pub's burglar alarm. She reached over for her phone. Three thirty in the morning.

Still barely awake, she pulled on the dressing gown and made her way to the bedroom door. The corridor was deserted, but she could hear footsteps from the landing above. Robbie appeared on the stairs. He looked dishevelled and had clearly dragged on his clothes hurriedly. 'I gave them one bloody instruction. It's as if they don't have a brain cell between the lot of them.'

Ellie followed him back into the bar. The room beyond was still in darkness. Robbie made his way unerringly to the panel of light switches and turned them on, before turning his attention to the alarm unit behind the bar.

The noise ceased suddenly, the silence almost as startling as the previous cacophony.

For a moment Ellie was dazzled by the brightness. Then she saw Robbie striding towards the open pub doors. The Fairweathers were standing just outside the entrance, gazing bewilderedly out into the snowy night.

'I thought I'd made myself clear enough. Which of you decided it would be fun to open the bloody doors?'

Ellie looked around the room. The answer to Robbie's question seemed obvious. There was no sign of Alison Evans.

Robbie had clearly reached the same conclusion. 'Oh, for Christ's sake, of course it was her. Is she completely bloody insane? Any idea why she might have taken it upon herself to go outside?'

Carrie Fairweather stepped forward. Like her husband, she'd remained largely fully dressed, and she'd now wrapped her sleeping bag around her shoulders like a scarf. There were snowflakes in her hair. 'I don't know what's happened. We were asleep until the alarm went off.'

Outside, the snow was still falling heavily. There was a set of footprints leading away from the entrance, but they were already being lost. Robbie stood in the doorway and shouted: 'Alison!'

The night felt eerily silent, all sound deadened by the thick blanket of snow. There was no response to his call. He tried twice more, then returned inside the pub. 'I don't like this. Nobody in their right mind would go out in weather like this. I'm going to get my coat and boots on and have a scout around.'

'We'll come with you,' Fairweather said.

'Your choice,' Robbie said. 'But you're not really dressed for this weather. We're high enough up that it can turn very nasty very quickly. That's why I'm concerned about your friend. By all means come and have a scout around the car park with me, but don't stray far and come straight back inside if you start to feel too wet or cold. I don't want to be searching for anyone else.'

'Understood. But I'll do what I can. I feel responsible for her.' Fairweather glanced towards his wife, leaving Ellie with the sense of something not being said.

Robbie gazed at him for a second. 'Aye, well, maybe take a bit more care of her next time, then. If it's not too late.'

CHAPTER TWO

'You okay?' Sheena asked.

Annie Delamere was curled up in her favourite armchair, a book open on her knee and a mug of coffee steaming on the table in front of her. She looked fine, Sheena thought, as long as you ignored the fact that it was four in the morning.

'Sorry. Couldn't sleep again. Tried really hard not to disturb you.'

'You didn't,' Sheena conceded. 'But when I did stir, I couldn't help noticing you weren't there.'

'Assumed you'd realise I'd come downstairs.'

'Oh, I did. I may not be a detective inspector like some people, but I managed to deduce that. I just wanted to make sure you were okay.'

Annie smiled. 'I'm fine. Well, maybe not fine exactly. But nothing to worry about. Just thinking about things.'

'Your mother?'

'She's definitely one of the things.'

'Ready to talk about it yet?'

Annie was silent for a moment. 'Maybe. As much as I can. But you need to get some sleep.'

'I've a rare day off tomorrow. Well, no constituency engagements, anyway. Just the usual piles of casework. Actually, that reminds me. There's a case I'd like your professional opinion on at some point.' Sheena was an MP who, while Parliament was in session, spent much of the working week living in a small rented flat in Pimlico. 'Not sure I'm going to get back to sleep

13

now anyway, so it's you or constituents' emails. Just let me get myself a coffee. You need a refill?'

Annie peered into her mug and swallowed the remainder of the contents. 'Why not?'

Five minutes later, the two women were sitting together on the sofa: Sheena upright, Annie with her head on Sheena's lap. 'This feels uncomfortably like a psychiatrist's couch.'

'With added benefits.' Sheena stroked Annie's hair. 'So what's the latest with your mother?'

'At a personal level, she's still not talking to me. I probably got it wrong when I went to see her after what happened in Meresham. She needed me then, and I couldn't open up to her.'

'Bollocks,' Sheena said firmly. 'She's never shown any warmth towards you. She's no right to expect any emotional support from you. She was lucky you were even prepared to see her.'

'She's still my mother.'

'And you're her daughter. But she never let that affect the way she treated you.' Sheena stopped. 'Sorry. The last thing you need is someone lecturing you about what you ought to be feeling.'

'It's probably exactly what I need. I've no idea what I'm feeling at the moment.'

'You've been through a hell of a lot.'

'It's been a challenge.'

That was one way of putting it, Sheena thought. She still wasn't sure how Annie had coped with the revelations of the preceding months. The discovery that her mother, a former assistant chief constable, had been guilty not only of serious corruption, but had also, decades before, been involved in the unlawful killing of teenage girl. As far as Sheena was aware, the complicated truth behind these events was still being disentangled, but any lingering trust between Annie and her mother had been shattered.

'So what's the latest? If you can tell me.'

Annie hesitated. 'It's tricky. I'm supposed to be kept at arm's length from the investigation, but Stuart Jennings has been good enough to give me the occasional heads-up in confidence. I feel awkward about breaking that confidence, even with you.'

'I'm not going to try to persuade you either way. I understand you want to do everything by the book. But you know that anything you tell me won't go further.'

'Of course I know that. And, to be honest, I really need to talk about it.' Annie paused, with the air of someone summoning up the will to continue. 'Stuart reckons the investigation is pretty much complete and they're about to submit the findings to the CPS.'

'Ah. And?'

'He tells me they think there are sufficient grounds for a prosecution.'

'Not good.'

'I genuinely don't know. If the evidence is there, it's the right decision.'

'Do you know what they're planning to charge her with?'

'I didn't think it was right to press Stuart on the details. There're plenty of options. Perverting the course of justice. Misconduct in public office.' She laughed bitterly. 'They're pretty spoiled for choice.'

'If they have the evidence.'

'I'm sure that's been their biggest problem, especially since most of the potential witnesses are dead. I can't imagine they're going to be able to do much with the original case. It was decades ago, my mother was just a child herself, and she's the only living witness to what happened. The corruption stuff is different. The fact that my mother took early retirement when she did suggests that the evidence is there.'

'But will they want to air that dirty linen in public?'

'I'd initially thought they wouldn't, just as they didn't at the time. My mother was close to retirement anyway. Others were discreetly shuffled into back-room roles. But I wonder if the climate's changed now. Our new chief constable's keen to wield his new broom. Most of those who were implicated are retired, so there's no risk of embarrassing anyone still in post. They can probably claim the recent investigation uncovered new evidence. In other words, it might suit them to make an example of my mother to demonstrate their determination to stamp out corruption.'

'A very belated slamming of the stable door, I'd have thought, but I take your point.' Sheena reached out to take Annie's hand. 'So what does this mean for you?'

'In theory, not much. I'm not responsible for my mother. In practice, who knows? If it does come to court, I'm going to have an uncomfortable few months. I've always had to live with suggestions that I've only reached the rank I have because of my mother's influence. Christ, if only they knew. If she's prosecuted, will everyone assume like mother, like daughter?'

'Of course they won't. Like you say, you're not responsible for your mother.'

'That's not how it works, though, is it? I mean, you're in one of the most cut-throat professions of all. Are you trying to tell me your colleagues wouldn't dish the dirt on you given half a chance?'

'They don't need half a chance, or any chance at all. With a handful of honourable exceptions, the parliamentary party is a seething nest of venomous vipers. Are you telling me the police are the same?'

'It's probably less dog eat dog, but not much. There are enough people who'd be happy to see me take a fall.'

'How soon will you know what the CPS have decided?'

'No idea. I don't imagine they work quickly.'

'So all you can do is get on with things. There's no point in worrying.'

'I keep telling myself that. I don't know if it helps.' Annie shook her head, as if trying to clear her thoughts. 'Anyway, what's this case of yours?'

'You're changing the subject.'

'Obviously. But it's not often you ask my opinion on a case.'

'You gave me some help on this one before. You remember Jude Parrish?'

'Vaguely. The woman with the abusive partner?'

'That's the one. He'd been physically and psychologically abusing her and their child for years. We eventually helped them find a place in a refuge. Partner was eventually sent down.'

Annie nodded. 'I remember. He was a nasty piece of work.'

'He was. And she's just discovered he's about to be released on parole. Nobody bothered to tell her, and she's scared witless.'

'That shouldn't have happened. She should have been kept informed and given the opportunity to contribute to the parole hearing. Sounds as if someone's messed up.'

'That's what I thought. I just wanted to get my facts straight before wading in. I'll look into it.'

'If there's anything I can do to help, let me know.'

'Thanks.' Sheena smiled. 'And, just in case you think you've wriggled off the hook, I'm going to say it to you one more time. If the blessed Margaret isn't prepared to talk to you, there's not much you can do about it. It's her loss. She's only herself to blame for the mess she's in.'

'Thanks, Shee. I know you're right. But it doesn't always feel like that. Especially at four in the morning.'

'I might put it another way. Margaret's successfully wrecked her own life, and she's tried hard to wreck yours. You can't let her do that.'

'That's definitely true.' Annie sat up and moved along the sofa, reaching for her coffee. 'I suppose that's one reason I feel guilty. She's my mother and I'm not supposed to feel this way. But I'm much happier without her in my life.'

CHAPTER THREE

Ellie pulled on her heavy waterproof and followed as Robbie trudged his way to the end of the car park. The snow was falling less heavily now and the visibility had improved. He waved his flashlight around, peering into the darkness for any sign of movement. 'Alison!'

They'd tried to follow the footsteps leading from the door, but the falling snow had already erased them. It seemed most likely that Evans had either walked straight out of the car park or made her way to the rear of the pub. On that side of the building the land dropped away, gradually at first and then more steeply, towards the valley. It was one of the pub's attractions: the spectacular view out over the dark waters of the reservoir to the hills beyond, but unlikely to be welcoming on a night like this.

Robbie had decided to check outside the car park first. Ellie watched as he shone his torch around more slowly, looking for any disturbance in the snow. There was nothing. The thick snow on the road down from the pub and to the right into the village was undisturbed. If Evans had come this way, she must have continued walking, allowing her prints to be covered behind her.

They made their way back towards the pub. Brian Fairweather was peering ineffectually into the darker corners of the car park. 'Anything?'

'Not so far,' Robbie said. 'As far as I can see, the snow's undisturbed. If she's gone that way, she must have just continued walking. But it doesn't seem likely.'

Fairweather looked towards the entrance to the car park, as if contemplating whether to set out after her. 'I can't imagine why she'd do that.'

'Me neither,' Robbie said. 'But then I can't envisage why she'd have come out here in the first place. I'm going to check around the back.'

He led Ellie along the side of the building. The ground was level enough until they reached the rear corner, then it began to descend gently. 'Alison!' he called again. 'Where are you?'

The wind was stronger on this side of the building: an icy blast against the skin, the falling snow whipped and swirling in the darkness. Robbie shone the torch around him, then took a few more cautious steps forward. From Ellie's recollection of the landscape, he'd be able to progress only a few more yards before the route became too risky to follow.

'Ellie,' he said. 'There's something down there. Come and tell me what you think, but take care. The ground's treacherous.'

She stepped tentatively forward until she was standing close behind Robbie. He was right. There was something there, perhaps thirty or forty feet below them. An unevenness in the snow that didn't look like a natural feature of the land. Robbie took another half step, moving cautiously, and raised the torchlight again.

Ellie was sure now. There was something there. It was already fully covered in snow, but the snow was thinner than on the surrounding ground and she could see traces of darker colours beneath the white.

She had little doubt that they were staring down at the body of Alison Evans. The only question was whether that body was dead or still alive. If she'd fallen from here, Ellie thought, she'd have rolled for several yards before the incline became more extreme. The final drop would have been faster and harder.

She could see that Robbie was wondering if there was some safe way to reach the body. He took another step and almost immediately slipped, clearly struggling to retain his balance. 'I can't see any safe way of getting down there.'

'Even if there was, how would we get her back up?' Ellie said.

'We couldn't. I don't have the equipment. Or the expertise, for that matter.' He pulled out his phone and dialled 999. Ellie listened as he explained the situation. He switched on the speaker so Ellie could hear the response.

'So the road up there's currently impassable?' the call handler said.

'At the moment, yes. I don't know if there's any chance of getting a snowplough up here?'

'Not much tonight, I'm afraid. Helicopter might be a possibility, but flying conditions aren't great at the moment. I'll see what we can do. We'll contact the mountain rescue too.'

'I only wish I could reach her myself.'

'You've done exactly the right thing, sir. Don't risk your own safety. We'll do whatever we can.'

Robbie took one more look around the car park, then led the way back into the bar. The warmth of the room took Ellie by surprise after the chill of the night air. Steph had emerged in their absence, rebuilt the log fire and presumably turned on the heating. Robbie walked over to the Fairweathers, who were sitting by the fire, mugs of coffee in hand. 'I'm afraid we may have found her.'

Brian Fairweather looked up. 'Where?'

'At the bottom of the slope at the back. She must have either been standing or walking at the top of the hill and slipped. The ground's treacherous. If she lost her footing, she'd have been gone in a moment.'

'You're sure it's her?'

'I can't be absolutely certain. There's something there under the snow and I don't know what else it could be. There are no sheep or other animals in that area. But I couldn't get close enough to be certain.'

'And you think she's…?' Fairweather clearly couldn't bring himself to finish the sentence.

'Again, I can't be sure. It would have been a big fall. But it might have been survivable.'

'We need to go and get her then. What are we waiting for?'

'How do you suggest we do that?' Robbie said.

'There must be a way.'

'No one here's an experienced mountaineer. We don't have anything but the most basic equipment.' He gestured down to his own sturdy walking boots. 'Even wearing these, I could barely keep my footing. If we tried to get down there, we'd end up with all of us lying beside your friend. I know it sounds brutal, but I can't allow anyone to risk it.'

'We can't just leave her there.'

'I've called the emergency services. Police, ambulance, mountain rescue. We need to leave it to the experts.'

'And what will they be able to do?'

'I don't know,' Robbie said. 'But whatever it is, it'll be a lot more than we're capable of.'

CHAPTER FOUR

'It's not going to last,' Zoe Everett said.

'You reckon?' Gary was busy at the cooker, frying sausages.

'It's thawing already. It'll be gone by this afternoon.' She stared pensively out of the kitchen window, watching the water dripping endlessly from the bushes at the top end of the garden. It had been snowing heavily when they'd gone to bed the previous evening, and they'd woken to a white landscape, unusual this close to the city. But the temperature had risen in the early hours and the snow was already disappearing from the garden paths and patio.

Zoe was slightly sorry. They had no reason to leave the house today and she'd almost welcomed the thought of being trapped by the elements. She needed that at the moment: the sense of being cocooned, with no pressure to take on any further responsibilities.

Not that there was much pressure on her in any case. Gary had been as supportive and helpful as any husband could be, even though she knew he'd been even more worried than she was. Her managers at work had been similarly sympathetic, allowing her the time off she needed and encouraging her not to worry unnecessarily about the day-to-day demands of the job. She'd expected that of Annie Delamere, of course, but she'd been more surprised and reassured to receive explicit support from Stuart Jennings. He'd always seemed uncomfortable when dealing with any kind of personal issue, but he'd gone out of his way to let her know he was fully behind her.

That was all good, and she'd received matching, if more formal, support from human resources. That wasn't entirely surprising. The force owed her a duty of care, particularly if there was any possibility her condition might be work-related.

The problem was that she still didn't know what her condition was, or even if she really had a 'condition' in the first place. There had been a number of incidents over the last year or so which had left her concerned about either her physical or mental health. The most extreme examples had been when her body had almost seemed to freeze, as if she'd lacked any sense of volition. On other occasions, she'd felt as if she'd been unable to maintain her balance or had been overwhelmed by a sudden sense of utter exhaustion.

At first, she thought little of the incidents, ascribing them to the pressures she'd been under in her job. She'd been involved in a couple of cases that had ended in significant risk to herself and Annie, and she'd thought that the trauma of those moments had perhaps triggered some kind of psychological reaction. Then their most recent major investigation had stirred up some unpleasant childhood memories, and she'd wondered whether that had added to her sense of mental dislocation.

She'd been offered counselling in the aftermath of the previous cases, but had always resisted, seeing it as a tacit admission of weakness. Although there'd been a considerable change in the culture of the force over the last couple of decades, it still tended to be a man's world, with women having to work twice as hard to make progress. She knew Annie felt the same, despite – or perhaps because of – the example of her own mother. But that, especially at the moment, was a whole other story.

In the end, it had taken the combined influence of Annie and Gary to persuade Zoe to take action. Annie had clearly been worried about what she was seeing at work – Zoe had been conscious she wasn't performing at her best – and even more concerned that Zoe might find herself incapacitated at some critical moment. Gary had shared those concerns, but was also worried that the real roots of Zoe's condition might be physical rather than psychological, that she might be suffering from some illness affecting her energy levels and balance.

She'd tried to dismiss the idea, insisting there was nothing wrong with her that some rest wouldn't put right. But she recognised that she was fooling herself. Her condition might be psychological or physical, it might be serious or relatively minor, but it was more than everyday tiredness or stress. 'Look,' Gary had said, 'just get it checked out. If it's something physical, it's probably easily treatable.'

'What if it isn't, though?' she'd said. 'What if it's something more serious? Something progressive, for example.'

'Then it's better we know about it sooner rather than later, isn't it?'

She had no ready answer to that, though part of her was silently saying, 'No, I'd rather not know. I just want to continue as I am.'

In the end she'd succumbed to Gary's exhortation, as much for his reassurance as for her own. She'd visited her GP, who'd taken her account more seriously than she'd expected – perhaps worryingly so, she thought – and arranged a referral. That had been followed by what seemed like an endless sequence of tests, culminating in a mildly terrifying MRI scan. The diagnosis, as far as she understood, was negative. The tests had found nothing. The more obvious potential causes had been eliminated. There were no signs of any abnormalities in the brain, no sign of anything indicative of even a minor cause for her experiences.

The consultant had said, 'I can't absolutely guarantee that there's no physical cause. There are a few further areas we can explore, and we'll continue to do that. But it seems increasingly unlikely. My best guess is that the root cause is probably psychological.'

'You think that's possible?'

'Easily. We're nowhere near to understanding the links between mental and physical health, but the experiences you've described could easily be associated with some psychological trauma.'

'A recent trauma?'

'Not necessarily. It might be linked to the risks you've encountered in your work. But it might be something much further back in your past. Perhaps something more deeply buried. It might be something substantial, but it might also be something that, at least from an adult perspective, seems relatively trivial.' He'd smiled. 'I'm sorry. I don't suppose that's much help.'

She'd smiled back, if only because she hadn't known how else to react. 'Not really. I mean, I'm reassured that it's not likely to be anything physical, but it doesn't really solve my problem.'

'I can see that. Unfortunately, I'm a neurologist, not a psychotherapist. I'll report back to your GP, and it's really up to her to decide what to do next.'

And that had been that. It was now back in the hands of the GP, who was doing her best to expedite matters but, as always, matters of mental health seemed to be given a lower priority than physical illness. Stuart Jennings was pursuing with HR whether there was any way to obtain further support through the force, but the available services seemed to be more generic and less targeted than Zoe was likely to need.

In the meantime, Zoe felt in limbo. For the moment, she was still on compassionate leave. But that had been a short-term arrangement to accommodate the round of medical tests. It couldn't continue, and Zoe had no desire that it should.

Gary was doing his best to help her, but she was finding his well-intended efforts increasingly wearing. She wanted him to behave normally, rather than tiptoe around her for fear of upsetting her or triggering some further physical reaction.

She was about to say something more to Gary, when she heard the chirrup of the landline phone in the hall. Her instinct was to ignore it. Hardly anyone called them on the landline any more, and the vast majority of the calls they did receive were from cold callers. But at the moment she felt that any interruption would be welcome.

She stepped out into the hall and picked up the phone. 'Hello?'

'Is that Zoe Callender?'

Zoe hesitated. She'd been married to Gary for over ten years. Who the hell would be using her maiden name? The voice didn't sound like that of a cold caller. The speaker was female, and sounded nervous, as if making the call reluctantly. 'I'm sorry,' Zoe said, 'who is this?'

There was a prolonged silence and for a moment Zoe thought the caller had hung up. Finally, the voice continued, 'It's a long story. You don't know me.' There was another extended pause, though this time Zoe could hear the caller breathing at other end of the line. 'The reason I'm calling is that – well, I'm your mother.'

CHAPTER FIVE

DC Andy Metcalfe was feeling pleased with life. Other men of his age might feel less content about being dragged out of the bed where their girlfriends still lay sleeping to be summoned into work on a damp, dreary Sunday morning in late November. But Andy was more than happy.

DI Annie Delamere was at the wheel of the car, and he was sitting in the passenger seat, gazing at the passing view, relishing every moment of what he was still young and inexperienced enough to view as an adventure.

Annie glanced across at him, as if sensing what he was thinking. 'Sorry to have to drag you out on a Sunday morning.'

'No worries. It's the job.'

'It certainly is.' She sighed. 'I can't say I'm exactly overjoyed to be here, but there you go.'

'You had other plans?' He didn't know a lot about Annie's private life, other than the little he'd picked up as office gossip. He knew her partner was female and apparently a Member of Parliament, which had initially seemed impossibly glamorous to Andy. But he'd met Sheena Pearson briefly at some office do, and she'd seemed genuinely warm and down to earth, chatting to Andy at some length about his job and background with what seemed like real interest.

'Not really. That was kind of the point. It's one of the few days when Sheena doesn't have a thousand and one commitments, so we were planning a lazy day at home. Inevitably, I'm the one who gets called into work.' She smiled. 'Still, like you say, it's the job.'

They'd left Buxton behind and were heading up into the hills. For the moment, they were still on the main road, twisting and turning between dry-stone walls surrounding snow-covered fields. The morning was clear and bright, the low sun glittering on the white landscape.

The road they were following was already largely clear of snow, although Andy assumed it had fallen heavily here overnight. Annie had taken a 4x4 from the pool, unsure of the conditions they might have to deal with once they turned on to the back roads.

'You said it was a suspicious death,' Andy prompted. 'Someone who'd fallen during the night. Sounded a bit strange.'

'I don't know much more,' Annie said. 'She was part of a small group who managed to get themselves stranded in a pub overnight.'

'Lucky them.'

'You'd think. But apparently, for whatever reason, one of them took it upon herself to go wandering out into the snow. She was eventually spotted at the bottom of the steep slope at the rear of the pub.'

'Sounds more like an accident.'

'That's what they assumed. They couldn't get down to her overnight because of the weather and we couldn't get up there, so it was this morning before we were able to reach her. She was already dead. But the paramedic thought it wasn't from exposure. He reckoned the cause of death was most likely a major trauma at the rear of the skull, which didn't seem consistent with anything she might have struck in the fall.'

'So what's he suggesting? That someone hit her over the back of the head?'

'That seems to be exactly what he's suggesting, at least as a possibility. There are several caveats, though. First, the guy who examined her was a paramedic, not a pathologist. He was the first to admit that his knowledge is limited and he could well be wrong. Second, the slope she fell down is still largely covered

28

in snow, so it's possible that there's a rock or something under there that might have caused the injury.'

'I guess.' Andy sounded almost disappointed. 'So we could be wasting our time?'

'We're not wasting our time. It's a potentially suspicious death, so we have to investigate until we've determined the circumstances.'

'Yes, I appreciate that, but...'

'But you're hoping for a nice juicy murder?'

'Of course not.'

'Don't be embarrassed about it. That's the job too. It's what gets a lot of us out of bed in the morning. Not that we want people to commit murder, but we want to see those who've committed serious crimes brought to justice. And we want to feel we're doing something worthwhile.'

Andy grinned. 'To be honest, I just want something I can get my teeth into. A job where I can prove myself.'

'You've already done that.'

'I hope I've done something, but I want to do more.'

'You will do. You've got what it takes, Andy. Trust me.'

Following the directions of the satnav, she turned off the main road on to a B-road leading up into the hills. There was more snow on the road here, but the passage of previous vehicles had cleared the surface sufficiently to render the road easily navigable. Their route rose steadily higher, the landscape opening up behind them.

'Have you been to this place before?'

'I think so. I was trying to remember. Sheena and I quite often head up here to go walking in the summer. I've a feeling we called here for a Sunday lunch. What about you?'

'Not really my sort of thing. I'm more urban.'

'That right?' She sounded surprised by his answer. Andy had previously mentioned that one of his real ambitions was to move out to the country.

'I would like to live out here,' he said. 'Well, maybe not here exactly, but not in the city. But coming out to places like this – especially to the pubs and restaurants – always makes me feel uncomfortable. It's not that anyone's antagonistic. Not often anyway. It's more that they – well, they notice you, if you see what I mean. They don't see that many Black faces so they're curious.' He stopped, conscious he'd said more than he intended. 'Or maybe I'm imagining it.'

'I doubt it. It's not the same, but I've occasionally noticed a reaction if Sheena and I show any affection for each other in public. Not usually anything hostile, but it makes us feel uncomfortable.' She peered through the windscreen. 'Think that's the place up ahead. There's a single-track road off to the left.'

The road looked more treacherous here, though it was clear that other vehicles had already passed this way earlier in the morning. The road turned sharply to the right, still rising, and they saw two pillars that marked the entrance to the pub car park. The road itself continued past the entrance towards the neighbouring village. Annie drew to a halt as a uniformed officer stepped out to wave her down. She brandished her ID towards him. 'DI Delamere and DC Metcalfe. I take it we've found the right place.'

'I'd have said so,' the officer confirmed. 'You can park by the pub entrance.'

'Any sign of the CSIs yet?'

'We're told they're on their way.' The officer sounded sceptical, as if the likelihood of anyone other than the uniformed branch turning out on a cold Sunday morning was small.

There were a number of official vehicles here already – several marked cars, an ambulance, a 4x4 with the insignia of the mountain rescue service. She pulled in close to the entrance.

'Decent-looking place,' Andy said. 'If you ignore all the police tape.'

'Bet it does a bomb in the summer.' Annie was staring out past the building, at the landscape beyond. 'Incredible view. I remember it now. We had a decent lunch. Friendly landlord. Everything you want in a country pub.'

At the entrance, another uniformed officer ushered them into the interior of the bar. A man and woman were sitting by the open fire. Andy took them to be the couple who'd been trapped here overnight. At the far end of the bar, a man – presumably the landlord – was standing, talking to a uniformed officer. Andy followed as Annie stepped forward to greet the officer. 'Paul.'

'Morning. Wasn't expecting you to be attending this one.'

'Luck of the draw. Good to see you again, though.' She turned back to Andy. 'This is Paul Burbage. We've come across each other before. One of the good guys.'

'Let me do the introductions,' Burbage said. 'Robbie, this is DI Delamere.'

'And my colleague DC Metcalfe,' Annie added. 'We've met before, Mr…'

'Crowther. Robbie Crowther. Have we?' He looked troubled at the possibility. 'I try not to have any more dealings with the police than I can help. It's not good for the reputation.'

'Not in an official capacity, as far as I'm aware. I've been up here as a customer. You do a decent lunch.'

'We try our best.' There was a note of relief in Crowther's voice, Andy noted with interest. 'Unpleasant affair, this.'

'I'm sorry we have to disrupt your business.'

'I can live with that,' Crowther said. 'I just keep thinking about that poor woman. I just don't know what she was up to.'

'That's what we need to try to find out,' Annie said. 'I take it those are her companions, over there by the fire.'

'Man and wife. Called Fairweather. They dined here last night with the deceased. They told me they'd driven over from Chesterfield. I don't know anything else about them, or what their relationship was with Alison Evans.'

'We'll need to take statements from them and from yourself, Mr Crowther. Who else is on site?'

'Just my wife, Steph, and our waitress, Ellie. Ellie Brompton. She got trapped here last night, as well.'

'We'll need statements from both of them. There was no one else here at the time the incident occurred?'

Andy thought he sensed a hesitation before Crowther shook his head. 'Most of our customers cleared out as soon as it became clear that the snow was getting serious. A few locals hung on for a bit longer, but even they headed off well before our normal closing time. It's only a couple of hundred yards into the village, but even that must have been hard going last night. Once we'd got everything cleared up in here, we went to bed and left our guests to it. Next thing I knew I was woken by the alarm going off, presumably because of Evans opening the front doors.'

'Had they been drinking a lot?'

'I wouldn't have said so. Not across the evening. From memory, they had a drink with their meal. But two of them were driving so didn't drink anything else. Then when they got back up here, after their problems with the car, Steph gave them a medicinal whisky each, and they ordered another couple of rounds just before I went to bed.'

'Okay,' Annie said. 'We'll get statements taken, and we can get things moving. In the meantime, Paul, you'd better show me the location of the deceased.'

CHAPTER SIX

Gary was in the process of dividing bacon and sausages between the two plates on the kitchen table. He looked up at Zoe's words. 'What?'

'She said she was my mother.'

'But your mother's dead.'

Zoe pulled out a chair and sat at the table. 'That's the point. She reckoned that wasn't my mother.'

Gary slid a fried egg on to each plate. 'Who wasn't your mother?' He finished serving the food and sat down opposite her, pushing one of the plates in her direction. 'I'm really not making any sense of this.'

'No, me neither.' Zoe picked up her knife and fork and played for a moment with the food, cutting herself a portion of sausage. Then she placed the cutlery down again. 'She said the people I'd always thought of as my mother and father weren't my natural parents.'

'What? That you were adopted?'

'I don't know what else she could have meant.'

'But you'd know if you were adopted, surely?'

'Would I? Only if I'd been told.'

'But surely your parents would have told you?'

'I don't know. I mean, I'd have hoped so. But – well, you remember my mum and dad.' Gary had met Zoe's parents a few times in the early days of their relationship. Zoe had always had the sense that they'd mildly disapproved of him, though they'd never said so explicitly and, in practice, had always been welcoming. Then, after she'd known Gary for

33

only a few months, Zoe's father had died unexpectedly of a heart attack. Her mother, never the strongest of characters, had seemed utterly bereft by her husband's sudden death and had passed away the following year. They'd been relatively elderly parents, but had died comparatively young, only in their mid-sixties.

Gary nodded. 'Not the most easy-going people in the world.'

'That's one way of putting it. They were – I'm not even sure what the word is. Staid? Old-fashioned? Not people comfortable talking about personal matters. I hope they'd have told me if I'd been adopted, but I can easily imagine they wouldn't.'

Gary speared a piece of bacon on his fork. 'So what did this woman on the phone say, exactly?'

Zoe's breakfast remained untouched. 'She told me her name was Elaine Simmonds. Then she just went straight into it. Began by telling me she was my mother. My birth mother, that is. She said she'd spent months trying to track me down. She'd finally identified me and had confirmed to her own satisfaction that I was the right person. She reckoned she'd done that some months ago, but hadn't managed to pluck up the courage to make the call.'

'So what prompted her to do it today? First thing on a Sunday morning.'

'She didn't really say. Not clearly anyway. To be honest, it was all a bit garbled. She sounded incredibly nervous, as if she was regretting making the call. I was a bit gobsmacked myself so I wasn't taking it all in.'

'Take your time. Whatever's behind this, it must be a shock.'

'She said she'd considered writing a letter rather than calling, but she'd decided that would be cowardly.'

'So what does she want, now she's plucked up the courage to contact you?'

'She just wants to meet me. She was very insistent that, at this stage, she doesn't want anything more than that. Just one meeting so she can finally see me again after all these years – that's how she put it – and see what sort of person I've grown up to be.'

'Or one chance to pull whatever scam she's trying to pull. One chance to spin you some line that'll reel you in. One chance to try some sob story on you.'

'I know, I know. But she sounded genuine.'

'If she is a scam artist, this won't be the first time she's done it. She'll have this patter refined to perfection.'

'I wasn't really thinking about any of that while she was actually talking to me. I was just too stunned by what she was saying. It sounded convincing. Her voice was trembling and she sounded like she could barely hold it together. If it was an act, it was a bloody good one. But, yes, it could easily have been just that. A bloody good act.'

'I don't think you can take any of this at face value, Zo. It would be a shitty trick to pull, but there are some unscrupulous people out there. Listen to me, lecturing a literal detective sergeant about unscrupulous people.'

She smiled. 'I'm not an idiot, Gary. I know exactly what sort of people are out there, and now the moment's passed, I can see it much more dispassionately. But the question remains. What if she was telling the truth? What if she is my birth mother? If there's even the tiniest possibility that's true, I can't just ignore her.'

'What if there's the tiniest chance that a Middle Eastern prince has just popped his clogs, leaving millions in his will and you're entitled to a share? Are you going to start responding to those emails too?'

'Bugger off, Gary.' She was still smiling. 'It's not the same and you know it.'

'I know that, but it's how the trick works. So how did you leave it?'

'She told me she'd give me time to think about it. She realised I'd be shocked by what she'd told me and that I'd need time to absorb it. She left me her number and asked me to get back in touch when I'm ready.'

'And what if you don't want to talk to her again?'

'She said she'd accept that too. She'd be sorry, but she'd understand.'

'It still sounds like a skilfully worked scam to me. Sure, she sounds like she's being thoughtful and not pressurising you into making a decision you might regret. But she's also leaving you time to ponder, knowing it'll play on your mind until you find out more. And when you do call her back, you'll probably be even more receptive to whatever she says.'

'On the other hand,' Zoe said, 'it does give me an opportunity to try to find out if there's any truth in what she's saying. If I was adopted, there must be some kind of record of that, surely?'

'It's not something I know anything about. But it's worth a try. What about your birth certificate?'

'I was just thinking about that. I can't recall ever seeing it.'

'What about when you applied for a passport?'

'I got my first passport before I went to university, and my dad did it all for me. When I replaced it, I just needed to send off my old passport. It was the same when we got married. You only needed your birth certificate if you didn't have a passport.'

'What about when you went through your mother's belongings?'

'I kept a file of official documents. It's up in the attic, I think. There was a copy of their marriage certificate, from what I recall. But I don't remember my birth certificate. I can have a look.'

'Seems to me that's the place for us to start. If we can find any hard evidence that this woman's lying, we'll know what to do.' He smiled suddenly. 'I don't suppose you told her anything about yourself?'

36

Zoe shook her head. 'We didn't discuss anything personal beyond what I've told you. She didn't want to take it any further till I'd had time to think. Why?'

'I'm just thinking that, if she is a fake, she may get a real shock when she finds out what you do for a living.'

CHAPTER SEVEN

Annie watched Danny Eccles standing at the top of the hill, peering nervously down towards where Alison Evans's body was still lying.

'There's no way you're getting me down there,' Eccles said over his shoulder. 'I'll have to send one of the youngsters down.'

'Like child chimney sweeps?' Annie said.

'Only with marginally more risk assessment.'

Eccles had arrived in his white van just as Annie was coming out of the pub entrance with Paul Burbage, having left Andy Metcalfe to take a statement from Robbie Crowther. Eccles was a senior CSI, normally cheerful enough but today looking as if he'd much rather be anywhere else. While he was talking to Annie, he was looking round, clearly sizing up the scene and what might have happened to result in Evans's body lying at the foot of the hillside. 'Assume you've ensured this area at the top of the hill has been undisturbed?' he asked Burbage.

'As far as possible,' Burbage said. 'I made sure the mountain rescue people and the paramedic took a detour to the left so they wouldn't trample on the area above the body. Robbie, the landlord, would have been out here when he first spotted the body, but other than that, it shouldn't have been touched.'

'Good lad. If there's anything significant, I reckon we're more likely to find it up here than down there. Whether there's anything worth finding is another question. The snow won't help, and the fact that it's thawing will help even less.' He sighed. 'I'll get someone down there to photograph the body and record whatever we can. Then we can get the body brought up and do the rest up here. We'll do the best we can.'

'All we can ask, Danny.' Annie stood to one side and looked down the slope. The body had fallen some distance, and the final part of the slope was relatively steep, but to Annie's untrained eye it looked as if the paramedic's judgement could well be correct. If Evans had simply slipped and fallen, the drop itself would have been unlikely to be fatal. The question, then, was whether the blow to the head had happened here at the top of the hill or somewhere in the descent.

She left Eccles to his work and walked over to join Burbage, who was talking to another of the uniformed officers. 'Just making sure we've got everything covered,' she said. 'What happened to the Fairweathers and Evans's cars? Danny would like to give them a going-over.'

'Robbie Crowther got one of the local farmers to drag Evans's out of the ditch, then we brought both cars back up here.' He pointed to the far corner of the car park. 'Over there.'

'Can you let Danny know? My next step is to speak to our friends inside. See what they've got to tell us about themselves and Alison Evans.'

The bright morning offered a marked contrast to the gloomy interior of the pub. Annie had found the place cosy and welcoming on her previous visit, but there was an odd melancholy about its out-of-hours atmosphere, despite the fire roaring in the hearth. The dim light, the scent of stale beer, the simple emptiness of the place, along with what she'd just witnessed outside, combined to create an unexpected sense of bleakness.

Robbie had taken Andy Metcalfe through to his small office at the rear of the pub so they could conduct their discussion in private. He'd suggested that Annie could use the living room he and Steph had on the first floor. 'It's not much,' he said apologetically, 'but it's comfortable enough and, apart from our bedroom and the spare room Ellie used last night, it's the only other private room in the place.'

Annie knew that the couple by the fire had been watching her since she'd first entered the pub earlier. For her part, she'd wanted to let them stew for a while before she spoke to them. If Alison Evans's death had not been accidental, then it was possible the perpetrator was one of those two people.

'Good morning,' she said. 'I'm DI Delamere. I'm very sorry we've had to keep you waiting for so long. First, I'm afraid I don't come bearing any good news. The paramedics have now been able to reach your friend and – well, there's nothing they could have done. Their view is that she died almost immediately as a result of the fall.'

'So it wouldn't have made any difference if we could have reached her last night?' the man said.

'It doesn't appear so. Obviously, we'll need a post-mortem to confirm the exact cause of death.'

'Why the hell did she go out there? What was she thinking?' the woman asked.

Annie regarded her with interest, trying to gauge what emotion might lie behind her questions. 'That's what we need to find out.'

'But you're not suggesting there was anything suspicious in what happened?' the woman said.

Annie waited a moment before replying, watching the couple's faces. 'I'm suggesting nothing at present. We simply need to investigate the facts. I'd like to speak to you both individually. I just want to hear your account of what happened last night.' She turned to the man. 'Perhaps you'd like to go first?'

She led him into the rear of the bar and Steph directed them up the stairs to the living room. It was a compact space, but Robbie and Steph had made the best of it, creating a cosy environment with an open fire – already lit and burning – a couple of armchairs and a sofa. There was a large screen TV and a wireless stereo unit, presumably linked to some music streaming service. A good place to escape the hurly-burly of the pub, Annie imagined. She took one of the armchairs and gestured for the man to take the other.

'It would be helpful if you could begin by telling me a little about yourself, just for background. Your full name, address and occupation, for example.'

'Brian Peter Fairweather. I'm a solicitor.' He gave an address, which she recognised as being just outside Chesterfield.

'You have your own practice?'

'With a partner. Courtney and Fairweather.'

'What kind of work do you do?' She couldn't recall coming across the firm in a criminal context.

'Conveyancing. Wills. Probate. Divorces. Family court work. Not necessarily the most exciting stuff, but it keeps the wolf from the door.'

'How did you come to know Alison Evans?'

This time she thought she detected a hesitation, as if he'd been caught out by her sudden change of topic. 'I didn't really. I mean, not well.'

Annie offered no response, forcing Fairweather to continue.

After a moment, he added, 'She was a friend of my wife's, really.'

He sounded, to Annie's ears, like someone trying to distance himself from the late Alison Evans. She wondered if there was any significance to that or whether it was just a semi-superstitious desire to dissociate himself from ill fortune. 'But you knew her well enough to invite her to join you last night?'

'Well, that was more Carrie's idea. Carrie got to know her originally because they both used to do volunteer work for the local Wildlife Trust. Carrie's into all that stuff – animals, conservation. They got on well enough. I think she felt sorry for Alison, who seemed a bit lonely. So Carrie invited her to join her and some friends on one of their nights out, and it developed from there.'

'So why did you invite her last night?'

'She'd been through a tough time in the last few months. She'd had to care for her elderly father and she'd apparently split up with her boyfriend. She was just at a low point, so Carrie thought an evening out might cheer her up. In practice, I'm not sure it was a good idea. It all just felt a bit awkward.'

'There's no easy way to ask this, Mr Fairweather, but how would you characterise her state of mind? From what you saw last night.'

She could see he was considering his answer carefully. 'There's no real way of knowing, is there? But if you want my honest opinion, I'd say she was depressed. Perhaps more than we realised.'

CHAPTER EIGHT

'Don't waste too much time. This lot won't be around for long.'

Martin watched his grandson Lucas trudge his way up the hillside, pulling the plastic sledge behind him. It was a pity really, he thought. Watching the falling snow the previous evening, Martin had been expecting to wake up to a crisp white coating that would at least last through Sunday. But even when Martin had risen, at seven a.m., the thaw had been well under way. As he'd shaved, he could hear the sound of water dripping steadily from the eaves of the house.

Luckily, Lucas generally woke almost as early as Martin, particularly at weekends. It was harder to drag him from his bed on a school day, but then Martin recalled that feeling only too well. This particular morning Lucas had appeared just as Martin was sitting down with his toast and coffee. Martin had poured him a bowl of cereal, and seen the disappointment in the boy's face as he'd stared out of the kitchen window. 'Snow's going.'

'In that case,' Martin had responded, 'we'd better get out there while it's still worthwhile.'

If nothing else, it had allowed Amy to have a lie-in. That was why he was here, after all. It suited both of them, or at least he hoped it still did. Occasionally, lately, he'd wondered if Amy might be getting irritated by his presence. There'd been the odd sharp or sarcastic comment when he'd been with them, and he'd felt that her initial enthusiasm for the arrangement had lessened as the months had passed.

It wasn't as if she saw that much of him. Probably no more than if they'd still been living at separate addresses. He had his own self-contained flat, and he kept out of the way. He generally joined Amy and Lucas for a late Sunday lunch, but that had been Amy's idea anyway. And he went round first thing to help get Lucas ready for school, but that was supposed to make life easier for Amy. It was the reason he'd suggested the set-up in the first place.

He supposed they were bound to go through their ups and downs. Amy was well aware of the contribution that Martin had made to the deposit and continued to make to the mortgage payments. If it hadn't been for Martin, she couldn't have afforded a place like this after the divorce. It was possible Amy resented that, but it didn't mean much to Martin. He had a decent pension. He had a few quid stashed away from the sale of his old place. He could afford to chip in with the deposit, and it was only right he paid rent for his use of the flat. When he popped his clogs, the money would all go to Amy anyway, so he might as well help out while she needed the support.

For Martin the best part – the only real part that mattered – was that he got to spend more time with his grandson. That would come to an end itself, of course. Lucas was already nearly six. In a year or two he'd feel too old to play with his ancient grandad and be off with friends of his own age. But for the moment, Martin could enjoy the simple joy that Lucas displayed as he came skidding down the hillside on his small plastic sledge.

Martin had made sure Lucas had told his mum where he was going before they'd set off, so there was no need to rush back. Amy could enjoy a lie-in, a relaxed breakfast or whatever else she might want to get up to on an undisturbed Sunday morning. Martin could enjoy Lucas's laughter and enthusiasm for life.

He helped Lucas pull the sledge back up the hillside, then watched as the boy repeated his short but joyful trip down the slope. The boy would be happy to repeat the same simple activity over and over again, seemingly never growing bored. Martin was just as happy to watch, though from time to time he allowed his gaze to drift away from Lucas to admire the surrounding landscape.

Martin never tired of this view. He'd spent most of his life living in the vicinity of the Peak District, but it had only been in the last decade that he'd lived at the edge of the National Park, first in his own house and now with Amy on the outskirts of Buxton. No longer a wage slave, and with Lucas his only real commitment, he could come out here whenever he wanted, drinking in the miles of openness, the wind-lashed moorland, the tangled patterns of dry-stone walling.

'Grandad! Watch!'

He looked back at Lucas who, for the purpose of variation, was planning to conduct his next trip face-down, on his stomach. 'Okay, show me what you can do!'

Lucas kicked himself away and came speeding down the hillside. Perhaps because of his changed position, his trajectory was less straight than before, veering off to the left, away from where Martin was standing. The sledge struck a patch of less even ground, and bounced slightly into the air, tipping over and tossing Lucas into the snow.

For a moment, Martin was afraid that Lucas might have been hurt. It took the boy a few moments to clamber back to his feet, but by the time Martin reached him, he was laughing. 'Did you see that, Grandad? I crashed! I need to do that again!'

Martin shook his head, amused by the boy's resilience. 'Well, take care. I don't want your mam blaming me because you end up with a broken leg.'

'I won't. The snow's soft enough.'

Martin helped Lucas to drag the sledge back up the hillside, and watched as he set off again, this time deliberately throwing himself off. Martin paused and watched anxiously for a moment, until he saw the boy jump triumphantly to his feet and wave. Martin made a show of applauding, as Lucas began to drag the sledge back up the hillside.

Lucas repeated the process several more times, his falls becoming increasingly exaggerated and melodramatic. He'd be getting himself wet, Martin thought. It was probably time to give him a ten-minute warning before they started the journey back. He turned and looked around him, once again drinking in the glory of the landscape. After the night's snow, the day was sunny and clear, and from this vantage point it was possible to see for miles. Martin scanned the landscape, trying to spot landmarks he recognised.

It was a few minutes before he realised that he had allowed his attention to be distracted. He looked down the slope, but could see no sign of Lucas. The brightly coloured sledge lay on its side in the snow, but he could see nothing of the boy who had been riding it moments before.

Martin hurried down the hillside, his anxiety rising. He told himself he'd looked away only briefly, that nothing could have happened to Lucas in that short time. Most likely, the boy was hiding down there somewhere, preparing to play some trick on his grandpa. Or he'd grown suddenly bored with his playing, the way young children sometimes did, and had made his way back down to the car.

Martin was telling himself all this as he jogged back towards where the sledge was lying. But he could already feel a clutch of fear in the pit of his stomach.

CHAPTER NINE

'I understand Alison Evans was primarily a friend of yours, rather than your husband's?'

Carrie Fairweather hesitated and Annie thought she detected some unease in the woman's expression. 'I suppose that's true,' she said finally. 'Though I wasn't really close to her. I'm not sure anyone was.'

The tone of Fairweather's response surprised Annie. In the circumstances, it seemed oddly dispassionate, emotionless. Annie was already forming an impression of Fairweather as someone likely to have strong opinions, and that made her wonder about the relationship between the two women. 'Yet you invited her to join you for dinner?'

'We thought it might help her. But it was a difficult evening.'

'Maybe you'd better start at the beginning. How did you come to know Alison Evans?'

'It's a longish story. By training, I'm a solicitor like Brian, but I specialised in criminal law. A few years ago, I started to get disillusioned with it for a variety of reasons. So, when Brian's practice began to take off, I opted for a change in career. I'd been volunteering at the local Wildlife Trust. Nothing grand. Mainly just helping to keep their reserves tidy, bits of maintenance and repair work, making sure there was nothing left that might be harmful or detrimental to the wildlife, that kind of thing. It had been an opportunity to get out of the house and get some exercise in some beautiful locations. Anyway, they had a staff position going, so I applied and managed to get the job.'

'What about Alison Evans?'

'She joined us as a volunteer quite recently. To be honest, I'm not sure it was really her thing. It was more hands-on than she'd expected. She wasn't impressed at being asked to tend a wildflower meadow on a wet Saturday afternoon. She only lasted a few weeks but we got to know each other. She sort of latched on to me. She stopped coming to the Wildlife Trust sessions, but kept in touch. We went for a drink a couple of times and then I invited her over to dinner with me and Brian. She seemed lonely, I suppose, and I felt sorry for her.'

'What sort of person was she?'

'A woman with a lot of problems. There's a lot I never found out about her, but she came weighed down with baggage. She always said she didn't want to talk about it, about her past or about what she'd been going through. But then she'd let slip just enough to make you concerned. To be honest, I think she used that as a way of inveigling herself into your life.' She shrugged. 'Maybe I'm being unfair. But I didn't feel entirely comfortable with it at the time, and the more I've thought about it, the more uneasy I feel. Her father was one example. He was elderly and in poor health, and Alison said she'd been effectively his sole carer.'

'You don't think that was true?'

'There were parts of what she told us that didn't quite hang together. Little details that weren't consistent. Things about her father's medical condition, for example. Then there was the boyfriend.'

'Boyfriend?'

'Looking back, I'm not sure he even really existed. They'd supposedly split up a few weeks before she first met me. Bit younger than her. Decent looking, fairly well-off. Perfect catch, or so she told me.'

'You're saying she made this up?'

'I don't know. But again, there were inconsistencies in the way she described him.'

'So what are you saying? That she was some kind of compulsive liar?'

'I honestly don't know. My guess is that she'd found a way of interacting with others that worked to her advantage. She made you feel sorry for her and you felt obliged to accept her as a friend, at least for a while.'

'Is that why you invited her last night?'

'We'd been worried about her, I guess.'

Annie sensed again that there was something Fairweather wasn't saying. 'How was she last night?'

'Let's just say it was a difficult evening. For all of us.'

'Your husband thought she seemed depressed.'

'He might be right. It might explain what happened.'

It might, Annie observed. But it left unanswered questions. Above all, if Carrie Fairweather was right, how did that explain the blow to the back of Alison Evans's head?

CHAPTER TEN

'Lucas!'

Martin stooped to pick up the abandoned sledge, then looked around. 'Lucas, stop messing around.' He could see in the snow the marks of Lucas's footprints. They led a few yards down the hillside towards the road. Beyond that, the ground became softer and wetter, much of the snow already melted. It was impossible to tell which way Lucas had gone.

Still clutching the sledge, Martin walked down the hillside, looking for anywhere Lucas might be hiding. There were few obvious places. At this point, this was open moorland, bleak and exposed to the elements, with no trees or undergrowth. Further down the hillside, there was a stretch of dry-stone walling. It was conceivable Lucas could have concealed himself somewhere behind that. But there was no gateway nearby, and Martin couldn't imagine how Lucas could have scaled the wall. More likely, he'd walked back along the moor towards the road.

Hurrying now, Martin reached a point where he could gain a clearer vantage of the road below. He could see his car parked a few hundred yards away, but still no sign of Lucas. There were no other vehicles parked near his own, although a couple of other cars were parked further down the hill, on the edge of the neighbouring village. At this point, the single-track road curved to the left, skirting the moorland where he was standing, before descending again towards Macclesfield. This stretch of road had been invisible to Martin further up the hillside, concealed by the contour of the hill. He tried to recall if he'd heard any traffic in those few minutes. Any passing vehicle should have been easily audible on this quiet Sunday morning, but he realised he was unsure. His attention had been too distracted by the view. Too distracted, he added silently to himself, to keep proper watch on Lucas.

But it had been no more than a minute or two. Nothing could have happened to Lucas in that time. He was here somewhere. Perhaps he'd managed to make his way to the road unseen and was concealing himself behind his grandad's car.

Martin jogged down the hill to the road, still looking around him. As he reached the corner of the field enclosed by the drystone wall, he peered over, hoping his first unlikely guess might prove to be true and that Lucas had somehow succeeded in concealing himself there. But the field was empty, the snow undisturbed.

Martin turned his attention back to the car. 'Lucas!'

He walked around the vehicle. The snow around the edges of the road was largely melted, and there was no way to tell whether Lucas had been there.

If Lucas wasn't at the car, it seemed unlikely he'd managed to reach the village in the time it had taken Martin to walk back. He would surely still be visible on the road. More likely, he was still back on the hillside somewhere.

Martin left the sledge propped against the car and then hurried back up the hill, still calling Lucas's name. He walked back past the point where the sledge had been and continued along the moor, looking for anywhere the boy might be concealed. Perhaps just some fold in the ground or hillock in which his small figure might be hidden. There seemed to be nothing. The snow here was thicker and more solid than further down the hill, and there was no sign of any disturbance. After a few moments, Martin was forced to concede that Lucas couldn't have come in this direction.

But where else could he have gone? If he'd headed up the hillside, Martin would have spotted him as he came down. In the space of a few minutes, Martin felt as if he'd moved from a momentary lapse in concentration to a seemingly unfathomable mystery. He turned and walked back in the opposite direction, his anxiety mounting by the second.

It was impossible. There was nowhere here for anyone, even a small child, to be hidden. Up to now, it had just been one of those moments that occur so often in childcare. The second when your child slips away from you in a crowded shop. When your child runs ahead of you in the street and turns a corner. All those times – and he recalled a few of them when Amy had been small – when your heart momentarily stops and you fear the absolute worst. But those moments never lasted. Almost immediately, you spotted or caught up with the child, chastised them for slipping away. It always happened so quickly that you never really stopped to think about the implications if, just this once, the ending had turned out not to be a happy one.

He hadn't even considered that possibility today, not even in those first few seconds. It had just seemed impossible that anything could happen to a child on an empty hillside on a Sunday morning. It had felt obvious that, at any moment, Lucas would pop up from whatever ingenious hiding place he had managed to find, and shout and laugh at his worried grandad.

That was what was really worrying Martin now. Even if there had been somewhere for Lucas to hide, Martin couldn't believe he could have maintained his concealment for so long. He'd have grown bored with the game and jumped out. Lucas couldn't even play hide-and-seek without revealing himself within minutes. Martin called Lucas's name several more times, increasingly loudly, but there was still no response. With sound partly blanketed by the snow, the morning was eerily silent.

Feeling sick to his stomach, Martin pulled out his mobile phone, his eyes searching for any sign of movement in the surrounding landscape. After another moment's hesitation, he dialled 999.

CHAPTER ELEVEN

Gary descended the ladder cautiously, the cardboard box balanced on his arms. 'I think this is the last one, but I'll double-check.'

Zoe took the box from him and carried it through to the living room, placing it on the coffee table beside the three boxes that Gary had already carried down. It was slightly depressing that this was what her parents' lives had amounted to. Other than Zoe herself, these four boxes contained all they'd left behind, most of which she had retained largely for sentimental reasons.

As she'd worked her way through the first box, she'd realised that in many cases she couldn't even recall what those reasons had actually been. Some of the items were interesting in their own right – photographs, old diaries, copies of old newspapers. But many were just official documents of one sort or another. Papers relating to the sale and purchase of the several houses her parents had occupied during their married life. An old school hymn book that had presumably once belonged to Zoe herself. Various documents relating to her father's work. Zoe must have once thought these papers were worth keeping, but now she couldn't imagine why. Even so, she knew that once she'd finished today, she'd dutifully pack everything back into the boxes. They'd be returned to the loft and no doubt sit there for years to come.

'No, that's it,' Gary said from the doorway. 'Just those four boxes.'

'That's what I remembered.' She was already feeling they were wasting their time, but she supposed it had to be done. Apart from anything else, it was the only action they could carry out before the start of the working week, and there was a chance it might provide them with the answer they needed.

Zoe wished now that she'd packed these boxes with more care. In the weeks after her mother's death, she'd been mainly concerned to get the task over with. Zoe had never felt particularly close to her parents. They were decent people who had always had – at least from their perspective – her best interests at heart. But they'd always seemed mildly baffled to have this young person living with them, as if they'd unexpectedly found themselves having to deal with a set of attitudes and values previously unknown to them. As a teenager, Zoe had thought that this was simply a manifestation of the generation gap. Most of her school friends had also complained about their parents, even though they were generally younger than Zoe's. Now, she was wondering whether that apparent lack of parental warmth might have had other roots.

The first box had yielded little of interest. In the second, Zoe found some photograph albums, alongside folders of loose photographs. The first album contained pictures of her parents in their younger days, faded colour images of seaside holidays and country picnics, probably from the 1970s. Some pictures showed only the two of them, while in others they were accompanied by friends or relatives. There were no annotations on the albums or the images themselves, no indications of where the pictures had been taken or who the other individuals in the photographs might be.

The second album was more interesting, because it contained the first pictures of Zoe herself. She flicked aimlessly through the pages, Gary peering over her shoulder. 'Beautiful baby pics?' he said. 'Or did you look like Winston Churchill?'

'That's what's beginning to strike me,' Zoe said. 'There aren't any pictures of me as a small baby. Not in this album, anyway.

Even in the earliest pictures, I look as if I'm already almost a toddler.'

'You think that's significant?'

'Who knows? Maybe the baby pics are in another album. It would seem a bit odd to have nothing, though.' She picked up the remaining albums and flicked through them. 'There's nothing here. It's odd.'

'Maybe it'll be in one of the other boxes. Or it went astray at some point in the past.'

'It's making me wonder, though.'

'Of course. But let's not jump to conclusions. It doesn't necessarily mean anything.'

Zoe continued to work through the boxes. The third box contained items that had belonged to her parents. An old handbag, now empty. Some ornaments. A few framed photographs, including a couple of Zoe herself, one as a child and one at her graduation. Again, nothing of her as a baby.

It was in the fourth box that Zoe finally came across some folders of more official-looking papers. There were all kinds of documents here, and in most cases Zoe couldn't conceive why her parents had hung on to them. Zoe recalled that she'd done little more than skim through the folders when clearing out her mother's house. Oddly, she'd found these stacks of bureaucratic trivia more poignant than many of the more obviously significant items. They provided such a vivid reminder of her mother's character. She'd been no hoarder, but she'd had an almost superstitious need to hang on to any official document 'just in case'. She'd seemed almost to believe that at some point a government representative would turn up on her doorstep to enquire whether she'd preserved her council tax bill from five years earlier.

Zoe worked systematically through the material, pulling out anything she thought might be of value. She might at least take the opportunity to put the documents in order.

In practice, the useful documents were few and far between, and apparently placed randomly into the folders. She found copies of her parents' marriage certificate and her father's death certificate, along with some of Zoe's examination certificates. There were documents that would once have been of value but were now obsolete – relating to her father's pension, a long-expired life assurance policy, some old building society account books.

Then, finally, in the third folder, Zoe found it. A brown envelope contained several pieces of paper and, among them, what appeared to be a birth certificate.

She was holding her breath as she spread the contents of the envelope out on the table. It was another moment before she released her breath and looked at Gary, who had been watching her quizzically.

'It's what we've been looking for,' she said. 'The answer was here the whole time.'

CHAPTER TWELVE

'Nice people,' DC Andy Metcalfe said, 'but I'm not sure how much I really got out of that. Maybe I asked them the wrong questions.'

Annie smiled. 'I'm sure you didn't. You're a good interviewer. I've watched you. You put people at their ease.' They were in Robbie Crowther's office, sharing the outcomes of their various interviews.

'Is that what I'm supposed to do, though? I thought I was supposed to pin them down with remorseless forensic questioning. I'm sure that's what they said at police college.'

'Maybe it was. There are times when it's necessary, but it's not usually the place to start. Most people will tell you a lot more if they're relaxed. I suspect the problem here is that they just didn't have much to tell you.'

'Didn't seem to have. The landlord, Robbie Crowther, gave me a blow-by-blow of what happened last night. The snow. This group getting stranded. Everyone going to bed. The next thing he knew, he was being woken by the alarm. Pretty much in line with what he'd told us over the phone.'

'And Alison Evans was already gone when he got downstairs?'

'That's what he said. The other two were standing by the open doors, trying to see what had happened to her.'

'Do we know what sort of time gap there was between the door being opened and Crowther coming downstairs?'

'Not precisely, but it can only have been a few minutes. He reckons the alarm would have woken him pretty much

57

instantly. He stopped to pull some clothes on, but that only delayed him for another couple of minutes. The young woman, Ellie Brompton, pretty much confirmed that. She was woken by the alarm as well. By the time she came out of her room, Crowther was already coming down the stairs.'

'So if someone did kill Alison Evans, they could only have done it in those few minutes, presumably.' In her interviews with the Fairweathers, she'd asked them for their account of what had happened in that brief interval. Their versions had been consistent and tallied with what Crowther had said. They'd all been woken by the alarm. There'd been a minute or two of confusion, then they'd realised the doors were open and Evans was missing. Their first reaction had been to go and look for her, and they'd initially headed out into the car park to see if they could see her, until Crowther had appeared and taken charge. Brian Fairweather had tried to help Crowther find her, but it had been Crowther alone who'd spotted the body.

On the face of it, it seemed as if there'd been very little opportunity for either one of them to have killed Alison Evans. The only real chance was if one of them had left with – or straight after – Evans, committed the murder and then almost immediately returned to the now-open entrance, perhaps before the other was fully awake. That seemed unlikely. Would it have been possible for one of them to have done that without the other being aware?

The other possibilities, of course, were that both of them were involved or that one of them was lying to protect the other. It wasn't impossible, she supposed. They'd had several hours to ensure their accounts were consistent.

Beyond that, they couldn't discount the idea that the killing had been carried out by some third party. But that would mean one of the three other people in the pub – Steph, Robbie Crowther or young Ellie Brompton – or some unknown figure who happened to be outside the pub on the night of a severe snowstorm. Those options felt even less likely.

All of this assumed that Evans had been murdered. That was still far from certain. All they really had was the opinion of a paramedic with limited expertise. They wouldn't know more until the post-mortem had been completed, and even then the answer might not be definitive. Even if the melting snow uncovered a suitably sized rock on the hillside, there could still be doubts about whether Evans had struck it in her descent or whether it had been used to kill her and tossed down afterwards. The weather would further degrade any forensic evidence that might help inform the investigation.

The next step would be to talk to the regulars who'd been in the pub at the end of the evening, but she wanted to consult with Stuart Jennings before proceeding too much further.

'Okay,' she said to Andy, 'I think we might as well let everybody go now. We're not going to get any more out of the Fairweathers today, and I imagine Ellie Brompton will be happy to get back home.'

As she was speaking, there was a tap at the door and, after a moment, Paul Burbage's head appeared. 'Sorry to interrupt, but I've just had a call. Looks like we've another possible incident on our hands.'

'What sort of incident?'

'Missing child. Over in the next valley. Kid went out sledging with his grandad. Somehow slipped away. Grandad searches but can't find him. It's probably one of those that'll turn out to be nothing, but given the kid's age and the weather, they're trying to get a team pulled together to conduct an urgent search. Want to know if we can spare anyone.'

'Best have a chat with Danny Eccles. Check what he still needs to keep the scene protected. But I imagine we can release some people now.'

'Will do. Thanks.'

'Missing child's got to be a priority.' Annie turned back to Andy Metcalfe. 'I'll give Stuart a call to update him and agree next steps.' She paused, thinking. 'If the uniforms are needed for this search, why don't you give the Fairweathers a lift back? Don't imagine they'll say much in front of you, but it might be useful to see how they behave together. And maybe get a sense of where they live, what sort of house.' She shrugged. 'We may be wasting our time, particularly if it turns out that Evans's death was accidental. But you never know.'

Andy nodded. 'You never do. Want me to come back to pick you up?'

She smiled. 'I'm not just using you as a chauffeur, Andy. I'm quite serious about keeping an eye on the Fairweathers. I'll find someone else to take me back.'

CHAPTER THIRTEEN

'First of all, sir, just take a deep breath and try to calm yourself a little. I fully appreciate your concern, but it'll be best if you can give me a clear account of what happened.'

Martin knew the police officer was right. He'd kept himself together until now. When he'd called 999, he'd managed to talk coherently to the call handler at the end of the line. He'd half-expected she might not take him seriously, tell him it was too soon to be reporting Lucas missing. But she'd noted Lucas's young age and assured Martin they'd send someone out as a matter of urgency. She'd offered to stay on the line in the meantime, but Martin had wanted to check at some of the nearby houses, in case Lucas had managed to reach the village without Martin spotting him.

He'd even managed to maintain some composure when he'd rang the bells of the first few houses. None of those he'd spoken to had seen Lucas and had no idea what Martin was talking about. A couple of the men had offered to help search, and a small group had been collected. They were now up on the hillside, checking out the area where Lucas had been last seen.

After that, he'd finally plucked up the courage to call Amy and tell her what had happened. She'd taken the news more calmly than he'd expected, reassuring him that Lucas would just be playing some game and was bound to turn up or be found before long. Martin hadn't been able to tell whether Amy really believed her own words, or if she'd simply been trying to reassure herself.

The police car had arrived shortly afterwards, and Martin was now being addressed by a burly middle-aged PC, who'd introduced himself as Dave Jackson, and a younger female PCSO called Fran Wilson. It was only at the sight of the two uniformed officers that Martin had finally broken down and found himself sobbing almost uncontrollably. 'It was my fault. I wasn't paying attention.'

'These things happen all too easily, sir. Kiddies can move very quickly. But he can't have gone far. We'll find him.'

'I keep telling myself he must be somewhere nearby.'

'Just tell me exactly what's happened. You're the boy's grandfather?'

'That's right. His name's Lucas. I'd brought him up here sledging. Youngsters don't get many opportunities these days, and I thought it would give his mum a break—'

'Have you informed her of what's happened?'

'I called Amy just before you arrived.'

'So you took Lucas sledging. Where exactly were you?'

Martin pointed to an area further up the hillside, where he could see some of the villagers tramping backwards and forwards. 'Just up there. I was at the top, and Lucas had been sledging down. Not very far. Just a few yards, really, but he was enjoying it. He'd done it a few times, then he fell off, which he thought was hilarious, so he was repeating that.' Martin paused, conscious he was on the verge of losing control again. 'I was keeping a close eye on him.'

'Then what happened?'

'Look, I just want to start looking for Lucas.'

'I appreciate that, sir.' Jackson exchanged a look with Fran Wilson that Martin couldn't interpret. 'And we'll start that urgently. We've got additional resources on the way. I just want to make sure we know where to look. You were watching Lucas…?'

'He was pulling the sledge back up the hill. I must have become distracted. I was enjoying the view. But I only looked away for a few seconds. When I looked back down, he wasn't there.'

'Where was Lucas when you last saw him?'

Martin pointed to where the villagers were conducting their search. 'Just about where they're looking.'

Jackson nodded. 'Okay, let's head over there and have a chat with our friends. Make sure they're not just tripping over each other.'

Even to Martin's untrained eye, the impromptu search party looked disorganised, little more than a group of well-intentioned individuals milling about and occasionally calling Lucas's name. Jackson called the group to him. 'Thanks for coming to help out, folks. It'll be really useful to have your support. We don't believe young Lucas can have gone far, so I'm sure we'll soon track him down.' He turned back to Martin. 'Can you show us exactly where you last saw him?'

'Just there. You can see the tracks from the sledge. The last time I saw him, he'd come off the sledge and was about to start pulling it back up the hill. I looked away for no more than a couple of minutes. When I looked back, the sledge was there but no sign of Lucas.'

It was clear that at least a couple of the villagers were sceptical of this account. They presumably thought he'd been more careless than he was suggesting. It just wasn't true, though, Martin told himself. Yes, he'd allowed his attention to wander, but only for a minute or two. But he knew now that, if it turned out that something really had happened to Lucas, no one would ever believe him. It didn't matter anyway. Even those few minutes had been unforgivable.

He waited while Jackson organised the villagers into a more disciplined search party, proposing that each of them should take an area to check. 'I assume you're all locals,' he said in conclusion. 'Do you know of anywhere in the immediate area where the boy might be hiding? He might think he's in trouble and be afraid to come out.'

The nearest man shook his head. 'There's nowt up here. No caves or owt like that. Not even a bush I can think of. Don't know where he can have got to. Mind you, they can be slippery at the age. Sometimes they get further than you think.' He looked up to where the slope grew increasingly steep. 'Don't reckon he can have gone much further uphill. If we spread out and start at the highest point he's likely to have got to, we can work our way down. If we keep ourselves coordinated, we shouldn't miss anything.'

'Sounds good to me.'

For all the police officer's reassurance, Martin was feeling a rising sense of despair. It was now over half an hour since Lucas had gone missing, and with every minute that went by the chances of finding him were diminishing. It took him a moment to realise that Jackson was speaking to him.

'Are you okay, sir?'

'Sorry, I was just thinking – well, you know.'

Jackson smiled sympathetically. 'I know. We'll find him. Look, if you feel up to it, you can join the search team with Fran.'

'Aye, that's probably for the best. I need to be doing something.'

Jackson gestured down towards the village, where another police car had just pulled into the roadside. 'It looks as if the first of the backup's arrived, so we can really get things moving.'

CHAPTER FOURTEEN

Gary was standing behind her, peering over her shoulder. 'Ah. Right.'

Zoe was staring at the piece of paper she was holding in her hands. 'I just saw the top document at first, and I thought that gave me the answer I was looking for. Then I saw the second one.'

'Why are there two? I don't understand.'

'Neither do I. When I saw Certificate of Birth, I assumed that was confirmation I wasn't adopted. Then I saw the Certificate of Adoption. Which seems to confirm the opposite.'

Gary picked up the two documents and examined them. 'This isn't a full birth certificate. It doesn't have any details of your mother or father on it. It's not like mine.'

'So what is it?'

'Let's find out. There must be stuff about adoption online.'

Zoe sighed. 'I'm not sure I can face it.' She gestured to the second document. 'Anyway, that seems to tell me everything I need to know. It turns out that the people I always thought of as my mother and father were nothing of the kind.'

Gary sat down at the table and took her hand. 'They brought you up as if they were. They did a good job of that. They didn't do anything wrong.'

'Except not tell me the truth. I think I'm going to find it hard to forgive that.'

'They'll have had their reasons, Zo. You shouldn't judge them too harshly.' He smiled. 'I'll go and make us a coffee, then we can try to find out what all this means.'

She made an effort to smile back. 'It feels like that's the last thing I needed, after everything that's been going on.'

'It doesn't change anything. You're still the same person you always were.'

'Am I, though? I mean, that's the point, isn't it? I don't know who I am now.'

'Coffee first. Then we can talk. Apart from anything else, the dust from those boxes is getting to my throat.'

That was the thing about Gary. His response to any crisis – whether physical, emotional or psychological – was to fall back on practicality. It could sometimes be infuriating, but it was one of the things she loved about him. It wasn't that he was unwilling or unable to deal with less tangible issues. It was more that he wanted to ensure he was on solid ground first.

Gary returned a few minutes later, bearing two mugs of coffee. 'First things first, let's try to find out more.' He pushed aside the boxes and walked over to retrieve his laptop from his work bag. 'I know it's not what you want to think about, but we need to understand what these documents actually mean.'

She nodded, though she felt sceptical. What the documents meant, as far as Zoe could see, was that her life to date had been built on a lie. A well-intentioned lie, perhaps, though that remained to be seen, but a lie nonetheless. She wasn't actually the daughter of the staid, reserved couple who'd brought her up. In some ways, that made sense. She'd always vaguely wondered how the combined genes of that couple could have produced the person she'd turned out to be. Her father had been mildly horrified when she'd joined the police. Not that he entirely disapproved of what he saw as a good solid career. It just wasn't the kind of good solid career he'd envisaged for his own daughter.

Gary had been flicking through various web pages. Finally, he looked up. 'It's all a bit confusing. There have been various changes over the years. But essentially, the process seems to be that, when the legal adoption process has been completed, the adoptive parents are issued with a full Certificate of Adoption.' He tapped the document on the table. 'That's this one. That replaces the original birth certificate for all practical purposes. In other words, this is what your father would have had to use to apply for your first passport.'

'So what's the other document?'

'As far as I can understand, that's what's known as a short-form birth certificate. That's given to the adoptive parents at the time of the adoption, but is just a confirmation of the child's birth details. Apparently, you can't normally use it for legal purposes.'

'But you could show it to your child to deceive them into thinking they weren't adopted?' In fairness, Zoe couldn't recall her parents ever actually doing that, but she wasn't currently feeling in a charitable mood.

'I suppose. The piece I was just looking at says that people can sometimes use them for other purposes – maybe proving their age for a sporting event or something – without having to disclose potentially sensitive information about their parents.' He paused. 'But this does seem to prove that the woman on the phone, this...'

'Elaine Simmonds.'

'Yes – that what she was telling you was at least partly true. That you were adopted.' He reached to put his arm around her. 'I'm sorry, Zo. This must be a shock.'

'It's not really the kind of thing you expect to face on a quiet Sunday. Let's put it that way.' She mainly felt numb, as if she couldn't even summon up the feelings to respond to what she had discovered. There was some anger, some bitterness, but beyond that there was nothing. 'But, yes, it looks as if she was right.'

'Partly right, at least. It looks as if she was right about you being adopted. That doesn't necessarily mean that she's your natural mother. That's a separate question.'

'But how could she have known otherwise?'

'There could be countless ways. She could have been a friend or an acquaintance of your adoptive or birth parents at some point. I suppose she could have been involved in the adoption process itself. I don't know.'

'Sounds a bit of a stretch.'

'Like I said, I don't know. I'm not saying she's lying to you. I'm just saying that you still need to be cautious. Just because the first part of her story turns out to be true, it doesn't necessarily mean it all is. Or, even if it is, it doesn't necessarily mean her motives in contacting you are honourable.'

Zoe knew Gary was right, but she wasn't sure it was what she wanted to hear, not at present. She was already feeling as if her life had been torn from her, as if everything she'd always thought she knew had simply dissolved. She felt as if she desperately needed something – some truth, some solidity – she could cling on to. If she'd lost the people she'd always assumed were her parents, she wanted someone to replace them.

But if this was some kind of scam, she supposed that was exactly how it would work. You take someone at the point of maximum vulnerability, and provide them with an alternative truth they grasp with both hands. She tried to force herself to think like the detective she was. What would she be telling someone else who'd found themselves in this position? She'd be advising them to find out more, but to tread carefully. 'I need to talk to her, though,' she said finally to Gary.

He had returned to the information on his screen. 'It looks as if you can apply for a copy of your original birth certificate. But you need to know your full name at birth to do it straight-forwardly. That would give us a way of checking if she's telling the truth.'

'Suggests it'd be worth talking to her first, though. See what she says. Get as much information as possible for us to check out.'

'You sure you're up to talking to her? It's a lot to deal with.'

'I can't just ignore her, can I? I can't just pretend none of this has happened.' Zoe was silent for a moment. 'I mean, it's been a shock and I'm still reeling from it. But in another way, weirdly, I feel better than I've felt in months.'

CHAPTER FIFTEEN

'Don't like the look of the weather,' the man beside him grunted. 'Bit black over Bill's mother's, as my mum used to say.' He gestured towards the summit of the hill.

He was right, Martin thought. The morning had been sunny, but the clouds to the north looked dark and potentially heavy with rain. If so, that wouldn't be good news. The search was hard enough anyway, and a rainstorm was unlikely to make it easier. The conditions would be even more hostile to young Lucas, wherever he might be. The only advantage was that it might help to clear some of the lingering snow, revealing more of the landscape.

The truth seemed to be, though, that there was almost nowhere Lucas could be concealed. Even if he'd fallen and hurt himself, his small body would have been visible. There was almost no vegetation on the moorland other than the scrubby turf, and only the occasional indent or hollow, mostly too shallow to have allowed Lucas to hide. They were now only a short distance from the village and had found no sign of the boy or any clue to his whereabouts. If seemed almost impossible. How could a child have disappeared so suddenly and yet so thoroughly?

Martin's attention had been focused on the search, and at first he hadn't registered the noise from further down in the village. It was only as he'd stopped to look up at the heavy sky that he'd realised there was some kind of disturbance. From where he was standing, he couldn't see who or what might be causing it.

'Someone's making a racket,' the man beside him said. 'You reckon they've found something?'

'Sounds angry,' Martin said.

After a few minutes, he saw a man emerge from behind the stone buildings of the village, accompanied by a uniformed police officer. The search line paused, as everyone looked up to see what was happening.

'I don't care,' the man was shouting back at the officer. 'This is my bloody son. Why didn't anyone bloody tell me?'

'With respect, sir—'

Tom, Martin thought. Presumably, Amy had called him and broken the news. It was understandable he'd be emotional, and in Tom's case, emotion tended to manifest itself as anger. He'd be angry with Amy for not telling him sooner. He'd be angry with Lucas for playing silly buggers and causing all this panic. He'd be angry with the police for not yet finding Lucas.

But most of all he'd be angry with Martin.

The police officer placed a hand on Tom's shoulder, but Tom shook it off and strode towards the search line. It took him a moment to spot Martin. As soon as he did, he placed himself in front of the older man, his face intimidatingly close. 'What the hell have you done?'

Martin involuntarily took a step back. 'I'm sorry. I didn't...' He wasn't even sure what he was intending to say. There was nothing he could offer to Tom, other than the desperate hope Lucas would be found.

Tom was jabbing a finger at him. 'You take the bloody kid out of the house without even bothering to tell his mother. You bring him up to this godforsaken shithole for reasons best known to yourself. Then you can't even take care of the bloody kid. You're a senile old fool who shouldn't be let out of the house.'

Almost none of this was true, Martin wanted to say. He'd often taken Lucas out if they both happened to be up early on a Sunday morning, usually for a walk or a trip to the local

71

playground. Amy had never complained previously, and he knew she'd enjoyed having the morning to herself. In any case, Lucas had told her where they were going.

The police officer had again placed his hand on Tom's arm, trying to draw him away. Tom swivelled and jabbed his finger at the police officer. 'I don't want him here. He's responsible for this. I want him out of here. I can look for Lucas.'

'Sir…'

'I can't be any clearer, can I? I don't want the old bastard here. I don't want him anywhere near my son in future. I don't want him to be any part of this.' He gestured around him, as though indicating the whole landscape. 'You should be bloody arresting him.'

'Look, sir, this isn't helping. I understand your feelings—'

'Oh, you understand my bloody feelings, can you? Is it your bloody kid that's gone missing? Just get this old bastard out of here, so we can get on with looking for Lucas.'

The officer sighed and turned to Martin. 'It might be better if you did leave us to this, sir. This is a distraction from what we need to be focusing on.'

'But I just wanted…'

'I understand that, but in the circumstances, it might be for the best.'

The officer was right, Martin thought. It was probably better if, at least for the moment, he took himself away. It tore at his heart, because he didn't want to leave until Lucas had been found. But this wasn't about Martin or his feelings. It was about finding Lucas. 'Okay, if you think so. I just want him found. I'm sorry, Tom. You're right. This is my fault.'

Tom glared at him but made no response. Martin walked past him, back down towards the village. He could head back to Amy and at least ensure she wasn't left by herself.

The only possible outcome, he told himself, was that Lucas would be found. He'd have discovered somewhere to hide after all, or been taken in by some kindly soul in the village who hadn't yet heard the boy had been reported missing. That would surely be the outcome. Something along those lines. It had to be.

The alternative didn't bear thinking about.

CHAPTER SIXTEEN

'Have you actually been home?' Stuart Jennings said. 'You must be knackered.'

Annie looked up. 'And a good morning to you, Stuart. Actually, I didn't get home too late in the end. Was able to enjoy the evening with Sheena. But she had to be up at the crack of dawn to get the first train to London, so I thought I might as well come in.'

Jennings lowered himself on to the chair opposite her desk and stretched out his legs. 'Seems to have been quite a weekend in that neck of the woods.'

'What's the missing child story? I've only just picked up on that.'

'It's not looking good. Young kid went missing yesterday morning. Out sledging with his grandad. Grandad reckons he only looked away for a minute or two, and that the boy couldn't have gone far. But as of last night, still no sign.'

'I wouldn't fancy the boy's chances, if he's been out all night at this time of year.'

'Exactly. From what I understand, they continued the search as late as they could and then restarted it at first light. But it's a long time if he's got no shelter. That's assuming the grandad's telling the truth.'

'You think he might not be?'

'Who knows? From what I understand, there was nowhere immediately around for the child to hide, so it seems odd he could have slipped away so quickly. If he doesn't turn up today, the investigation may be landing on our desks.'

'Let's hope they find him. And not just because we could do without the additional workload.'

'Amen to that. What's next with the Alison Evans case? How soon will we get the post-mortem?'

'I'll try to get them to expedite it. But you know what it's like.'

'Tell me about it. Whatever the outcome of the post-mortem, it's still a suspicious death until we can prove otherwise. Even if the injury happened in the fall, she could have been pushed.'

'Quite. The question is what she was doing out there in the first place.'

'We're assuming she went out voluntarily?'

'I'm assuming nothing. But I don't see how anyone could have dragged her out unwillingly without disturbing the others.'

'The other possibility is she took her own life.'

'The others said she'd been in a low mood for some time. She seems to have been an odd character. Carrie Fairweather thought she was a compulsive liar. Someone who made up stories to get attention. We need to know more about her. If nothing else, try to find out how much truth there was in the stories about her father and her ex-boyfriend.'

'Do we have any information on the boyfriend?'

'Nothing. Not even a name.'

'What about the father?'

'That should be easier to check out. Again, the others didn't know much except that he lived in Derby somewhere. But we should be able to get details from Evans's birth certificate and track down more information. I don't know how much it'll tell us, but it might help to confirm how much Evans had been telling the truth.'

'It's a start, though. If she was a compulsive liar, she might have got herself into any kind of trouble.'

'We need to find out more about the Fairweathers too. They seem straightforward enough, but there might be more there than meets the eye. I'm not entirely clear why they invited Evans to join them on Saturday night. They reckoned they just wanted to cheer her up, but something didn't quite ring true.'

'Perhaps she didn't give them much choice. Some people make it hard for you to say no.'

'Maybe. I know that feeling all too well from dealings with my mother. When I was younger, she could get me to do anything she wanted. A mix of bullying and guilt-tripping. Took me years to realise what she was doing. Speaking of whom, I take it there's no more news?'

'Not yet. As I understand, the case should be going to be DPP's office this week. How long it'll take them to make a decision is anyone's guess. I'm not sure I'm supposed to, but I'll tip you the wink if it looks as if anything's about to hit the fan.'

'Thanks, Stuart. I really appreciate that. There's nothing much I can do about her now, but it would be good to be forewarned. I'm really not looking forward to how this is going to pan out. Whatever the outcome, it won't be good news.'

'I'll do what I can to protect you from any fallout.'

'I appreciate that too. But I don't need protecting. I just want to be treated fairly. I don't want to be punished for the sins of my mother. That's not unreasonable.'

'Not remotely unreasonable. All I can advise is to watch your back.'

'I'll do my best.' Annie found she was increasingly warming to Jennings. When he'd first joined the team, their relationship had been wary. Annie had felt the usual unease that accompanies dealing with a new boss, trying to gauge his preferences and motivations. Jennings had seemed uncomfortable slotting into a well-established team, and also, Annie suspected, in managing a couple of fairly strong-willed women.

But as the months had passed, she'd realised he generally did have the best interests of the team at heart, even if his manner was awkward at times. She'd decided he was essentially a private, perhaps even shy, man. Even after all these months, she still knew little about his own private life. He was married and had two children, a boy and a girl, still at primary school. But she knew that only because he had a photograph of them on the desk in his otherwise sparsely decorated office.

But when she or others had needed support, he'd been there for them. He'd helped her deal with the fallout from her mother's past. He'd helped Zoe deal with her recent troubles. Day to day, he was skilled at shielding them from those further up the hierarchy, helping to preserve the space and freedom they needed to get on with their jobs.

As if he'd been reading her mind, he said, 'How's Zoe at the moment?'

'She seems okay. She's still going through these rounds of medical tests, but so far they've found nothing, as far as I'm aware.'

'That's something, I suppose.'

'Definitely. But it means she still doesn't have any answers.'

'Maybe it is something psychosomatic.'

'It could be. But that doesn't necessarily make it any easier to resolve.'

'If there's anything else I can do, just let me know. When's she due back?'

'She's got another week of compassionate leave. But she's champing at the bit to return. As far as work's concerned, she just wants to get on with it.'

'We just have to be careful. If she has another one of those attacks or whatever they were, it might put her at risk.'

'I know that, and so does she. That's why the medical tests are so important.'

'I'll stop fussing. We can't afford to lose people like Zoe. At the end of the day, we've a job to do.' Jennings looked up at the clock on the office wall. 'Speaking of which, I was supposed to be at a finance meeting five minutes ago. I'd better head up before they start making decisions without me.'

CHAPTER SEVENTEEN

'Anything?'

Amy placed her phone back on the table in front of her, then gave a tiny shake of the head. 'Nothing new. I can't believe it.'

Martin shook his head. 'Neither can I. It seems impossible.'

He'd wondered whether he even should be here. He might be the last person she'd want to have around. But there was no one else who could sit with her. She seemed almost oblivious to his presence except when, as just now, he addressed her directly. She seemed less distraught than he might have expected, but that was probably just because she was clinging on to the possibility of good news.

'How was Tom?' he asked.

Amy sighed. 'How do you think he was, Dad? He was the way Tom always is. Furious. I mean, supposedly worried. But mainly furious, because that's Tom. I don't think he cares a jot about Lucas. He's more interested in using this to get back at me.'

Martin nodded. It was how he'd always seen Tom, and he sometimes wondered why it had taken Amy so long to realise what he was really like. Or perhaps it hadn't. Perhaps she'd known all along but hadn't wanted to admit it. Certainly not to Martin, who'd made his disapproval of Tom clear from the start. He wondered whether Tom had ever been violent with her. She'd said not, and Martin had seen no evidence that she wasn't telling the truth. But he found it hard to believe that Tom's constant anger had never boiled over into something more physical.

It was nearly twenty-four hours since Lucas had gone missing. The size of the search party had grown over the previous day, with more police drafted in, joined by more volunteers. The police had also been encouraging locals to check their own houses and gardens, in case Lucas had somehow managed either to hide himself or to get trapped somewhere. By this point, given the scale of the search activity, it seemed unlikely that Lucas was being cared for by some well-meaning villager.

By now, Martin thought, the police would be considering more sinister explanations for Lucas's disappearance. Soon Martin's own role in the events would no doubt come into question. The police would be wondering whether it was really possible for Lucas to vanish so completely in those few minutes. If the boy wasn't found, this kind of investigation would always begin close to home.

Amy's phone buzzed again on the table. She hesitated a fraction of a second, as if saying a silent prayer, then took the call. Martin heard her say, 'Yes. No, I understand. Yes, he is. No, no problem.' Much more quickly than Martin had expected, she hung up.

'Tom again?' It was obvious that, whoever the caller had been, they had delivered no further news.

'No, that was the police.'

'But nothing new?'

'That wasn't the reason for the call, though they said there was nothing new to report. They were calling to check whether you were here.'

'Me? Why?' Martin could already feel a clutch of anxiety in his stomach.

'Because they want to talk to you, Dad. They're on their way over.'

CHAPTER EIGHTEEN

Sheena Pearson had been an MP for over eight years now, but she still felt uncomfortable in the Palace of Westminster. She occasionally looked with mild envy at some of her colleagues who'd been working – in some cases almost living – in the place for decades. They seemed at home here, steeped in the atmosphere, the traditions, the absurd ceremonials.

On her first day, she wandered around, lost and baffled, though the parliamentary staff had done their best to make her feel at ease. That sense of alienation had never really departed. She had no doubt that many of the more established Members, even in her own party, looked down on her because she was, in no particular order, female, relatively young and northern.

She wasn't the only person who felt that way, and she'd developed friendships with other MPs from the recent intakes who, she knew, shared her sentiments. At least they could exchange their collective experiences and feelings, but she couldn't help thinking it really didn't need to be this way. Practices were slowly being reformed, but the pace of change seemed little more than glacial.

In the end, she'd more or less managed to make the place work for her. She had a small but practical office in Portcullis House. She'd established a supportive team, both here and in her constituency. She'd learned how to work with the anti-quated bureaucracy of the House. Above all, she'd learned, at least in small ways, how to play the system. Who to speak to if she wanted to get things done. Who the real influencers were. Who could pull the right strings or press the right buttons.

Often, these people were not those you might expect or those in official positions of authority.

She'd also gradually worked out what her role as an MP entailed, or, perhaps more accurately, what she wanted it to entail. There was no real job description or role profile. There was a one-page summary of what the role ought to involve, covering its contribution to the legislature, to the constituency and to the party, but no real guidance as to how those various aspects of the job should be carried out. Some of the content of that document Sheena found mildly depressing – the assertion that 'members appear in the Chamber to speak rather than to listen,' and the frank acknowledgement that, most of the time, parliamentary debate 'has only a marginal effect on major decisions'. The document concluded that MPs' roles are 'largely tailored to their own needs, capabilities and ambitions'. Thanks a bunch for that, pal, Sheena had thought at the time.

So she'd had to work it out for herself. She'd watched and talked to other MPs she admired – not necessarily a hugely expansive group – and learned from their experiences. She'd tried different approaches and worked out which were likely to deliver the most benefit. Above all, she'd concentrated on what might deliver most benefit to those she was representing. People like Jude Parrish, who'd been the main focus of her thought that day.

Sheena had spent much of the morning in meetings, and had asked Emily Caddick, her parliamentary assistant, to carry out some research on her behalf. They were sitting in the lobby of Portcullis House, with coffees and sandwiches in front of them, discussing what Emily had discovered about the impending release of Ben Yardley, Parrish's ex-partner.

'First, Jude Parrish is right. Yardley's due out on licence in a couple of weeks. He's currently in Sudbury prison, preparing for release.'

'They don't think there's a risk to the public?'

'That's the assessment. He's been a model prisoner, apparently. Kept his head down and got on with it. Spent most of his time studying. Granted parole at the first time of asking.'

'And the terms of the licence?'

'Main condition is to keep well away from Jude Parrish and the child, as well as all the usual stuff.'

'They think he'll stick to the terms of the licence?'

'I asked the question bluntly. They said there was no reason not to think so. He's shown remorse for what he'd done. He claims he's had time to reflect, and now realises that what he'd thought at the time to be reasonable behaviour was actually unacceptable.' Emily smiled. 'I'm paraphrasing, but not much. They read out the relevant section of the parole report to me.'

'Forgive me if I look cynical,' Sheena said. 'I saw him in court. When he was found guilty, he looked genuinely surprised. I don't think it was an act. He sincerely believed he'd done nothing wrong. He was even more shocked at the sentencing, as if he'd never expected a custodial sentence, though I assume his lawyer would have warned him. I'm all for forgiveness and giving the benefit of the doubt...' Sheena took a mouthful of coffee.

'But?' Emily prompted.

'I can't really see it. He didn't strike me as the introspective type.'

'Prison can change people.'

'I'd be delighted to be proved wrong. Especially for Jude's sake. But he struck me as a smart manipulative young man. Even Jude thought for a long time that his behaviour was perfectly reasonable, that she was the one in the wrong. That's the way these people work, isn't it? I wouldn't be remotely surprised if he's managed to pull the wool over the eyes of the people assessing him for release.' She shook her head. 'Why didn't Jude Parrish know this was happening? I'm sure she was registered with the Victim Contact Scheme. It was something I checked at the time. She should have been informed of the parole hearing and given the chance to provide a victim statement. This shouldn't have been sprung on her out of the blue.'

Emily flicked back through the pages of her notebook. 'When I asked that question, there was a bit of a kerfuffle. It seems to have been a cock-up. At first, they told me she hadn't been registered with the Victim Contact Scheme.'

'I'm sure she was.'

'You're right. I asked Carla to check in our files.' Carla MacDonald was the administrator in Sheena's constituency. 'It was advice you gave her, and you checked it had happened. So I called back and told them she definitely was.'

'And their response was?'

'A long silence at first. Then they said there was no record on the files. They're looking into it, but it sounds like it was a breakdown in communications.'

'And some poor overworked probation officer will no doubt take the blame. We get so many stories like this. Public services working on a shoestring. People do their best, but things fall between the cracks.'

'Whatever the reason, it meant that Jude Parrish didn't get informed about the hearing and didn't get the chance to submit a victim statement. Luckily, the Community Offender Manager had thought to include restrictions in the licence to prevent Yardley from approaching her.'

'That's something. I don't want to drop anyone in it, but we need to find out how this happened and make sure it doesn't happen again. But that's for another day. Is there anything we can do about Yardley's release?'

'Given that Jude Parrish wasn't given an opportunity to contribute to the parole hearing, she can request a reconsideration of the decision simply on procedural grounds. That might delay his release, but I don't know if it'll make much difference in the end. The board were made fully aware of the nature of Yardley's offences, and took that into account in making their decision. They just felt that, based on the assessments, he was unlikely to reoffend or be a risk to the public.'

'I'm the last person to want anyone to languish in prison unnecessarily. But this one worries me. We'd better get back to Jude Parrish and see what she wants to do. She may prefer to get his release over with and hope the protections work okay. I know she finds it stressful having to deal with this. It's got to be her decision.'

'I'll see what she says.'

'Thanks, Em. And thanks for all you've done on this. Just wish we had more hours in the day.' She glanced at her watch, seeing that she was already running late for her next appointment. 'Or at least fewer pointless meetings.'

CHAPTER NINETEEN

'First of all, I'm sorry to say we've nothing new to report as yet. We've expanded the search area and drafted in more support.'

Martin had been unsure what to expect when he'd opened the door. He'd half-expected they'd have sent out some stone-faced detective to grill him about Lucas's disappearance. But the person standing on the doorstep had been a uniformed female PC, a woman probably in her late twenties, who looked as awkward as Martin was feeling.

His second thought, on seeing a female officer, was that she'd actually come bearing bad news. She'd obviously sensed his reaction, hence her opening words. 'But we will keep you and his mother fully informed. Do you mind if I come inside?'

He led her into the living room, where Amy was already sitting. Martin forestalled any anxiety on Amy's part by saying, 'Nothing new, I'm afraid.'

Amy nodded. 'At least it's not bad news. Can I get you a tea or coffee?'

The officer shook her head. 'No, that's fine. It would be useful if I could talk to your father alone, though.'

'We can go through to my place,' Martin said. 'We've a kind of granny flat set up. Or in this case a grandad flat.' It was a line he'd used jokingly before, and he'd said the words without thinking. It was only as he spoke that he realised the word 'grandad' had caught in his throat.

'That sounds good. Then we don't need to disturb your daughter.'

Martin's flat was accessed internally through a door off the hallway. He ushered the officer through and directed her towards his small living room. 'How can I help you?'

'Let me introduce myself. PC Gill Doyle. I just want to have a chat with you about the circumstances of Lucas's disappearance.'

'Circumstances?'

'We want to make sure we have as much information as possible about what happened.'

'I explained to the officers when they first got there...'

'We do appreciate that. But at that stage we'd hoped to find Lucas without any difficulty. That obviously hasn't happened, so we need to make sure we've not missed anything that might help in finding him.' She smiled sympathetically at him. 'Believe me, Mr Pritchard, I wouldn't be spending your or my time on this, if we didn't think there was a possibility it might be useful.'

'Yes, of course.' Martin felt slightly dizzy, as if his usual mental bearings had been taken from him. 'What can I tell you?'

'Perhaps the best thing would be to start from the beginning. When you first saw Lucas that morning.' Doyle had taken out a notebook and was carefully noting down the details of the interview.

'I'm always a pretty early riser. Must have been up about seven thirty. Lucas gets up early too, at least when it's not a school day. If his mum's still asleep, he comes through here because he knows I'll be up. I think he appeared about eight on Sunday. I was just eating some toast, so I made him some cereal and got him a drink. Is this helping?'

'Just carry on, Mr Pritchard. It's possible that anything might turn out to be useful. So you had breakfast with Lucas. Then what?'

'He was excited by the snow. We don't get much of it these days, and this was the first really heavy snowfall he'd seen. I could see the snow wasn't going to last long, so I suggested heading out once we finished breakfast.'

'To go sledging?'

'I'd bought him a sledge the previous winter when we had a bit of snow, but there was never enough for him to use it properly. I thought this might be the only chance he got this year.'

'And you let your daughter know where you were going?'

'I never take Lucas out without making sure she knows. I told Lucas to go and tell her before we set off.'

'You're sure he did that?'

'Pretty sure. He's good about that sort of thing. But I also left her a note. I knew that if she was half asleep, she might not have taken in the details of what Lucas had told her, so I wrote her a note and left it by the kettle, where she'd see it. And of course she has my mobile number anyway, if she was worried for any reason.'

Doyle was still scribbling in her notebook. 'Then you took him up on to the moorland?'

'I got him into his shoes and coat – not always the quickest task with Lucas – then we set off.'

'Why did you go where you did?'

'It's the most suitable spot round here for youngsters. I used to take his mum sledging there when she was small. I thought there might be other people already there – it's usually quite a popular spot – but it was too early.'

'You didn't see anyone else around?'

'Not another soul.'

'There were no other cars?'

'I didn't see any. Once we were on the slope, we were out of sight of the road, so some might have gone past, but I didn't register anything.' He paused. 'There's not much else to say, really. We walked up the slope, me dragging the sledge, found a suitable starting point and Lucas sledged down. He did that, well, quite a few times. That's what they're like at that age. Once they're stuck into something, they just want to do it over and over again. Then he started falling off. Accidentally, the first time, then on purpose. He thought it was hilarious.'

'Tell me about his disappearance. If it's not too painful.'

'It's not easy to talk about. There's no question in my mind that this is my fault. I don't think I was negligent – or at least I hope to God I wasn't – but I did allow myself to become distracted. Just for a minute or two, but it was obviously enough.'

'Tell me what happened.'

'There's nothing really to tell. I was just admiring the view. It had been a while since I'd been up there and I'd forgotten how impressive it was. When I looked down again, Lucas had vanished.'

'How long do you think you'd been looking away?'

Martin was silent for a moment, trying to get the events clear in his own mind. 'It felt like just a few seconds. But it's hard to be sure, isn't it?' Even to his own ears, his words sounded unconvincing.

'So it could have been – what? Two or three minutes? Or longer?' For the first time, Doyle's tone sounded accusatory.

'Not more than a couple of minutes, I'd have thought.'

'What did you do after that?'

'At first I thought he'd either just wandered out of sight or was hiding somewhere. I assumed he was playing a game. There didn't seem to be anywhere for him to go.'

'How long did you search for him? I mean, before you contacted anyone else.'

'I don't know exactly. Fifteen or twenty minutes, I suppose. Long enough to check he wasn't hiding anywhere obvious. Then I called 999. I didn't know if they'd take me seriously, but, well, I'm glad to say they did. Then while I was waiting for the police to arrive, I went into the village and knocked on some doors, in case anyone down there had seen him.'

Doyle was still writing in her notebook. 'I just want to get the timeline straight in my head. You said Lucas came in to see you around eight. What time do you think it was when you left the house?'

'About eight thirty, I'd guess.'

'How long did it take you to get up there?'

'It's about a twenty-minute drive.'

'So you'd have been there around nine?'

'That sounds right.'

Doyle flicked back a few pages in her notebook. 'Your 999 call was taken by the control room at 10:32 a.m. Does that sound right?'

'Well, it must be, if that's what they're saying.'

Doyle nodded, as if his response had confirmed some suspicion on her part. 'So if you were searching for Lucas for some twenty minutes before that, it suggests that he first went missing at around 10:10 a.m.'

'I suppose.'

'So if you arrived around nine a.m., you must have been playing with Lucas for over an hour before he disappeared.'

'That all makes sense. I couldn't say how long we'd been playing. I was just watching Lucas. Watching him enjoy himself.' He felt the words catch in his throat as he spoke. 'I didn't keep track of the time.'

'You spent the whole time doing that? Just watching Lucas sledging down the hill, over and over again?'

'That was all he wanted to do. You know what kids are like at that age. They're either happy to keep doing the same thing over and over, or they get bored very quickly. This was the first time he'd ever been sledging properly, so he was just taking the opportunity to keep doing it as long as he could.'

'I don't know much about young children,' Doyle said. 'One day, maybe. But I'm sure you're right. It just seems rather a long time to keep doing the same thing.'

'I can only tell you what happened. Look, I'm sorry but I don't really see the point of these questions. What do you think's happened to Lucas?'

'I don't know, Mr Pritchard.' She sounded weary. 'I'll be honest with you. We've searched the vicinity very rigorously

89

indeed. It seems increasingly unlikely that he simply wandered off. We have to consider other possibilities.'

Martin was staring at her, a sick feeling in his stomach. 'Such as?'

'At the moment, we're conducting searches in all the houses in the village. We'd also like to conduct a search here.'

'Here? Why here?'

'It's routine in situations like this, Mr Pritchard.'

'Are you suggesting that I might be involved in Lucas's disappearance?'

'We have to explore every avenue, Mr Pritchard. One of the reasons I'm here is to seek your – and your daughter's – permission to carry out a search. We'd rather have your agreement than have to take a more formal route.'

'I'll need to speak to Amy. She's going through hell as it is.'

'That's why I wanted to speak to you first. I thought the question might come better from you than from me?'

'I'll go and check with her. But we don't really have a choice, do we?'

'Not really, I'm afraid. We'd just rather make it as easy as we can.'

Martin wanted to feel angry, frustrated. He wanted to tell Doyle that the police were wasting their time. That they should be out there searching the moorlands rather than chasing shadows. But he felt as if the ground had been snatched from under him. He no longer knew what to believe.

'I'll go and see what she says.'

CHAPTER TWENTY

Zoe paused in the doorway. The place was busier than she'd expected on a Monday lunchtime, and she gazed around the occupied tables, trying to identify someone who might be Elaine Simmonds.

'Table for one?' a voice said from behind her.

Zoe turned to find one of the young waitresses beaming amiably at her.

'Actually, I've arranged to meet someone. I'm not sure if she's arrived already. We've not met face to face before, so I don't know...'

The waitress nodded and pointed across the room. 'The lady over there said she was waiting for someone. Could she be the person?'

The woman in question looked slightly younger than Zoe had expected, although certainly old enough to be her mother. She was well-dressed and fitted easily into the middle-class ambience of the cafe. If this was Elaine Simmonds, she wasn't exactly what Zoe had been expecting. On the other hand, Zoe wasn't entirely sure what she had been expecting. 'She might be. Thanks. I'll go and check.'

As Zoe eased her way through the tables to the corner where the woman was sitting, she looked up. 'Zoe?'

'So you must be Elaine. Don't say you recognised me.'

'The last time I saw you, you looked very different.' The woman seemed nervous, Zoe thought. 'Much smaller, for a start. You've turned out very well.'

Zoe seated herself diagonally opposite Simmonds. 'I'm not sure about that. But I'm doing all right. You're looking well yourself.'

'Well, that's a long story.' Simmonds looked around anxiously. 'I hope you didn't mind coming over here. I thought this would be a good place to meet. It's usually busy enough around lunchtime so you can talk easily, without feeling the world's listening in.'

When Zoe had phoned Simmonds the previous day to confirm she was willing to meet, she'd assumed the meeting wouldn't take place for at least a few days. She'd been mildly taken aback when Simmonds had asked whether she might be available the following day. Gary had suspected it might be a tactic to wrong-foot Zoe, but Zoe had felt that, if she was going to meet Elaine Simmonds, she might as well do it as soon as possible.

She hadn't really cared much about the venue, and had happily accepted Simmonds's suggestion that they should meet in the cafe at the Chatsworth Estate's farm shop. She'd visited a few times with Gary, so it didn't feel completely alien territory. 'It's a nice place,' she said now. 'Do you live near here?'

'Just outside Bakewell.'

They were briefly interrupted by the waitress coming to take their order. Simmonds had insisted that this should be her treat, so Zoe limited herself to a sandwich and a pot of tea. She didn't want to be any more indebted to this woman – even in the most trivial of ways – until she knew much more about her.

When the waitress had departed, Zoe said, 'This has all been something of a shock, but I'm sure you realise that.'

'I've thought about nothing else for the last few weeks. I don't know if I should have handled it differently.'

'I don't want you to take this the wrong way, but I've done some checking up. It's not that I'm doubting your word, but I did want to ensure I wasn't being misled.'

Simmonds nodded. She was an attractive woman, Zoe thought. She presumed Simmonds must at least be in her early fifties, but she looked younger. Her clothes appeared, to Zoe's inexpert eye, expensive and well chosen to match her dark hair and pale colouring. 'I'd be surprised if you hadn't carried out some checks, given your occupation.'

'You know what I do?'

'I understand you're a police officer. A detective.'

The information was hardly a secret, and no doubt could be found by anyone who had Zoe's name. Even so, she found herself surprised that Simmonds had already learned so much about her. 'We're taught to be sceptical.'

'Quite right. So what did you find out?'

'So far, I've only confirmed that I was adopted. My adoptive parents went to some lengths to conceal that truth from me. It hadn't even occurred to me that I'd never actually seen my birth certificate.'

'I'm sure their intentions were good.'

'I imagine they thought so, anyway. They were very, well, let's say conservative.'

They fell silent while their drinks were delivered. Simmonds took a sip of her coffee, gazing at Zoe. 'I hope they were good parents to you.'

'They were. They had their quirks, like all parents. But they were kind to me. They brought me up well. I've nothing to complain about. I just wish they'd felt able to be more open about this. At my age, it's a shock to discover you're not who you always thought you were.'

'You're the same person you always were. Nothing changes that.'

'Rationally, I guess that's true. It's not how it feels at the moment. And as things stand – and, again, I hope you'll take this in the spirit it's intended – I've only your word that you're my mother.'

'Though, no doubt, you'll be checking that out.'

'Of course. In the meantime, I'm happy to take you on trust and listen to what you have to say. Why did you want to track me down? Especially after all these years.'

'There's a reason for that, which I'll come to. I've struggled with this. I decided years ago it wouldn't be right for me to intrude into your life. I'd made my decision at the time, and you've had to live with the consequences of that, for good or ill. I felt I couldn't have it both ways. I couldn't hand you over to a new life, then try to bring you back when it suited me. I still don't want to pressurise you into taking this further. It's entirely up to you to decide whether you want to see me again after today.'

'That may depend on whether you're telling me the truth, of course.' Zoe tried to defuse the bluntness of her words with a smile.

'I appreciate that. But you'll find that I am. I'm happy to take each step as it comes. For the present, I'm just delighted we've been able to meet.'

Zoe was wondering where to take this next. Gary had warned her not to go too far, not to allow herself to become too emotionally embroiled with this woman until they were sure she was telling the truth. It was no doubt sound advice, but Zoe felt there were things she needed to know.

'So what is the story, then? Why did you have me adopted?' Everything she said sounded too blunt, too bold, but there was little she could do about that. She needed to know the truth, or as close to the truth as she could get.

'It's not a very unusual story. I was very young. Just seventeen. My mum was a single parent and struggled to make ends meet. I was basically just a troublemaker in those days. Hated school. Hated everything, basically. My friends were all people my mum heartily disapproved of, probably for very good reason. Then there was Liam Crane. My boyfriend, or at least that's how I thought of him. I'm not sure he shared the same cosy view. Few years older than me. Early twenties. And, though I didn't realise it at the time, a nasty piece of work. Not with me, not initially. That came later. But he wasn't averse to giving a good beating to other men who crossed him. Not by himself, of course. Always with a little coterie of hangers-on to back him up.'

'Sounds like a charmer.'

'Funnily enough, that's exactly what I thought he was. Cool, mature, in control. It never occurred to me he was basically just a thug. He'd already served a custodial sentence for assault, though I didn't know that. You can probably guess the rest. The relationship developed. I was desperate to get away from my mum, so moved into some rented flat with him, working my socks off waitressing and the like so we could pay the rent, while he mainly lounged around at home. After a while, he started to get violent. I walked out and went back to my mum's.'

'Good for you. So then what happened?'

'Liam came round and tried to force me to go back to him. My mum saw him for what he was and defended me, even in the face of all his threats. We both thought he was bluffing.'

'Why did he want you back anyway?'

'Partly because I provided the income he couldn't be bothered to earn. But that was never the point with Liam. The point was I'd crossed him. I'd exercised my own free will rather than doing what he wanted. He didn't particularly want me, but he wanted to be obeyed.'

Zoe noticed that Simmonds had barely touched her sandwich. She carefully cut her own into a smaller portion and then chewed on it before offering a response. 'Are you saying he wasn't bluffing?'

'Liam wasn't a bluffer. If he'd allowed his bluff to be called, it would have destroyed whatever credibility he had. He wasn't going to let me get away with challenging his authority.' She picked up her sandwich and stared at it for a moment, as if unsure of its purpose, then dropped it back on to the plate. 'Anyway, shortly after that I discovered I was pregnant with you. I'm sure Liam wasn't the father. I had another very brief relationship almost immediately after I left Liam. Just a one-night stand with some guy I met in the place I was working.'

'So if you don't think Crane's my father, what's the issue?'

'The issue is that Liam convinced himself he was. It gave him another grievance. He came round yet again, banging on the door, shouting the odds. Then I was attacked when leaving work one night. It looked like a mugging. My handbag was taken, and was found later with some cash and my bank cards missing. But there were three of them, which seemed over the top for mugging a solitary waitress. More to the point, I let them have the handbag straightaway – it wasn't like I had anything of great value – but they continued to attack me. I was given a pretty savage beating.'

'Jesus. I'm sorry.'

'It's a long time ago now.' She gestured towards her own face. 'At the time, I thought this was ruined for good. A broken arm, cuts and bruises. The worst part was that I was terrified it would affect the pregnancy, but fortunately that wasn't an issue.'

'You must have recovered well. There are no signs I can see.'

'I was lucky. It took months, but I did recover.'

'What happened to Crane?'

'Nothing. Not about that, anyway. I was afraid to make too much of his involvement, in case he decided to take further revenge against me or my mum. I told the police I didn't know who was behind it. They treated it as a straightforward mugging. The only upside was that Liam left me alone after that. He'd made his point.' She pushed her sandwich away from her, untouched. 'But I was still terrified about what would happen when you were born. That Liam might try to harm you. It was enough to change my views about adoption. I didn't want to spend my life – or for you to spend your life – scared of Liam. I talked it over and over with my mum, and in the end I decided there was no alternative. It would mean you could start a new life. It would keep you safe. And you were likely to end up with far more advantages than if I'd brought you up.'

Zoe was silent for a moment. 'What happened to Crane?'

'Everything you'd expect. He might have escaped justice for what he did to me, but it caught up with him soon enough. He was involved in all kinds of stuff. In the end, he was convicted of GBH and sent down again. After that, he was in and out of prison a few times, and ended up doing a long stretch for manslaughter. Something like his attack on me, a beating that was meted out by him and a couple of his cronies to someone who'd crossed them. They did enough damage that the victim died. Liam was lucky to avoid a murder charge, but with his track record, he was still given fifteen years.'

'You said at the start that you had a reason for tracking me down now?'

Simmonds raised her head and looked around the room, as if she were suddenly conscious they were sitting in a public space. When she spoke again, her voice was lower, as if she was concerned about being overheard. 'The reason is Liam Crane.'

'What about Crane?'

'This is mostly second- or third-hand. I've not had any direct contact with Crane since all those years ago. At least until… well, I'm come on to that. I'd hoped he didn't even know where I lived. But I'd kept in contact with one or two people that he knows. He got out of prison a year or two back. He's kept his nose clean since then, or at least he hasn't been caught. But he's still the same Liam Crane, and from what I'm told, he's not in a good way. Most of his old scams have dried up, and someone like Liam's never going to find – or probably even look for – legitimate work. He's a bitter man. He blames everyone else for his problems, just as he always did. And he's looking for, well, not even revenge, I don't think. He's looking for recompense.'

This all sounded overly dramatic to Zoe. She'd dealt with plenty of villains in her time, and most of them were petty small-time nobodies. 'Recompense?'

'He thinks he's owed.'

'I'm not sure I understand. Owed what?'

'Owed for what he's lost, I suppose. Owed by the supposed friends and contacts that he thinks have let him down. Owed by his past business partners for the money he thinks they've scammed him out of. Owed by people like me and his no doubt other countless partners for denying him the life he thinks he deserves. In short, owed by the universe.'

'Where do I come into this?'

'You come into it because, from what I hear, you're one of the debtors.'

'Me? I don't owe him anything. I'm sorry. I really don't understand.'

'He believes you're responsible for stealing from him his only opportunity for fatherhood.'

'That's ridiculous. An hour ago I didn't even know he existed.'

'None of this makes sense or is rational. The truth is that, for all his bravado, Liam can't really cope with life. He's smart enough, in a streetwise way. But he's always bluffed his way through, using violence and intimidation to get what he can't get in any other way. But he thinks he's better than that. He's a man with a massive chip on his shoulder, and during his time in prison he's no doubt allowed his grievances to fester. He blames everyone else for the mess he's in, and now that includes you.'

'Why would it include me? I mean, why would he take an interest in me now?'

'Because he's obsessive.' Simmonds fell silent again for a moment before continuing. 'Again, this is just second- or third-hand. But I work in the legal field myself now, and I've had some dealings with people who came across Liam inside. What I've heard is that, while he was in prison, he fell in with some of these men's rights types. You know, the kind who've managed to persuade themselves that all their problems in life don't stem from the fact that they're sad inadequates but from the fact that it's men who are really the poor oppressed minority.'

'I've come across them,' Zoe said. 'Usually protesting about the fact they're not being allowed access to their children just because they've a history of domestic violence or abuse.'

'Exactly. Well, from what I hear, that's Liam now.'

'I'm a bit too old to be at the centre of a custody battle.'

'This isn't a joke, Zoe. It really isn't. I know Liam. I know what he's like even now. He's a vicious bastard. I know what he did to me all those years ago, and I know what he might be capable of doing to you.'

For the first time in the conversation, Zoe felt a first clutch of fear. It was the way Simmonds's tone had changed. Previously, she'd been nervous, a little tense, but nothing more. Now, it was as if, just for a moment, she'd allowed her real emotions to show. She was scared herself, Zoe thought. Beneath the polished, prosperous exterior, there was genuine fear.

'He doesn't even know me,' Zoe said. 'He doesn't know who I am or where I am.'

Simmonds stared back at her, and it was as if the burble of noise around them had suddenly died away. 'He does, though,' she said. 'He does know. That's why I'm here. He knows because he made me tell him.'

CHAPTER TWENTY-ONE

Annie drove through the village, following the directions she'd been given, and turned into the car park of the village hall. The place was already half-filled with marked cars and a couple of police vans. It was clear that a substantial contingent of officers had been allocated to the search.

Stuart Jennings had called her as she was driving back from meeting the pathologist who had conducted the post-mortem on Alice Evans. Jennings's opening questions had been about the pathologist's conclusions, and he'd sounded dispirited by her answers. 'He's sure, is he? That we're looking at murder?'

'Murder or manslaughter, anyway. It was all couched in the usual caveats, but I wasn't left with much doubt. He reckoned the head injuries were unlikely to be consistent with simply striking something during the fall. More likely caused by a blow from a relatively sharp instrument.'

'I was hoping you might come back with some good news.'

'I'm only the messenger. I imagine Alison Evans wasn't overjoyed to be killed either.'

'It's just that we're going to have a hell of a lot on our plate. You know I reckoned this missing child case might be heading in our direction. It looks as if I was right.'

'They've not made any progress then?'

'Nothing at all. They're continuing the search of the countryside, but getting less optimistic by the hour. If they haven't found him out there by now, it's unlikely they're going to. They've moved on to checking the houses in the village, but again so far without success. So now they're moving on to other possibilities.'

'Such as?'

'First, that he might have been snatched by some motorist passing through the area. In which case, he could be anywhere and anything might have happened to him. If he was just taken opportunistically, we could be in for a very long haul. The second possibility is some kind of family involvement.'

'Is that likely in this case?'

'It's usually the first place we look, isn't it? And the family background sounds fairly tangled.'

'So you reckon it's going to end up on our plate?'

'I've just been told so. Obviously, the search will continue so it might come to nothing, one way or another, but for the moment it looks as if it's heading our way.'

'You can't run two major investigations.'

'Too right, I can't. Trouble is, we're facing the usual resourcing issues. We're all supposed to work miracles. The powers that be are currently running round like the proverbial decapitated poultry to identify a suitable SIO, but in the meantime they've asked me to get things moving. I'm just heading up to have a chat with the officer currently running the search. Since you're out and about already, why don't you join us? We can get a sense of what's needed. Two heads are better than one and all that.'

She'd thought about pointing out that her journey from Derby to police HQ didn't take her anywhere near the location of the search. But she'd welcomed the fact that he was actively seeking her input. It was a sign of how their relationship had developed since his arrival. 'Sure. Just tell me where to go.'

The village hall had been temporarily commandeered by the police as a makeshift headquarters for the search, with volunteers from the village providing refreshments to those involved. The hall itself comprised a single large space, with a small stage at one end that was presumably used for various local events, and a kitchenette by the entrance. Tables and chairs had been set up around the room, a couple of which were occupied by a mix of uniformed officers and villagers taking a break from the search. Jennings was sitting at a table just below the stage, talking to a uniformed sergeant. He looked up as Annie entered and waved her over to join them.

The sergeant pushed himself up from his seat and held out his hand to greet her. 'Dick Pargetter. You must be DI Delamere. I've just been hearing about you.'

'Annie, please. And don't believe a word Stuart tells you.'

'That's a pity because it was all positive.' Pargetter was a slightly rotund figure, almost a caricature of a village bobby, with his neat haircut and amiable features. 'Good to meet you, even in difficult circumstances.'

'I take it there've been no further developments?'

'Nothing. I've pretty much given up on the idea that the boy just wandered off. We'd have found him by now, one way or another.'

'What about the family? Has the grandfather been interviewed?'

'Aye. He's sticking by his account. We're in the process of searching the house where he and the boy's mother live.'

'You told me on the phone that there were some issues in the family,' Jennings said. 'What sort of issues?'

'That's the other thing that made me decide to refer it back. There's some history there. It was something we first picked up from the grandfather when we were getting permission to search the house. As we were leaving, he asked if we were searching the boy's father's house. Said we might be better off focusing our attentions there.'

Jennings raised an eyebrow. 'Rather than wasting your time searching his?'

'Well, that's what we thought at first. But then I checked the files and discovered that the father does have a record. Relatively minor stuff, but he did serve a short custodial sentence for common assault. There were also a couple of domestic call-outs by the boy's mother. In both cases, she'd claimed he was abusing her, then backtracked when the officers visited.'

'Not necessarily a nice guy, then?' Jennings said.

'I'd already formed my own impression of him. He turned up early on in the search and started abusing the grandfather. Maybe understandable enough, but he's been throwing his weight around since. Not made himself popular with the volunteers from the village, even though they're obviously cutting him a lot of slack.'

'Reasonable for him to be on edge, surely?' Annie said.

Pargetter shrugged. 'Of course. Except that, according to the boy's mother, he hasn't really had any kind of relationship with the boy previously. Seems that young Lucas was the product of a fairly short-lived relationship. Father was reluctant to take any responsibility for the boy, and the split was pretty acrimonious. But recently the father's been saying he wants access rights.'

'Is that right? Without any success, presumably?'

'Certainly so far. He's not named on the birth certificate so he doesn't have any automatic rights, and I can't imagine any family court would support his application. The mother's never pursued him for any child support, mainly because she wanted nothing to do with him.'

'So how come he turned up for the search?' Annie said. 'Who told him Lucas had gone missing?'

'The mother, apparently. She reckons she was out of her mind with worry by that stage, and she felt she ought to tell him. She hadn't really thought he'd do anything, but she reckons he seemed more affected by the news than she expected.'

'I take it someone's interviewed the father?' Jennings said.

Pargetter nodded. 'Story consistent with what the mother told us. Says she phoned him on Sunday morning to break the news. His first reaction was to head over to join the search. He acknowledges he was a bit heavy-handed with the grandfather, but claims it was just because he was so worried. Claims he's been desperate to be a proper father to Lucas, but the mother's blocked him at every turn.'

'Maybe with good reason,' Annie said, 'if he was abusive towards her.'

'He denies all that. Reckons the incidents when we were called out were just heated arguments. But he would say that, wouldn't he?'

'So both the father and the grandfather are potentially worth investigating,' Jennings said. 'The question is, if we assume young Lucas didn't just wander away, what could have happened to him? If the grandfather's involved, I guess anything's possible. We've only his word for the timings or even for the fact that Lucas came up here at all.'

'What about the father?' Annie said. 'If he's behind this, how could he have snatched Lucas? Assuming the grandfather's account is accurate, there is only a short window in which it could have been done.'

'I was looking at that,' Pargetter said. 'If you stand where the grandfather claims he was standing, there's a fairly long stretch of the road that's invisible to you. It would be possible for a car to have stopped there without being seen, if it turned up after the boy had started sledging. If the boy wandered in that direction – or was encouraged to wander in that direction – it's conceivable he could have been taken without the grandfather being aware. Especially if the grandfather was distracted for a bit longer than he thinks. He reckons he's no memory of hearing a car, but it's possible he didn't register it, if by then he was more focused on looking at where Lucas had gone.'

'So that could potentially put the father in the frame,' Annie said, 'or it could suggest someone just snatched Lucas opportunistically. It would have had to be the act of a few seconds, but it wouldn't be the first time that's happened. I assume there were no other witnesses?'

'Nobody,' Pargetter said. 'The grandfather reckons he'd expected there to be one or two other people up there sledging, but it was relatively early. There doesn't seem to have been anyone out and about in the village.'

'Convenient for the grandfather, maybe,' Jennings commented. 'He might have picked this spot because he knew it was likely to be quiet. But we're getting ahead of ourselves. This is all speculation. We need to get this kicked off properly.' He turned to Pargetter. 'For the moment, you'd better continue the search. We may still find Lucas. I'll get everything sorted and get the inquiry launched. You've done a good job so far, so that gives us plenty to build on. I'll kick it off as acting SIO but I'm expecting that someone else will take it over, as I'm already in the middle of another major inquiry.'

'Aye, I heard that,' Pargetter said. 'That poor lass over at the pub. Sad business. You don't suspect foul play over that one, do you?'

Jennings exchanged a glance with Annie. 'Too early to say yet. But it's an unexplained death.'

Pargetter looked appropriately sceptical at Jennings's response. 'They seem to be suffering from a bout of ill luck round these parts, anyway. Let's hope they're wrong about trouble coming in threes.'

'I bloody well hope so,' Jennings said. 'I don't reckon we've the resources to handle a third investigation.'

CHAPTER TWENTY-TWO

'That's all you can tell me? You've really no idea?'

'I don't know what to say to you, Margaret. I'm keeping you fully up to speed as far as I can, but they're playing their cards very close to their chests.'

'And meanwhile I'm left here twisting in the wind?'

'That's how it is, Margaret. You know that. You've been on the other end of this stuff often enough.'

Margaret Delamere couldn't deny that. It was a familiar technique. The power of silence. Giving suspects just enough rope and waiting till they felt like hanging themselves. She didn't know if this was exactly what was happening here, but it certainly felt like it.

She was standing at the window of her penthouse flat, gazing down at the Derby cityscape. It was a long while since she'd actually enjoyed this view. When she'd first moved into the flat, it had felt like a liberation, a visible manifestation of the freedom she was enjoying in retirement. At that point her life had been on the up. Everything was going her way. She was acquiring a reputation, a profile, building a whole new career in the media.

Then, quite suddenly, all that had come crashing down. The media career – which, she now realised, had never been anything more than a mirage – had fizzled away. She was nothing but a retired senior police officer. And now a senior police officer being investigated for corruption. Everything was gone.

She'd hoped at first that they'd just brush the history under the carpet, the way they had before. But it was a changed world.

The new chief constable had things to prove and wasn't afraid to air dirty linen in public. Just as long, she thought, as it was his predecessors' dirty linen rather than his own.

'You've really heard nothing more?'

Her solicitor, Lawrence Rodgers, gave an exasperated sigh at the other end of the line. 'Believe me, Margaret, as soon as I hear anything, I'll be straight on the phone to you. All I know is that it's now with the CPS.'

'And we've no idea how long they're likely to take before making a decision?' It was a pointless question. She'd had plenty of dealings with the CPS. She knew full well that the decision would take as long as it took. That was how these things worked. She was asking these questions only because she was desperate to regain some semblance of control.

'We've been through this endless times, Margaret. No, I've no idea. I've asked the question repeatedly. I've made it clear how stressful this is for you. But they've a job to do and they'll do it how they want to. Nothing you or I say is going to change that.'

'I know you're doing everything you can, Lawrence. I appreciate that. It's just...' She trailed off, unsure how to finish the sentence.

'I understand. It must be torture for you. I presume you've had no luck in getting any information through other channels?'

He meant Annie, Margaret thought. He knew she had a daughter in the force, and he'd suggested before that she might be able to find out more from informal sources than he could through official routes. She'd told him then that she had no desire to embroil her daughter in this mess any more than she was already.

What she hadn't told him was that she'd barely spoken to Annie since all this had happened, and at present she had no intention of doing so. It was too late. They'd had their chance at reconciliation, and they'd not taken it. Margaret had never been an affectionate mother, and she and Annie hadn't been close. Now, it felt as if what little relationship they had shared was irretrievably fractured.

'I've no desire to put my daughter in a difficult position,' she said to Rodgers. 'I suspect I've made her life quite difficult enough already.'

'Well, I've told you all I can tell you for the moment, Margaret. Obviously, I'll keep chivvying them, but they work at their own pace. I will let you know the moment I hear anything.'

'I know you will, Lawrence. And I appreciate you're doing everything you can. I'm very grateful.' There was no point in alienating Rodgers as well, she thought. She'd managed to drive away pretty much everyone else. Her former colleagues were understandably treating her as a pariah, afraid their own reputations might be tainted by association. Her contacts in the media had melted away overnight, and the phone hadn't rung since the news had broken.

She ended the call and walked back into the kitchen. On the work surface by the door there was an unopened bottle of single malt. Beside it sat several boxes of painkillers. She'd been amassing them over the preceding weeks, buying a packet or a couple of packets every time she went shopping.

It wasn't that she had any intention of doing anything with them, she told herself. It was more that she was testing herself, proving she really did have the resilience to get through this.

She walked over and picked up the bottle of whisky, resisting the urge to unscrew the top. She placed it back on the worktop, sliding it back against the tiling. Then she turned and walked over to fill the kettle.

Not today, she told herself. Not today.

CHAPTER TWENTY-THREE

'He threatened you?'

'He didn't need to. Not explicitly. That's not Liam's way.' Elaine Simmonds was speaking more quietly now, as if afraid she'd be overheard, though the burble of chatter around them was undiminished.

'When was this?'

'A couple of weeks back. He called me one evening. Out of the blue. Unknown number, obviously, but stupidly I took the call.'

'That must have been a shock.'

'A complete shock. He was someone I never expected or wanted to hear from again. I'd gone out of my way to make sure he wouldn't easily be able to contact me.'

'So how did he?'

'I don't know exactly. He has his ways. I'm guessing he threatened people until someone was too scared not to tell him what he wanted to know. There aren't many people from those days who know my number and I'd hoped I could trust them, but Liam can be very persuasive when he wants to be. I should have just cut the call and blocked the number. But I know Liam's not one to take no for an answer. If I'd crossed him, he'd have moved heaven and earth to track me down.'

'What did he say?'

'He didn't seem interested in me at all. He didn't even ask what I'd been up to. His opening question was, "Do you know where she is?" I didn't even twig what he was talking about at first. It took a few minutes of me asking who he meant and him repeating the same question, increasingly angrily, before I finally realised he meant you.'

'And by this point, you did know where I was.'

'I'd finally tracked you down a month or two before. I was still going backwards and forwards, trying to decide whether to contact you. I don't see how he could have known that. I think he just assumed we'd have made contact by now. At first, I tried to deny knowing where you were. But he knew straightaway I was lying. Basically told me that if I didn't tell him the truth, I'd regret it. I held out at first. But I was terrified. I know full well what Liam's capable of. I told myself there couldn't be any harm in just giving him your phone number. But I regretted it as soon as I'd spoken. If Liam wants to track you down, he'll find a way.'

'But what does he expect from me anyway?'

'He wants you back in his life. He wants to be your father.'

Zoe almost laughed. 'But he's never been in my life. You say he's not even my real father. Why would he think he's any right to be part of my life now? For that matter, why would he think I'd want him to be? I didn't even know he existed until today.'

'Those are questions you'd have to ask Liam. He's convinced himself he's your father and he thinks he's owed something.'

'But I'm not just something,' Zoe said. 'Even if he was my father, I'm not some chattel he can just demand when it suits him. I'm an adult human being. He has no rights whatsoever. And if I'm blunt, neither do you. I don't owe anybody anything.'

Simmonds held up her hands. 'You don't need to tell me any of this. I hope I've made it clear that, as far as I'm concerned, it's entirely your decision whether you see me again. If you decide not to, I'll be sorry, but I'll leave it there. But you may find that Liam's a different matter.'

'I don't care what he is. From everything you've told me, I've no intention even of seeing him. Did you tell him what I do for a living?'

'He asked, and I wasn't sorry to tell him. I thought it might dissuade him from approaching you. But he seemed to find it funny.'

'He won't find it so funny if he tries anything. If he approaches me, I'll tell him to bugger off. If he doesn't, I won't hesitate to take legal action. He could very quickly find himself back in prison.'

'I'm sure you can look after yourself,' Simmonds said. 'At least you're forewarned. But he's not someone who thinks about the consequences of his actions. He won't even consider the risk of going back inside.'

'I need to think about all of this. Give me time. I promise I will be back in touch with you, though I don't know what my decision will be.'

'You mean you want to check me out.'

'That too. I'm not saying I don't believe you, but I'm too old and cynical to take things on trust.'

'I'm not offended. I'd expect nothing else. I'd do the same in your position.'

Zoe sat back and looked at the other woman. This meeting hadn't gone the way she had expected. She'd imagined Simmonds would be keen to talk about herself, to explain what her life had been like since she'd had Zoe adopted. She'd said she'd done well for herself and now worked in the legal profession, but she'd given Zoe no other clue as to what she'd been doing in the intervening years.

Zoe decided that, for the moment, she didn't want to know. She didn't want to find herself being drawn any further into Simmonds's life until she'd at least confirmed the woman was telling the truth. She looked pointedly at her watch. 'I'm sorry. I probably should get going. I promised my husband I'd get some shopping on the way back so we've got something to eat for tonight. Are you sure you don't want to split the bill?'

'My treat.' Simmonds reached out and, before Zoe could move, took Zoe's hand in hers. 'Take your time in making a decision. I'm not here to pressurise you. But in the meantime watch out for Liam. It may be that he's all mouth and he does nothing about it. When he stops to think about it, even he might realise that tangling with a serving police officer isn't smart. But, frankly, that's not Liam. He's impulsive, and he's never been one to listen to reason. If he wants to see you, he'll come.'

'If he does, I'll deal with him. But thanks for the warning.' Zoe pushed herself to her feet. 'It really has been good to meet you. I will be back in touch, I promise.'

'Take as long as you need. I'll be waiting.'

Zoe felt, just in that moment, that what she wanted to do more than anything was to sit down, accept this woman as her mother and continue the conversation. She could feel a mix of emotions – sadness, hope, anxiety – welling up inside her, and she knew she couldn't trust herself to say more. Instead, she nodded her farewell and then, while she could still help herself, turned and left the cafe.

CHAPTER TWENTY-FOUR

'Thought you might want something to keep you awake, given you're still here.' Annie stood in the doorway of Stuart Jennings's office, brandishing two mugs of coffee.

'You must be psychic,' Jennings said. 'I was just thinking that if I didn't get a shot of caffeine, I'd be falling asleep at my desk.' He frowned. 'In fact, it's possible I did fall asleep at my desk. Is it morning already or are you still working at stupid o'clock as well?'

Annie sat herself down in front of Jennings's desk and slid the mug across to him. 'There's plenty to do and I've not much to rush home for at present.'

'Ah, yes. Parliament's in session, isn't it? Do you two ever actually get to see each other?'

'We make the most of it when we do. We both knew what we were signing up to.'

'Do you think Sheena will stick at it? Being an MP, I mean. It strikes me as pretty all-consuming.'

'Like being a police detective, you mean? Well, in Sheena's case, the choice may not be entirely hers. She's not got a huge majority. But she's very committed. I can't see her stopping unless she's voted out.' She eyed Jennings with curiosity. 'What about your own wife and kids? How do they feel about you working these kinds of hours?'

'I can't pretend Kirsty's over the moon about it. But, like you say, we knew what we were signing up for. And we make the most of the quiet times too.'

Annie knew she was unlikely to extract much more about Jennings's domestic life. 'How's the work going, anyway?'

'I'm putting pressure on the powers that be to resolve the SIO situation. I just can't run two major inquiries, along with all the other stuff that's on my plate. I'll do what I can to get the Lucas Pritchard case up and running as a matter of urgency. That's the really time-critical one. It's more than possible that Lucas is still out there somewhere unharmed.'

'What do you want me to focus on?' Annie asked. 'Do you want me involved in the Pritchard case?'

'I've just been thinking about that. My feeling is that you should stick with the Evans inquiry. I need someone reliable to keep that show on the road until I can devote more time to it, and you've been involved from the start. You can run an inquiry as well as I can.'

Compliments from Jennings weren't common, and Annie was more than happy to accept this one, even if he was soft-soaping her into taking on the additional responsibility. 'Good of you to say so.'

'It's the truth. And that'll free me up to focus on Lucas Pritchard till we get someone else identified. Thought I might bring across Chris Statham as DI, if he can be freed up. What do you reckon?'

Annie didn't know Statham well. He had a reputation as an effective operator, but she'd found him a little abrasive for her taste. He was basically a blunt, plain-spoken Yorkshireman who never missed an opportunity to call a spade a bloody shovel. Annie suspected it was largely an act, but she'd seen him put other people's noses out of joint on a couple of occasions. 'Not exactly my cup of tea,' she said, 'but he has a decent reputation.'

'Can't say he's exactly to my taste either, but he gets the job done, which is really what I need at the moment.'

'He'll do that all right. I take it there've been no more developments with Lucas?'

'Nothing. As on the previous night, they continued the search as long as they could, but nothing new. Pargetter reckons the enthusiasm is waning among the volunteers. They know they're probably wasting their time now, and that it's more likely the answer lies somewhere else. We'll keep it going for another day or two. We're going to ramp up the media coverage tomorrow in the hope that might prompt some information. It's been pretty well covered already in the local media and that's generated plenty of calls but, as always, only a handful that seem potentially useful. They've completed the searches of the mother's house, the grandfather's flat and the father's place, but that's yielded nothing of significance. We need to find out if there are any other relatives or friends who could potentially be involved, and we need to have some further chats, particularly with the grandfather and father.'

'None of which helps if he was snatched opportunistically by some stranger.'

'That's the nightmare scenario. But those cases are pretty rare. More usually, there's some family or friend connection.'

'You have to the play the odds. There's no other option.'

'We're checking the ANPR cameras in the area to see if there's any chance of identifying any vehicle that might have passed along that route at the appropriate time. That might give us something. Assuming the grandfather's telling the truth, we've got a fairly clear time slot to work with and there shouldn't have been too many vehicles at that time on a Sunday morning. The downside is that that spot's in the back of beyond and there aren't likely to be many cameras in the vicinity.' Jennings yawned. 'The coffee's wearing off already. What are your next steps on the Evans case?'

'The CSIs have finished at the scene and we've completed all the local house-to-house interviews. I was just reading through the interview notes again. It all feels painfully thin at the moment, but we'll have to look at it in much more detail now we're more certain we're talking about a crime. I reckon the biggest point in our favour is that Evans's killing must have happened very quickly. There were really only a very few minutes between the alarm being triggered by the opened door and the landlord coming down the stairs. Even if Evans's associates aren't telling us the whole truth, they can't alter those facts.'

'Doesn't take very long to hit someone over the head,' Jennings observed. 'Or to push their body down the hillside.'

'True. But it does limit the options in terms of what happened. Given the timescales, it was either utterly opportunistic or carefully planned. If she went out of her own volition, someone could have followed her and taken the chance to kill her. If someone persuaded or forced her to go out, it suggests the person did so with the express intention of murdering her. There wouldn't have been time for an argument or anything of that nature that might have provoked the killing.'

'I take your point. Either way, it suggests a cold-blooded murder rather than, say, a crime of passion or a fight that got out of hand.'

'Exactly. And, as things stand, we've only a very limited number of suspects.'

'The Fairweathers?'

'We can't entirely write off the Crowthers or Ms Brompton. But it's hard to see what motive they'd have had, or for that matter how they'd have contrived to do it.'

'You don't think there could have been any third-party involvement? I mean, that she was killed by some passer-by.'

'Again, we can't discount the possibility, but it seems unlikely. On a night like that, no one's likely just to be wandering by. I'd have thought the only possibility would be one of the villagers – maybe one of those who stayed after the snow started falling – but nothing significant's emerged from the house-to-house interviews. I don't know why any of them would have been out and about in the small hours in that weather. Or what motive they'd have had for harming Alison Evans.'

'On the face of it, the whole thing seems pretty baffling,' Jennings said.

'I suspect the answer's going to lie somewhere in Evans's background. She seems to have been an enigmatic figure.'

Jennings swallowed the last of his coffee and shuffled the papers in front of him. 'Still no word on your mother, by the way. I checked again today and it's still sitting with the CPS. I take it you've heard nothing from her?'

'Not a word. I've left her a couple of messages, but she's not returned the calls. That's her choice.'

'She's okay, though?'

'I hope so. I don't think there's much more I can do. I've made it clear I'm open to talking. But I can't force her.'

'I'm sorry.'

'It's not as if we've ever really been close. But I never thought it would end like this.'

'It's not ended yet.'

'Maybe not. We'll see.' She took another mouthful of coffee and then climbed to her feet. 'I'll leave you to it. I probably won't stay too much longer. I've done everything I can for the moment.'

'Wish I could say the same. Feel as if I'm drowning here.'

'Anything I can do to lighten the load, just let me know.'

'You may regret saying that. But thanks. I'll call it a night myself before too long. My brain's beginning to freeze up.'

'Well,' Annie said, 'tomorrow's another day.'

'So they say,' Jennings replied. 'Though sometimes it feels as if it's just the same day over and over again.'

CHAPTER TWENTY-FIVE

Zoe Everett waved a greeting to the receptionist as she passed through the entrance lobby and then, brandishing her electronic pass to open the interior door, she made her way down the corridor to the Major Investigation Team offices. It was a route she'd followed almost every weekday morning for years, but she'd never felt so nervous and uncomfortable.

It was partly because she wasn't strictly supposed to be here. It was possible that Annie, or more likely Stuart Jennings, would tell her to head straight back home. But over the preceding days she'd come to realise that the enforced time off wasn't doing her any good. She'd rather be back in the office, working.

At least, that was what she kept telling herself. It was partly the reason, but the full truth was even simpler. After what she'd heard from Elaine Simmonds the previous day, the thought of being in the house alone unnerved her. Zoe had shown plenty of bravado in her responses to Simmonds, but she was only too aware of the risks that a potentially violent man like Liam Crane might pose to a solitary woman.

She'd been tempted not to tell Gary what Simmonds had said. She knew that his first reaction would be to protect her. But it was possible that Crane might be a threat to Gary too.

In the event, his reaction had been calm and rational. 'The whole story sounds dodgy to me. But even if it's true, I can't see this Crane character turning up at the door of a detective sergeant mouthing threats. He can't be that much of an idiot.'

Zoe pushed open the door of the open-plan office that housed the Major Investigation Team. It was still early and most of the desks were unoccupied. Even Annie, usually an early starter, hadn't yet appeared. However, an unfamiliar man was sitting at one of the desks just across from Zoe's. He looked up as she entered. 'Morning. I was told no one was using this desk. Is that right?'

'I think so. Sorry...'

The man rose and held out his hand. 'DI Chris Statham. I don't think we've met.'

'Zoe Everett. DS,' she added, recalling the occasions when male officers had mistaken her for a secretary. 'Are you joining us?'

'Temporarily. From over the border in Notts. I hope you won't hold that against me.' Major Investigation was now configured as part of a regional Special Operations Unit, and it was increasingly common for work to be conducted on a region-wide basis.

'I'll try not to. What are you working on?'

'This missing child. Lucas Pritchard.'

Zoe was aware of the case from the media coverage, but hadn't yet spoken to anyone internally about it. 'I've been away. First day back today, so not fully up to speed with what's going on.'

'You and me both, then. I'm waiting for a briefing from Stuart Jennings on the case. There seems to be a lot on at the moment, what with that and this Alison Evans's murder.'

'It always comes all at once. I'll have to see what I'm allocated to.'

'They seem to be desperate for resources, so I'm sure your return will be greeted warmly.' Statham sat back down at the desk and tapped frustratedly at his keyboard. 'Do the computers here always take so long to connect to the network? Bloody thing.'

'They get there eventually.'

'I bloody well hope so.' He stabbed again at the keyboard.

'I'd recommend not breaking it. It'll take you weeks to get a replacement.' The voice came from the doorway. Zoe looked up to see Annie Delamere watching Statham with an amused smile.

Then Annie looked from Statham to Zoe. 'This morning's full of surprises. Wasn't expecting to see you yet, Zo.'

Zoe glanced at Statham, not wanting to say more in his presence. 'Long story. I couldn't keep myself away.'

Annie nodded, clearly taking the hint. Instead, she walked over to greet Statham. 'Morning, Chris. Not seen you for a while.'

'They keep us chained to the desks over there. How are you, Annie?'

'Not so bad. Other than drowning in work, as ever. I bet Stuart's pleased to see you over here.'

'He sounded a bit fraught yesterday. All hands on deck stuff. But I'm sure it'll be a pleasure working with you all.'

'We'll do our best. Sorry we can't do anything about the computers, though.'

'If the worst comes to the worst, I can always drop it out of the window. I understand Stuart's set up a briefing first thing.'

'That's what I understand too. He's going to brief the whole team about both of the ongoing major inquiries so we can work out how best to allocate the available resources. We may need to draft in more from across the region.'

'Good luck with that. Everyone's stretched paper thin. Presumably, the priority's got to be the Pritchard case.'

'Definitely. As long as there's still a chance for the poor kid. It's not too late.'

'I suppose not.' Statham sounded sceptical. 'Not yet.'

'Anyway, welcome on board, Chris. Anything you need, just ask. Can't promise you'll get it, but always worth a try.'

'How about a coffee?'

Annie smiled. 'Kitchen's just along the corridor. Couple of pounds a week in the kitty, and then feel free to help yourself.'

Statham nodded. 'Well, like you said, always worth a try.'

CHAPTER TWENTY-SIX

Martin Pritchard carefully locked the front door behind him and made his way down the short garden path to the street. He didn't really know where he was going. Maybe to the cafe in the village to get himself a coffee and sit in solitude for a while. Except that everyone in there would know who he was, and they'd all be staring at him and gossiping. There might even be some abuse. There had been a bit of that already. Anonymous letters pushed through the letterbox, accusing him or Amy of all manner of things. Someone shouting at him in the street when he'd been on the way back from the supermarket.

He didn't know what made people behave like that. Jumping to the most awful conclusions, judging without any grounds or evidence. Couldn't they see how much he and Amy were suffering, without adding to that pain? But that wasn't the way these people thought. They just wanted to assert their own moral superiority by thinking the worst of others.

Some of their neighbours would no doubt have seen the police searching the house and assumed the worst. Martin imagined the police were harbouring their own suspicions. They'd already made it clear that they were sceptical about his account of what had happened that Sunday morning. He couldn't quite believe it himself. And it didn't really matter anyway. Martin knew he was to blame. He hadn't harmed Lucas himself but he'd allowed this to happen. He'd never forgive himself for that.

He paused at the gateway and looked around, relieved that the street was deserted. Martin and Amy lived in a small relatively new-build estate at the edge of the village. Some attempt had been made – presumably a condition of the planning permission – to render the houses in keeping with the older, more picturesque buildings that largely comprised the rest of the village, but Martin knew the estate was resented by some of the older residents. The likes of Martin and Amy were seen as unwelcome incomers, even though Martin had lived in the area all his life.

After a moment's thought, Martin turned and walked away from the village centre, heading uphill towards the moors. All he wanted was time to himself, an opportunity to sit and think. He suspected Amy needed the same.

Head down, he continued trudging up the road until the village fell away behind him and he was walking in open country. The landscape here was largely empty moorland, strung with dry-stone walling and dotted with sheep. Martin turned, looking back down towards the village and the dark valley beyond. There were lingering traces of snow in the corners where the sun didn't reach, tucked beneath the dry-stone walls or in nooks on the hillside. Today, though, was a fine winter's day, the sky a clear blue, the low sun casting undulating shadows across the landscape. Martin walked away from the road and, finding a comfortable-looking spot, sat down on the hillside to regain his breath.

He barely registered the sound of the vehicle behind him. He became aware of it only when he heard the engine stop and a car door opening. Then a voice: 'Hey. Old man.'

Without rising, Martin twisted around to see Tom striding towards him. He was looking, as Tom always did, angry.

'I thought it was you, sitting there.' He was only a couple of feet away from Martin, glaring at him. 'Christ, you can't even be bothered to stay and look after your own daughter at a time like this. What sort of person are you?'

'I've…' Martin trailed off. He knew there was no point in engaging in any argument with Tom.

'You've what? Maybe it's time to tell everyone just what it is you have done.' Tom reached down, grabbed Martin's jacket by the lapels and dragged the older man to his feet. 'Rather than sending the police on a wild goose chase.' Tom jabbed him in the ribs. 'I was on my way to see you, but it's better we have this conversation out here. That way Amy doesn't need to hear it.'

'I don't—'

'It was you who set the police on to me, wasn't it? You who suggested they should search my place.'

'I didn't—'

'What was that? Some kind of smokescreen to save your own skin? You knew I had a record. You knew that as soon as they were aware of that, they'd stick me at the top of their list of suspects. You knew that would take the heat off you.'

Martin wanted to say that this wasn't how it worked. The police would have become aware of Tom's criminal record soon enough, whatever Martin might or might not have said, and close family members would always be high on the list in a case like this.

'Don't you think you've done enough damage, old man. I don't know how you can live with yourself. I don't know what you've done. Whether you've harmed Lucas yourself or whether you just didn't take proper care of him – the result's the same. You're responsible for whatever it is that's happened.' He was still jabbing Martin's chest, punctuating every word. 'I made that quite clear to the police. No one's going to make me take the rap for this. I told them you're the one they should be looking at.'

Martin still couldn't speak, couldn't find the words even to try to defend himself. At that moment, he felt almost as if he wanted Tom to vent his anger, for him to mete out the punishment that Martin knew he deserved. In the end, though, Tom just pushed him backwards, and he fell, sprawling on the grass.

'I hope to God they find him,' Tom said. 'Not just for his sake, but for yours too. If anything's happened to that kid, I'll make you bloody well pay.' He stared at Martin with contempt, then turned and walked back to his car. 'That's a promise, old man,' he called back as he opened the car door. 'And if you do know anything you're not saying, you'd better spill it to the police now, because I'm not going to give you another chance.'

Martin lay on the ground, his eyes closed, listening as the door slammed and the car turned to drive away. When he was sure that Tom was gone, he dragged himself back to his feet and made his way slowly back down the hill towards the village.

CHAPTER TWENTY-SEVEN

Annie Delamere paused at the front door and looked up at the house. Not a large place, but decent-looking and plenty big enough for someone living alone. She assumed these terraced houses had been built as workmen or miners' cottages, but most had been renovated as the town had become increasingly gentrified. This house looked slightly more neglected that some of its neighbours, but in broadly good condition.

She pulled out the keys and unlocked the front door, and then, with a glance around her at the empty street, she opened the door and stepped inside. She paused to take in the interior of the house. She was standing in a narrow hallway, the stairs ahead. There were two doors to her left, and a further door at the end of the hall, which she guessed led to the kitchen. Essentially, a two-up, two-down which, like many of these houses, had been extended at the rear. The place looked to have been redecorated relatively recently in a largely neutral style.

So far, they'd failed to track down any next of kin for Alison Evans. Already, their investigations had seemed to support at least some of Carrie Fairweather's suspicions. They'd so far been unable to find any trace locally of anyone matching her father's name. It was still early days, but there were at least grounds to question Evans's account of her own life.

Evans's handbag had yielded some further clues. There had been a staff ID for the county council, and they'd confirmed she'd worked there in an administrative role. She'd been seen as a reliable and conscientious worker, but also something of a loner, not particularly well-liked by her colleagues. Beyond that, her employer had been able to tell them very little. They had sent over a range of documents from her personal file, including her original application form for the job, which provided some further background.

Evans had been a local woman: born and brought up in Chesterfield, educated at local primary and secondary schools. She'd left school at eighteen, despite having what appeared to be good A-Level results, and had taken a range of largely administrative jobs, mainly in the public sector.

The handbag had also contained various other items, including the set of keys that Annie had used to access the house. The house itself was rented through a local agency, who had been able to provide little more information other than to confirm that Evans had been an unproblematic tenant, paying her rent on time.

Annie pushed open the door to her left, and peered into a small and unremarkable living room. There was a sofa and a single armchair, a small occasional table, and a disproportion-ately large TV set. More strikingly, there seemed to be very little evidence of any personality. There were a couple of paintings on the wall, but Annie guessed those had been placed there by the landlord. There were no photographs or ornaments, no books or magazines, no evidence that anyone had ever occupied this room. To Annie's eyes, it felt odd, even slightly disturbing.

She moved on to the adjacent room and found it was set up as a small dining room, with a table and four chairs in the centre. There was an old-fashioned cabinet against the far wall, containing drawers and a couple of cupboards. Annie walked over and pulled open the top drawer. There was little inside, other than a stack of official-looking documents – a council tax bill, some recent utility bills, correspondence from Evans's bank. The next drawer contained various user manuals relating to electrical items in the house, again presumably left there by the landlord. The remaining two drawers, like the cupboards, were empty.

Annie was finding the place increasingly discomforting. Admittedly, her and Sheena's house tended to be at the opposite extreme, cluttered with items that reflected their personalities and experiences. But this place seemed almost eerie in its absence of any sense of a unique human life. It felt as if Evans had never really occupied the place or had, for some reason, cleared it out prior to that final night.

The kitchen did at least provide evidence of previous occupation, even if again it gave little indication of what Evans had been like. The fridge contained just a handful of items, all of them fairly basic – a bottle of semi-skimmed milk, an unopened block of mild cheddar, some eggs, butter. The cupboards were similarly sparsely filled – a box of cereal, an unopened pack of rice, a similar pack of pasta, a couple of tins of tomatoes and a tin of baked beans. A bread bin on the work surface contained a part-used sliced white loaf. There was a gas cooker which looked as if it had barely been used, a toaster and a kettle. As in the reception rooms, there was nothing that gave any sense of a personality. Even the pinboard on the wall by the fridge was empty. There was a pedal bin by the rear door. Annie opened it and peered inside, wondering whether she might gain a better sense of Evans from what she'd discarded, but the bin bag had clearly been changed recently and the bin was empty.

Annie made her way upstairs. Immediately ahead of her was a small bathroom. Like the kitchen, it was spotlessly clean. There was a mug holding a toothbrush and a tube of toothpaste, and a bar of soap on the sink. A supermarket own-brand shampoo stood on the side of the bath. Annie pulled open the medicine cabinet over the sink and peered inside. There was only a pack of aspirin, an unopened pack of cotton wool and a similarly untouched pack of tampons.

She continued her search in the first of the two bedrooms. This was clearly the bedroom Evans had used, and for the first time there was at least some sense of a personality, if only by default. The bed was made up with a brightly patterned duvet.

There was a bedside cabinet which held a lamp and a glass. The only other items of furniture were a dressing table and a wardrobe. On the dressing table, there was a hairbrush and, more interestingly, a small framed photograph. It showed a man, probably in his late twenties or early thirties. Could this be the supposed boyfriend? Annie turned the frame over and carefully unclipped the back so she could extract the photograph. She had hoped there might be a name or some other information on the rear, but there was nothing. She replaced the picture and positioned the frame back on the dressing table, taking a photograph of it with her phone, before opening the drawers below. The top drawer contained a make-up bag with a few items inside, a pair of nail scissors and a box of tissues. The lower drawer was empty.

Finally, Annie turned to the wardrobe and opened the doors. By now, she was half-expecting it might turn out to be empty or to contain only a few unused items. But the contents were, by contrast with most of the rest of the house, relatively conventional. There were a few dresses, skirts and blouses, along with a couple of pairs of jeans and some T-shirts. The drawer below contained a selection of underwear, and there were several pairs of shoes at the bottom of the wardrobe. Everything looked plain and simple, and most of the items were familiar high-street brands. There was still little that was suggestive of any distinctive personality.

Annie made her way through to the second bedroom. This was smaller and looked unused. The bed was stripped to the mattress, and the wardrobe and dressing table were both empty. Presumably, Evans had used this only as a guest room. Perhaps not even that, if she had no visitors.

The whole place was making Annie increasingly uneasy. Except for the photograph and the clothes – themselves largely anonymous – there was nothing here that gave any sense of the person Evans had been. The few other items Annie had found could almost have been the basics that a generous landlord might provide for a newly arriving tenant. There was something not right about this.

As Annie made her way downstairs, she reflected on the items she hadn't seen in the house. There was no laptop, tablet or other computer. It might simply be that Evans had not owned one. That was relatively unusual now that so many day-to-day transactions were carried out online, but it was possible that Evans had used her phone. There were no personal letters, no diaries or notebooks.

She returned to the kitchen and unlocked the back door. The space beyond was little more than a courtyard. There was little to be seen out here either, other than a garden bench that had probably been supplied by the landlord and, at the rear of the garden, two bins. Annie walked over and peered inside. The first bin, for general waste, was empty. The second bin was designated for recycling and contained nothing but a couple of empty tomato cans and some plastic milk cartons.

Annie wasn't sure what she'd expected to find here, but she'd expected something. Something that might provide her with an insight into Alison Evans's personality or help to identify a motive for her killing. But the house seemed devoid of character. Perhaps that had simply been the way Evans was – a blank canvas on to which she could paint her own personal fantasies.

Annie walked through to the dining room and reopened the drawers of the cabinet and peered inside. It seemed barely conceivable that Evans had no paperwork other than this small stack of official correspondence. Was it possible that she'd cleared out anything more personal in the period before her death? But why would she have done that?

Or could someone else have cleared the house after her death? That might explain the absence of a tablet or laptop. But again why on earth would anyone have wanted to do that? Because Evans had some information they wanted, or because she had some information they didn't want anyone else to have? It was possible, though Annie couldn't imagine why anyone would be interested in Alison Evans.

It seemed unlikely she'd discover much more in here. She made her way out of the house, locking the front door behind her. She hesitated for a moment, then walked over to the adjoining house and rang the doorbell. There was no response. She tried the doorbell once more and waited for another couple of minutes, then she walked along to the house on the other side of Evans's.

This time the door was opened almost immediately. An elderly man peered at her suspiciously from behind the safety of a chain.

She held her warrant card out for him to read. 'I'm sorry to bother you. DI Annie Delamere. I'm investigating a spate of burglaries in the area, and I just wanted to ask you a couple of questions. I can do it from out here,' she added, seeing that her explanation hadn't lessened the man's evident suspicions. So far, although a media statement had been issued about a suspicious death, Evans had not been publicly named, pending the identification of any next of kin. She hoped the man wouldn't stop to wonder why a spate of burglaries might merit a visit from a detective inspector.

The man looked her up and down, then said, 'You might as well come in. Brass monkey weather out there.'

He released the chain and she followed him into the house. It was almost the polar opposite of Evans's, with every available shelf cluttered with a lifetime's accumulated possessions. The effect was welcoming and cosy, in sharp contrast to the stripped-back bleakness of the house next door. She followed him through into the living room and took a seat on the sofa, refusing the offer of a cup of tea. 'As I said, it's just a couple of questions. First, have you seen anyone coming or going in the house next door over the last day or two? Number 14, that is.'

'Has she been burgled then?'

Annie decided it was time for a small white lie. 'We haven't been able to contact the householder yet. We think they must be away. But we had an anonymous call about someone suspicious leaving the house. I've had a quick look round but there doesn't seem to be any sign of a disturbance.'

'Away, is she?'

'Do you know the householder?'

'Not really. I don't have any contact details, if that's what you mean. I've said hello to her a few times since she moved in, but that's about it.'

'But you've not seen anyone else going in or out?'

'That's why I was surprised when you said she was away. I thought I'd heard someone moving about in there yesterday.'

'You're sure it was yesterday?'

The man regarded her with a degree of scorn. 'I've not lost my marbles yet. It were definitely yesterday. Sometime in the afternoon. I noticed it because she's usually at work during the day.' He shrugged, apologetically. 'These are pretty solid houses, so it's hard to be sure, but I thought I'd heard something.'

'What did you hear?'

'Not much. Just a bit of banging and clattering. I didn't really think owt of it.'

'You didn't see anyone leave?'

'Sorry. Watching TV. Like I said, I didn't think much of it at the time.'

'That's very useful. You haven't heard anything today?' It occurred to Annie that the man might have heard her own movements in the house.

'Nowt.'

That was interesting, Annie thought. She hadn't made any particular attempt to be quiet while she'd been examining the house, and she'd been opening and closing drawers and cupboards. Whoever had visited the previous day had presumably made considerably more noise.

'Well, thank you. That's been very useful.' She pushed herself to her feet. 'I won't take up any more of your time. By the way, what day's your bin collected here? The general waste bin, I mean.'

'Tomorrow, as it happens. They do it weekly with the general stuff. Why?'

'I just wondered,' Annie said vaguely. 'But it's nothing important.' She wasn't sure whether it was important or not, but, given that both the pedal bin and the dustbin had been empty, it suggested that either Evans had thrown away nothing in the days prior to her death or that whoever had entered the house had even removed any rubbish.

Which suggested that someone was very keen indeed to get their hands on something they thought might be in Evans's possession.

CHAPTER TWENTY-EIGHT

She gazed fixedly at the camera, her face expressionless. 'What I'm saying is that someone out there knows what's happened to Lucas. And whoever that person is, they must have friends or relatives with suspicions. I'm begging of you. If you're the person who took Lucas, please tell us where he is. And if someone you know is acting strangely or suspiciously, please call in and tell the police. I just want to get Lucas back...' She stared at the camera for a moment longer, then swallowed hard as if to prevent herself from sobbing. 'I just want him back.'

Stuart Jennings waited while a female police officer led Amy Pritchard out of the room, away from the cameras and the flash photography. 'Thank you for listening to what Ms Pritchard had to say. I'd urge you in the media to use all available channels to get the message out there. As she said, someone knows the truth and we need to find out urgently who that someone is. Our lines are open, and we'd welcome calls from anyone who believes they may have information pertinent to our inquiry, however minor or trivial it might seem. We'll treat all calls with appropriate discretion.'

There was a barrage of questions after that – several of them implying criticism of the police's lack of progress to date – which Jennings handled with apparent openness while, as far as Zoe could see from the sidelines, revealing little of substance beyond what had been agreed beforehand. He was good at this stuff, she thought. In the workplace, he was sometimes prone to dithering or bluster when faced with a difficult decision, but there was no evidence of that today. He answered the remaining questions, then raised his hands to bring the session to a close. 'All the details, including the numbers to ring, are on the media release,' he concluded. 'Please, please encourage your readers, viewers and listeners to respond to this if they believe they have anything to tell us. Thank you, ladies and gentlemen.' He rose and made his way down from the podium to where Zoe and Chris Statham were standing. 'Let's talk downstairs.'

While the assembled group milled around the exit of the conference room, Jennings led Zoe and Statham through a side door and down the backstairs to his office. 'Where's Amy Pritchard?' Zoe asked.

'Someone's looking after her and feeding her tea,' Jennings said. 'I'll go along in a few minutes to see how she is. She did well.'

'Pitch perfect,' Statham said. 'Almost suspiciously so.'

'You reckon?'

'I don't know. It was a very effective performance. But we can't take anything at face value, can we? When the delivery's as spot-on as that, it makes me uneasy.'

'If it was a performance, she's a good actress,' Jennings commented. 'But I take your point, Chris. We've seen that before.'

'Just something to bear in mind.'

'We can have a proper debrief when I've seen Amy Pritchard. Anything else I should be aware of before I speak to her?'

'Not really. Search is continuing, though I think we're coming to the end of the line on that. Search at the Pritchards's produced nothing. Neither did the search at the father's. Nothing even slightly suspicious, let alone incriminating. Father was difficult to deal with, apparently. Resented having his house searched. Kept implying that it must be Martin Pritchard who'd directed us towards him.'

'You think he's got something to hide?' Jennings asked.

'We'll see. But he's the kind of guy who could kick off an argument in an empty room. You know the type.'

'Only too well. Anything else?'

'Not much so far. We're continuing the house-to-house stuff in the neighbouring villages. Checking all the relevant traffic cameras. Just got to keep plugging away.'

'We'll throw whatever resources we can at it over the next few days. If we don't make a breakthrough soon…'

'I know. We're pushing as hard as we can.'

Jennings nodded. 'I'd better see how Amy Pritchard is. Will catch up properly when I'm done.'

Statham watched until Jennings had left the room, then turned back to Zoe. 'What do you reckon to Stuart?'

'He's fine,' Zoe said warily. 'Why do you ask?'

'Just getting my feet under the table. Wondered if there was anything about him I ought to know. Likes, dislikes, any particular management quirks.'

Zoe was wise enough to remain cautious until she'd got to know Statham better. 'Don't know what to tell you, really. He's efficient, gets on with the job. Good at handling the media stuff, like today. He takes time to listen to what you have to say and takes it seriously. I've found him very good to work for. Very supportive.'

'I understand he's been very supportive of you, anyway.'

It was clear that Statham kept his ear to the ground. 'He's been helpful.'

'That's good to hear. We all need to work together on this one.'

She offered no response. She was still unsure what to make of Statham, but she was going to have to work with him. There was no point in either of them making it more difficult than it needed to be. They had to stay focused.

If nothing else, she thought, they owed that to Lucas Pritchard.

CHAPTER TWENTY-NINE

Gary Everett had just got in from work when the doorbell rang. He swore gently under his breath. He'd had a hectic day, a slow drive home, and was looking forward to nothing more than stretching himself out on the sofa in front of the TV.

He made his way through the house and opened the front door. The man standing before him was relatively short – certainly compared to Gary's own stature – and slightly squat. He had a shaved head, and was dressed in a leather jacket, T-shirt and jeans combination that looked too young for him. Most of all, he was heavily built, with the kind of muscle pattern that suggested not just serious working out, but also more than a few doses of steroids.

'Yes?'

There was no preamble. 'I'm looking for someone called Zoe Callender.'

Gary hesitated, perhaps a moment too long. 'I'm sorry. There's no one of that name here.'

'You're sure about that? I was told on good authority that she lives here.'

'I know who lives in my own house.' Almost immediately, Gary regretted both his words and his tone. There was no point in antagonising this man, especially if he was the person Gary suspected him to be.

'That right? Thing is, I'm not sure I believe you.'

'Believe what you like.'

Gary started to close the door but the man had already inserted his foot in the doorway. 'I don't like people lying to me.'

'Look,' Gary said, 'I don't know who you are or what you want. But you can't just turn up on people's doorsteps and start shouting the odds. If you don't leave, I'm calling the police.'

'I thought she was the police. For what it's worth, all I want is to have a word with her.'

'There's no one of that name here,' Gary repeated. He had no intention of revealing Zoe's whereabouts to this man if he could help it.

'You keep saying that,' the man replied. 'I still don't believe you.'

'I'm still saying believe what you like. Just don't do it here. If you don't leave in the next thirty seconds, I'm dialling 999.'

'How long do you reckon they'd take to get here?' The man laughed. 'I mean, do you feel lucky, punk?'

Up to now, Gary had been feeling wary and nervous, conscious that this man was likely to be stronger and more ruthless than he could ever be. Gary wasn't a cowardly man and he kept himself in shape, but he was no fighter. But suddenly, his anger overwhelmed his prudence. What right had this man to turn up at his door and start threatening him? Whatever the consequences, he couldn't just back down. 'Well, let's see, shall we? And if you try to do anything in the meantime, that'll just add to the list of charges.'

The man was still grinning. 'I suppose if she is the police, they might come running more quickly.'

'Thirty seconds.'

The man leaned forward and for a moment Gary thought his bluff would be called. Then the man stepped back, removing his foot from the doorway. 'I'm not here to cause trouble. Just pass on a message. Tell Zoe her dad called round, and he wants to see her.' He reached into his pocket and pulled out a torn scrap of paper he'd presumably prepared in case there'd been no one in. He handed it to Gary. 'You'll do that, won't you, son?'

Gary didn't trust himself to offer a response so instead he simply closed the door in the man's face. He turned the deadlock and then walked through to the kitchen to bolt the back door. He'd half-expected the man to ring or knock again, but there was only silence behind him.

Gary finally looked at the piece of paper. The scrawl looked semi-literate, printed out in upper-case letters. It said simply: 'Your dad called. Liam Crane. I want to see you.' Below that was a mobile phone number.

Gary was tempted to throw the paper in the bin, try to forget this had ever happened. But he didn't have the right to do that. Zoe would have to decide what she wanted to do next. All he could do was offer advice and support.

He picked up his mobile and dialled Zoe's number.

CHAPTER THIRTY

Annie's original plan had been to return to headquarters after she'd completed her visit to Alison Evans's house. The inquiry team was depleted for the moment, with officers diverted to the Lucas Pritchard investigation, but that didn't mean she shouldn't be delegating the hands-on work where she could. She'd visited Evans's house herself because she'd wanted to get a sense of it, see what it revealed to her about Evans's life and personality. Well, it had told her plenty, but that had simply clouded the picture still further.

On a whim, she decided that, as she was in the area, she should speak again to Carrie Fairweather. The Fairweathers, along with the others who'd been in the pub that night, had been made aware that the case was now formally a murder investigation, but no further information had yet been provided to them. The intention had been to re-interview all those who'd been in the pub over the next couple of days. On the other hand, there might be benefits in turning up unannounced on Carrie Fairweather's doorstep, particularly if her husband was at work. Annie was still struggling to see the Fairweathers as serious suspects for the murder, but the pool of potential suspects remained very limited.

The Fairweathers's house was very different from the pokey terrace that Annie had just left. It was in a pleasant-looking residential estate to the west of the town. Aspirational rather than seriously upmarket, but definitely a place suited to a middle-class professional on the way up. The house itself was a detached new-build, with a decent-sized and well-maintained front garden. There was a car parked in the drive, which Annie supposed was an encouraging sign. Presumably, at least one of the Fairweathers was at home.

Even so, there was no immediate answer to the doorbell. Annie tried once more, then peered into what she took to be the living room window. It was only mid-afternoon, but the sun was already setting behind her. The room beyond the window was unlit and Annie could make out nothing but the grey shapes of the sofa and armchairs. She took a few steps back and looked up at the house. It occurred to her that, despite the presence of the car, she could see no lights inside. By now, the afternoon was growing sufficiently gloomy that any occupant would surely have turned on a light. It seemed as if there was no one home after all.

She was turning to leave when a second car pulled into the driveway, parking behind the first. The car door opened to reveal Brian Fairweather. He gazed at her quizzically for a moment before his face cleared. 'DI Delamere?'

'I was in the area,' she said, 'so I thought I'd see if either of you was at home. We were planning to contact you about a further interview, so it seemed worth chancing my arm.'

'Of course.' There was a note of scepticism in Fairweather's voice. 'It's an awful business. You're sure it was murder?'

'We can't be certain of anything until we know more about the circumstances. But we've sufficient evidence to justify treating it as a murder inquiry.'

Fairweather was looking past her at the house. 'Carrie should be in. I phoned her a while ago to tell her I was likely to be back early. I've just been to see a client in Baslow, so there didn't seem much point going back into the office.'

'There was no response to the doorbell,' Annie said. 'And I can't see a light on in the house. I assumed she must be out.'

'That's odd.'

'Maybe she's just popped out for some reason.'

'There's nowhere to pop out to,' Fairweather said. 'Not without the car. One of the downsides of this place. We don't even have a convenience store within walking distance. Maybe she's having a lie-down or something. Do you want to come in and wait? Or talk to me?'

'Thanks. If nothing else, we can discuss when you can come in to be interviewed.'

As Fairweather unlocked the front door, he turned back to Annie. 'I still can't believe anyone could have killed Alison. It just seems incredible.'

As he spoke, Annie was looking past him through the now-open front door. In the gloom, she wasn't entirely sure what she was seeing, but it was enough to make her feel uneasy. There was something else too. At first she couldn't work out what it was, but her experience and instincts were telling her she shouldn't let Fairweather enter the house until she'd checked it out. She placed a hand on his arm. 'Excuse me, Mr Fairweather. Could you let me go in first?'

'I don't see why...' He turned and read her expression. 'Is something wrong?'

'I don't know. But I'd like to check it out before I allow you inside. Please, could you wait out here?'

'I don't...' But she'd already gently manoeuvred him back on to the drive, and she could tell he'd realised she was being serious. She made her way down the hallway, not wanting to dazzle herself by turning on the lights until she had an idea what she was dealing with.

What she'd seen was something lying on the floor, just inside the open door of the room at the far end of the hall. She'd been able to make out no other detail, but she had a good idea what it could be. She realised now that what had also provoked her unease was that the house had felt colder than it should have, a chill breeze from within brushing her skin as she'd stood in the doorway.

Moving cautiously, she made her way to what she now identified as the kitchen. Carrie Fairweather was lying on the floor, her limbs splayed awkwardly on the cold floor tiles. There was no one else in the room and, as Annie had guessed, the back door was standing open. Annie crouched down to check Fairweather's pulse. She could detect nothing. It would be for the paramedics to confirm, but she had little doubt that Fairweather was dead. Still on her knees, Annie pulled out her mobile and called the control room to request an ambulance and a response team.

She shone the torch on Carrie Fairweather's face. Her eyes were closed and her expression was one of shock. The cause of death wasn't immediately apparent, although there were crimson marks on her neck which suggested some kind of strangulation.

'DI Delamere? Is everything okay?'

She looked up. Brian Fairweather was in the front doorway, peering down the corridor towards where she was crouching. She rose hurriedly and, pulling the kitchen door partly closed behind her, strode down the hall towards him.

'What is it?' he said. 'What's happened?'

'I'm sorry,' Annie said. 'I'm afraid I've some very bad news.'

CHAPTER THIRTY-ONE

'Christ, this is all we need.'

Annie watched Stuart Jennings stride up and down the driveway as if trying to walk off his pent-up emotion. They were outside the Fairweathers's house, the evening pulsing with blue lights. Danny Eccles and the other CSIs were already at work inside the house, but as yet they had no further information about the cause or nature of Carrie Fairweather's death.

Jennings finally paused and walked back towards Annie. He tended to be like this when faced with something unexpected. It would take him a few minutes to calm down and become his usual decisive self.

Brian Fairweather had been taken away to stay with a brother in Belper. They'd need a statement from him in due course, but he'd seemed in no condition to respond coherently. That might have been an act, of course. Fairweather had to be at least a potential suspect in his wife's killing. It was conceivable he'd committed the murder and then left by the back door, returning later to 'find' his wife's body. That seemed convoluted, though. He couldn't have known that Annie would turn up to act as a convenient witness, so it wasn't clear what else would have been achieved by that subterfuge. She was also forced to concede that, if he'd been feigning his shock and grief, he was a much better actor than she might have expected.

'We won't be able to keep this one under wraps,' Jennings said. 'We've been able to play down the Evans killing for the moment and keep the focus on the Lucas Pritchard case.'

'At least this seems to remove any question that Evans's death was accidental. One death might be an accident, two looks like something more than carelessness. The question is why anyone would want to kill the two women.'

'Maybe Fairweather witnessed something that night.'

'If she did, why didn't she tell us?'

'Or maybe she didn't, but the killer was worried she had. Or perhaps she had something to hide as well. It's all just speculation, though. You reckon you didn't get much from Evans's house?'

'I found it slightly creepy. There was so little of her there. The question is whether that's just how she was, or whether someone had stripped the place deliberately. I'm inclined to think the latter, given that even the rubbish seemed to have been cleared away. I'm going to get the CSIs to give the place a proper once-over.'

'By the way, I've double-checked with Danny Eccles. No mobile was found on Evans's person or in the coat and bag she'd left behind in the pub. It might have got lost further down the slope, but we've found no trace of it so far.'

'So that, combined with the absence of any laptop or tablet in the house, is at least intriguing. As if there were aspects of Evans's life that someone didn't want us to know about.'

'Still all speculation, though. We need something more solid.' He paused as Danny Eccles appeared at the front door, white-suited as ever. 'How's it going in there, Danny?'

'We'll be a good while yet.'

'Anything so far?'

'Not really. Except we can be reasonably sure we're talking murder. She didn't just keel over from natural causes.'

'You know how to cheer a man up, Danny,' Jennings said gloomily. 'Cause of death?'

'For the doc to confirm, but looks like strangulation. There are some nasty lesions on the neck. I'd say she was taken by surprise. Something thrown round her neck from behind. A rope or a narrow belt maybe. But we've found nothing so far that might have been the murder weapon.'

'What about time of death? Any ideas?'

'Not precisely. But not too long ago. There was still some warmth in the body, so I'd say only a few hours.'

'Any sign of a break-in?'

'We haven't really had a chance to look around yet. We've been mainly working on the body. But there's nothing obvious. The back door was open, but it didn't look as if it had been forced.'

'Thanks, Danny. We'll let you get back to it.'

Jennings, in his usual manner, had already effectively ended the conversation and was turning to return to his car. 'If there's nothing I can do here, I'll head back to HQ and try to chivvy up some additional resources. The only silver lining to this cloud is that it means I can put even more pressure on the powers that be to come up with some more goods. They'll realise this one's going to hit the fan.'

'I'll hang around here to keep tabs on what Danny's coming up with, but I'll do what I can to get things moving. I reckon this just makes it even more important that we find out more about Alison Evans. The answers to this seem most likely to lie with her.'

'Feels like it's going to be a long night.'

'You can say that again. But then, just at the moment, there doesn't seem to be any other kind.'

CHAPTER THIRTY-TWO

Margaret Delamere rolled over in the double bed and peered at the bedside table. She was old enough still to have an old-fashioned wind-up alarm clock to wake her, rather than relying on her phone. Not that she bothered to set it much these days. She usually had nothing to get up for, and certainly nothing to drag her out of bed first thing. In any case, she barely needed the alarm any more. Whether she liked it or not, she generally found herself awake around six a.m., knowing nothing would get her back to sleep again.

Sure enough, it was just 6:15 a.m. She lay there for a few moments, trying to persuade herself that this time she really would be able to turn over and go back to sleep. But she knew it wasn't going to happen. After a minute, she climbed out of bed and dragged on her dressing gown.

As she entered the kitchen, she paused and gazed at the whisky and boxes of pills on the worktop. She'd tried to force herself to throw the tablets away, but she couldn't bring herself to do so.

She made a coffee and went to the living room. Dawn was still some way away, but through the window she could see the lights of the city centre. She picked up her tablet, which she'd left recharging on the table, and sat down on the sofa.

This was her routine every morning now. An aimless flick through the newspaper headlines online. An hour or so of anodyne morning TV until she felt ready to make herself some basic breakfast. A shower or a bath before she dressed. Then a day doing more or less nothing and talking to no one. All she was doing was waiting for something to happen, for the CPS to decide what to do with her case. Until then, she was stuck in limbo, her past worthless, her future unknowable.

As she flicked through the newspapers, a story caught her eye. It was the kind of provocative nonsense she might once have spun out into a lengthy diatribe on a political discussion show. This particular story concerned the so-called men's rights movement, a form of activism based on the idea that the real victims in society were now men. Despite the usual tenor of her opinions, she'd never had much sympathy with this kind of argument, if only because she'd had sufficient experience of male privilege during her time in the force. That wouldn't have prevented her from trotting it out in the old days, but it meant she barely skimmed through the story in front of her.

Even so, as she scanned down the paragraphs, a name caught her eye. Liam Crane. That was an echo from the past. It must have been getting on for twenty years ago now. It had been during the brief period she'd spent in CID. She'd never felt particularly comfortable as a detective – she hadn't felt it suited her skills or temperament – and she'd returned to operational roles as soon as she'd been able.

When she'd encountered Liam Crane, though, Margaret had been a detective sergeant involved in investigating a particularly nasty incident of assault. The victim had been attacked in a backstreet after a night of drinking. The assault had appeared premeditated, rather than an attempted robbery, and had been carried out by at least three individuals. The assumption had been that the perpetrators had been known to the victim, and the attack linked to some kind of grudge.

Liam Crane had come into the picture very quickly. He already had a record and was well known to the police as a small-time hustler. He'd been involved at various points in drug-dealing, loan-sharking and a variety of other dubious enterprises. The word was that Crane had believed the attack victim had crossed or scammed him in some kind of business deal.

The police had had little doubt that Crane had been behind the assault, but they'd had problems pinning him down. Crane himself denied all knowledge of the incident, and had concocted some alibi with his then girlfriend and a couple of his mates, quite possibly those who'd also been party to the assault. It was the flimsiest of stories, but the police hadn't managed to find any witnesses able, or willing, to challenge his account. Equally, there was no forensic or other evidence that would prove Crane's guilt.

They'd interviewed him several times but he'd stuck rigorously to his story, almost daring the police to show he was wrong. Margaret had been involved in a couple of the interviews and had taken an instant dislike to the young man. He'd seemed genuinely to believe he was untouchable.

Slowly, though, his account began to crumble. The investigating team tracked down a witness who'd spotted three young men, matching the description of Crane and his two mates, hanging around on a nearby street corner shortly before the assault. The witness said that the group had seemed both aggressive and drunk, and he'd hurried away before they'd caught sight of him.

It wasn't much and Crane had initially laughed it off. His girlfriend and companions were more circumspect, recognising that this might be only the first of multiple pieces of evidence that could tie them to the incident. One of the mates finally admitted he'd been out on the street with Crane shortly before the assault, but insisted that Crane had left them before the time of the attack. The girlfriend had also partly backtracked, admitting some uncertainly about exactly when she'd left Crane and his mates that evening, and finally acknowledging she probably hadn't been with them at the time of the assault. The investigating team put more pressure on Crane, implying that his mates were on the point of setting him up as the fall guy.

Margaret had been involved in the interviews with Crane's two associates. It had only been a matter of time before one admitted that they'd both been aware of Crane's intention to carry out the assault. The second followed shortly afterwards, saying that Crane had asked them both to provide an alibi for him. She remembered one of them saying, unconvincingly, 'We tried to stop him, but Liam does what he wants.' Both continued to deny being involved in the assault itself.

She and her colleagues hadn't really believed that. Under pressure, Crane had finally admitted his guilt but, to Margaret's slight surprise, hadn't tried to implicate his two friends. Either they'd been telling the truth after all or Crane had decided it would be more useful to have something over them. Either way, the police weren't too concerned. Crane was their primary target. He was a nasty piece of work with a string of convictions for violence already under his belt. As far as Margaret had been concerned, getting him off the streets had been a matter of public safety. She'd been gratified to see him sent down for a substantial period, not least because the sentencing had briefly wiped that bloody smirk off his face.

As her own career had prospered, she'd never expected to encounter Liam Crane again, and it had taken her a few moments to work out why the name had sounded familiar. The figure in the picture in front of her was recognisably the same man – the same smug expression, the same cocky demeanour – albeit a couple of decades on. The shock lay in seeing him portrayed as the spokesperson for this so-called Men First organisation. She hadn't envisaged Crane as a professional lobbyist, even for a dodgy bunch like this. On the other hand, she supposed she could understand it. He was articulate enough – assuming that was a loose synonym for mouthy – and he'd always had strong, if generally ill-formed, opinions. Above all, he'd seen himself as one of life's victims. It didn't matter how much harm he'd done to others. In his own head, he was the one who was really hard done by.

The newspaper interview was fairly uninformative, little more than a string of clichés about men increasingly being treated as second-class citizens. 'I've nothing against equality,' he concluded, 'but that's what's now being denied to men. It's time we fought back and reclaimed our rightful place.'

It was only Margaret's personal knowledge of Crane and his background that added a chilling edge to his words. He talked vaguely in the interview about 'taking action' and 'making our presence felt'. Unless he'd changed substantially, the only way Liam Crane could make his presence felt was through physical violence.

Maybe he'd put all that behind him and really was a reformed character. Margaret supposed it did happen, though she'd always been sceptical about the idea of rehabilitation. Once a scumbag, always a scumbag in her eyes.

As Margaret laid her tablet aside, she wondered whether she should take some action, at least alert the authorities to the inappropriateness of this man being allowed to lead rallies or address crowds. But no one would take her seriously anyway. She was *persona non grata* within the force and none of her former media associates – she no longer thought of them as friends – would welcome her call. The only person who might listen to what she had to say was Annie.

She picked up her mobile, seriously tempted to dial Annie's number. There was nothing stopping her. Annie might not be pleased to receive the call, but she'd at least take Margaret seriously.

Margaret sat for a few moments, cradling the phone in her hand.

Maybe later, she thought. Maybe I'll call her later.

CHAPTER THIRTY-THREE

'I'm beginning to think you're spending the nights here.'

Annie looked up and blinked, her mind still not fully in gear. Stuart Jennings was looming over her desk, looking depressingly full of energy. 'I'm sure I went home at some point. Can't remember much about it, though. Except that I must have got some sleep.' It was still only seven a.m. She'd left Carrie Fairweather's late in the evening, once it had been clear that the CSIs had given her all they were likely to at this stage. At home, she'd fallen into bed and slept almost immediately, until she'd found herself wide awake at around 5:30 a.m. At that point, she could think of nothing else to do other than return to the office.

'Don't overdo it, will you? I'm pushing hard for more staff. Trouble is, the buggers are pushing back, the way they always do. But we'll get there. Did you get much more from Danny Eccles and his chums last night?'

'Not much. He's pretty confident she was strangled. They've checked the house and there was no sign of any break-in, so it looks as if this was either someone she voluntarily let into the house, or someone who forced or scammed their way in. No obvious sign of the murder weapon at the scene, but now Danny's finished, I've initiated a thorough search of the house, garden and immediate vicinity. But almost anything might have been used to strangle her and it probably wouldn't have been difficult to dispose of. Various fingerprints in the kitchen, mostly Brian's and Carrie's, as you'd expect. But a few others, which we'll get checked out. We need to see if forensics can tell us anything, but that'll take a while.'

'What about the husband?'

'We'll interview him as soon as he seems in a fit state. We need to check out his alibi. I spoke to his business partner last night, and he confirmed that Fairweather was in the office in the morning. He left there about one p.m. for a client meeting in Baslow. Obviously, we haven't had a chance to speak to the client yet, but the partner confirmed the meeting was genuine. It was scheduled for two p.m. and he reckons it must have gone ahead as planned or the client would have phoned to see where Fairweather was.'

'Unless Fairweather cancelled or postponed the meeting without telling his partner. And an hour seems a long time to drive from Chesterfield to Baslow, even if we assume Fairweather arrived on time,' Jennings commented.

'True. And his route would have taken him more or less past his house. On the other hand, the partner says that Fairweather's paranoid about being late for business meetings so he does allow plenty of travel time. It wouldn't be uncharacteristic of him to allow an hour, apparently. But obviously, we need to check when he actually arrived.'

'The other question, if we're assuming the two deaths are connected, is what would be the link with Alison Evans. From what you said, Fairweather barely knew her, except through his wife.'

'That's what both he and Carrie Fairweather told me. Which brings me to one curious thing I discovered this morning.'

'I know that look. You've been saving this up, haven't you?'

Annie raised her hands, her expression one of wide-eyed innocence. 'I just thought you'd want the details on Carrie Fairweather first.'

'Go on, then. What's your great revelation?'

'It's not much. But it is odd. You remember I told you how little personal stuff there was in Evans's house? No real sense of a personality.'

'And?'

'The one personal item I did find there was a framed photograph in the bedroom. I'd assumed it was an image of the mysterious boyfriend. I'd asked for a search on the identity but that's barely kicked off as yet. So this morning, while I was waiting for the rest of the world to wake up, I carried out my own amateur reverse image search on the internet. And it didn't take me long to find him.'

'So who is he?'

'I've no idea. But the image is a stock photograph of some photogenic man used to illustrate countless media articles over the years. Earliest use I can find seems to have been in an Italian advert.'

'So this wasn't an image of Evans's boyfriend?'

'I suppose it's possible that her boyfriend was an Italian model, or whatever this guy is or was. But the image in her photograph is exactly the same as this stock picture. It seems strange that the only image she had was one that's appeared in countless articles and adverts.'

'So why would she have this in her bedroom?'

'Seems to me there are two possibilities. We know Evans was a fantasist, and maybe she was as capable of lying to herself as anyone else. Perhaps she'd conjured up some imaginary boyfriend, complete with imaginary photograph.'

'That's a pretty creepy idea. What's the other possibility?'

'I'm not sure it's any less creepy. You remember I said that Evans's house seemed so lacking in anything personal that I had the sense someone had cleared it out.'

'Christ.'

'Exactly. I'm wondering now if that clear-out was so thorough, it even included removing the real image of Evans's boyfriend and replacing it with that of our handsome friend here.'

CHAPTER THIRTY-FOUR

Annie looked around at the largely empty room. Stuart Jennings was gradually succeeding in his quest to bring more resources on to the Alison Evans inquiry, but, even with the news of Carrie Fairweather's killing, it was a slow process.

Her instinct was that the real answer to the killings lay with Alison Evans. They were following up the usual lines of enquiry with Carrie Fairweather, but so far there seemed to be nothing exceptional about her lifestyle that might provide a motive for her killing. Annie felt it was more likely that Carrie Fairweather had been collateral damage in something Alison Evans had been involved in. There was too much in Evans's life that felt out of kilter – the general lack of friends or acquaintances, the mysterious boyfriend or partner, the seemingly pathological lying.

The only problem was that, as yet, they had no way of delving into that background. Her colleagues at work had been able to offer nothing but the most superficial information, and could provide no leads to friends or relatives who might have known Evans better. In the absence of any phone or computer, they had no means of checking for any contacts, emails or messages that might shed more light. Carrie Fairweather had seemed to know no more than Evans's work colleagues, and her husband claimed to know less. Her house had yielded nothing of significance other than the faked photograph. They had so far found no neighbours with anything more than the most superficial knowledge of Evans or her movements. There seemed to be nowhere else for them to go.

Feeling disconsolate, Annie began to work through a range of administrative tasks that she'd accrued over the course of the previous days, thinking she might at least try to achieve something before the day was out. Sheena was due to return from London that evening but would be getting a relatively late train. Annie had arranged to pick her up from the station, with the intention of collecting a takeaway on their way home, so she had nothing to rush back for. She sighed and called up the relevant files on her computer.

Annie spent the next hour or so completing the largely routine tasks almost without engaging her brain. It was only when someone gave a discreet cough from behind the screen that she realised how much time had passed. She looked up, grateful for the interruption. Andy Metcalfe was standing in front of the desk, grinning awkwardly.

'Sorry, you looked engrossed,' he said. 'I didn't want to interrupt.'

'More that I was in a trance,' she said. 'The admin mindset.'

'Ah, I know that mindset all too well.'

'Grab a seat. What can I do for you?'

'A bit of a development, actually. Nothing major but it might help.'

'At the moment, anything would. Go on.'

'It's about the house-to-house interviews on Alison Evans's street. To be honest, it's all seemed a bit hopeless. We'd already spoken to the immediate neighbours and the people in the houses opposite, and didn't get much. But it looks as if we might have finally found something.'

'What sort of thing?'

'One of the houses on the other side. Not directly opposite, but a few houses along. Someone we'd not spoken to before because he's been away. Anyway, turns out he had a few things to tell us.'

'The sort of nosy neighbour we're always deeply grateful for?'

'Not the usual stereotype, to be honest. Fairly youngish guy. Shaun Norris. Lives with his girlfriend. Just seems the type who keeps an eye on what's going on. Also, someone who makes an effort to get to know his neighbours, at least as far as they'll allow. Which in Evans's case wasn't very far.'

'Why am I not surprised? So what did he have to tell us?'

'First of all, he saw a man coming out of her house on the Sunday evening after she was found dead. This was before we'd identified her in the media, while we were still trying to track down a next of kin, so he didn't think much of it, even though the man was carrying two full-looking bin bags, which he loaded into his car.'

'What time was this?'

'He reckons about eightish. He'd been to collect a takeaway, and he'd been keen to get it back while it was still hot.'

'He didn't worry that this man might have been burgling Evans's house?'

'He recognised the man. It was someone he'd seen a few times at Evans's house. He'd known Evans lived alone, but she had a couple of male visitors.'

'A couple?'

'Norris works from home a lot of the time and has a desk in the spare bedroom at the front of the house. So he spends a large part of the day looking out at the street. He's seen this guy several times, mostly in the afternoon. But there seems to have been a second male visitor. Norris assumed the other man must have been some kind of boyfriend or partner. He'd seen him leave the house with Evans a couple of times and they behaved like an item.'

'Was Norris able to give us a description of either man?'

'Of sorts. It was the usual story. He'd not really paid too much attention to their appearance and his house is a little way away. So it was mostly the usual average height, average build sort of stuff. He reckoned both men were clean-shaven. The supposed boyfriend looked to be a bit older than Evans, fair-haired but hair a bit thinning. Fairly formally dressed when Norris saw him, wearing a suit.'

'What about the other man? The one he saw on the night after her death.'

'Probably about the same age as Evans. A bit more heavily built, but Norris had the impression it was muscle rather than fat. Less formally dressed on the occasions Norris had seen him.'

'You said he was loading some full bin bags into the car. I don't suppose Norris remembers the registration?'

'Sadly, no. He had no particular reason to. He hadn't thought there was anything suspicious about him. It was only yesterday, when they got back, that he and his girlfriend found out Evans was dead. He remembered the make of the car, though. A SEAT León. Black.'

'It's something. We might be able to identify it from cameras in the vicinity. What about the other man? Did he have a car?'

'Norris never saw one, but again, he wasn't particularly looking.'

'If nothing else, this does seem to confirm that Evans's house was cleared out. And, maybe more surprisingly, we have two possible candidates for the mysterious boyfriend. As far as we've been able to ascertain, Evans doesn't seem to have introduced him to anyone else. Presumably, no one else on the street mentioned either of these men?'

'Not so far. We've been back to some to ask if they remember seeing anyone on that Sunday evening, but everyone just seems to have been watching TV. No one else recalls seeing any visitors at Evans's house. But Norris appears to be a reliable enough witness.'

'The whole thing's a good step forward, anyway. Well done to you and the team, Andy. Next step is to identify the car. Evans's house is pretty central, so there must be some cameras in the surrounding area. If we can find that – and if the reg is genuine – it'll be a real breakthrough.'

Andy was looking justifiably pleased with himself. Annie was growing increasingly impressed by him. He'd been responsible for a couple of major breakthroughs in recent investigations. He was a bright, enthusiastic young officer who could be relied on to carry out any assigned task with an impressive thoroughness. Annie could imagine he'd have made sure that no corners were cut in the house-to-house checks and that every lead was followed up.

'Anyway, thought you'd want to know as soon as possible,' Andy said. 'I'll get on with the camera stuff next.'

'Thanks, Andy. Feels like we might be starting to get somewhere. Good luck.'

CHAPTER THIRTY-FIVE

'We need to do something, Zo,' Gary said. 'We can't allow this to go on. It's scaring the hell out of me.'

'We don't even know if anything's really happening.'

'Come on, Zoe. The phone rang four times this evening before you got back. Every time I picked it up there was just silence.'

'It might have just been some kind of automated marketing call. We get loads of them on the landline. It's more or less all we do get.'

'This didn't feel like that. I was convinced there was someone at the other end of the line.'

'Did you hear breathing? Anything like that?' Zoe wasn't sure why she was being so resistant to what Gary was saying. She supposed it was partly her usual discomfort with seeking support from others. She'd already asked enough of Stuart Jennings and her colleagues in the force. The last thing she wanted was to go back with yet another problem.

'It wasn't like that,' Gary acknowledged. 'There was no breathing, no physical sign that anyone was there. I just had a sense that it was more than the line always going dead.' He stopped, clearly recognising the weakness of his claims. 'That's not the point, Zo. The point is that this Liam Crane turned up on the doorstep yesterday, and he could come back at any time. He might be waiting out there right now.'

'He's not out there right now,' Zoe said. 'There was no one out there when I got back. If he'd been anywhere around, I'd have seen him.' She wasn't sure this was true. It had been well into the evening when she'd finally got home from work, following an extensive debrief with Chris Statham and other members of the team, and there were plenty of places Crane could have concealed himself in the darkness. But if he had been out there, why hadn't he accosted her as she'd climbed out of the car?

'That doesn't mean he won't be back. He wanted to see you, Zoe. He was prepared to force his way into the house, if necessary.'

'But he didn't. As yet, we don't have any grounds for taking further action. A few silent calls doesn't give us enough.'

Before Gary could respond, the phone in the hall rang again. The sound startled her, as they received almost no calls on the landline. The last one had been the unexpected and disturbing call from Elaine Simmonds.

'I'll answer it,' Gary said.

'Let me. If it really is Liam Crane, he'll just go through the same silent routine. If he wants to talk to me like he claims, let him talk.'

'Zoe—'

Ignoring Gary, she walked into the hall and, after a moment's hesitation, picked up the phone. 'Yes?'

'Zoe Callender?' The voice was deep, with a strong Estuary English accent.

'I'm sorry?'

'I want to speak to Zoe Callender.'

'Who is this?'

'It's your father.'

She noted the use of the second person. 'I don't understand.'

'Don't play games, Zoe. That husband of yours will have told you I visited yesterday. He gave me a load of bullshit, but I'm not an idiot. What's your name now, anyway?'

There was no point in trying to deny what he was saying. If she tried to play dumb or hung up, he'd soon be back on the doorstep. 'What is it you want?'

'I want to talk to you, Zoe. I've every right to. I'm your father.'

'I don't even know who you are.'

'Christ, I'm your father.'

'So you say. But my father's dead.'

'I know Elaine's told you about me.'

'I don't know who she is either. Some woman who claims she's my natural mother, but I've no evidence for that either.'

She could almost feel the mounting anger at the other end of the phone. 'For Christ's sake, Zoe. All I want to do is talk to you. Is that too much to ask?'

'At the moment, yes. I don't know who you are. I don't know what you want. Even if you really were my father, you've never been any part of my life and I don't really see why that should change now.'

'I don't want anything but to talk.'

'About what?'

There was a moment's silence, suggesting Crane hadn't thought about how to answer that question. Which, Zoe thought, perhaps told her all she needed to know. Finally, Crane said, 'Just about us. You. Me. The future.'

'There isn't a future.'

'I'm your fucking father.'

The change in tone had been unexpected and startling. Zoe said, 'Again, even if you were my father, I wouldn't be your property. I don't know how I can make it any clearer. I don't want to speak to you again, not now, not ever. If you come round here, trying to harass us, I'll call the police. And then I'll take out a restraining order. You'll be back inside before you know it.'

'You're going to regret this, Zoe.' The tone had changed again, this time to something quiet and threatening. She couldn't trust herself to respond, so she simply ended the call. She stood for a moment, expecting he might try to call back, but the phone remained silent. She turned to see Gary in the doorway of the living room.

'You did the right thing.'

'I know. But you're right. He's a dangerous man. I don't like the thought of him out there.'

'So what are we going to do about it?'

'I'm not sure. I'll have a chat with Annie tomorrow. I guess it might be possible to get the local response team alerted so they'll take it seriously if we do call them.'

'Don't they take every call-out seriously?'

'You know what it's like. They're stretched to the limit. They can't easily tell which calls are genuinely urgent. They'll know I won't call them out unless they're really needed.'

'It doesn't give me a lot of comfort, to be honest.'

'I don't think there's much more we can do at the moment. We'll just have to wait and see what happens. Maybe he'll take the hint.'

'He doesn't strike me as the type to take "piss off" for an answer,' Gary said gloomily. 'But we'll see.'

Zoe followed him back into the living room. The call had left her genuinely shaken. She'd expected she'd have been able to deal with Crane if it came to it. She'd had experience of dealing with so-called hard men and she knew there was often little behind the bluster. But Crane's changes in tone had unnerved her, particularly the coldness of the final threat. It had sounded like the voice of a genuine psychopath, someone capable of doing real harm. If Elaine Simmonds had told her the truth, that was exactly what Crane appeared to be.

Gary had sat himself back down on the sofa, the TV playing quietly in front of him. She walked past him and over to the window. She pulled back the edge of the curtain and peered out. The window looked out on to their drive and then, beyond that, the street. There was a street light directly opposite, casting pale light on to the road, but otherwise the darkness was complete. She could see nothing, no sign of any movement. But somehow the night seemed more threatening than before.

CHAPTER THIRTY-SIX

'You take a seat in there and make yourself comfortable.' Sheena Pearson gestured towards the small meeting room at the rear of the first floor of her constituency office. 'I'll make us a couple of coffees and then we can get started. How do you take it?'

Jude Parrish looked terrified, her slim body taut as if she was expecting to receive a physical blow. But then, from her own account, she'd received a few of those over the years. She blinked at Sheena's question, as if unsure how to respond. 'White, no sugar, please. I mean, if it's no trouble.'

When Sheena returned with the coffees, Parrish was sitting at the table, looking no less tense than before. She mumbled her thanks as Sheena slid the mug across to her, then said, 'It's very good of you to take the time to see me again. I'm sorry if I'm being a nuisance.'

'This is what I'm here for. I'm only sorry there isn't more I can do.'

Parrish nodded meekly. Sheena suspected that Jude Parrish's expectations of life were very low. Living with an abusive and psychologically manipulative partner had probably reinforced that.

'Let's start with the good news, such as it is.' Sheena was trying her hardest to sound upbeat, but she needed Parrish to leave with a realistic understanding of what support was available. 'First, you clearly should have had an opportunity to contribute to the parole hearing. That was a serious administrative error. But it does mean that, because there was a failure of the process, we can ask for a re-hearing. And I can help you with the submission.'

'Does that mean they won't be releasing Ben?'

'I'm afraid not, though it may mean his release is delayed. The reality is that the original parole board were aware of the background and all the facts of the case when they reached their decision. I suspect they're unlikely to change it. By all accounts, Yardley has been a model prisoner.'

For the first time in the meeting, Sheena detected a spark of anger in Parrish's eyes. 'Is that what they told you? Ben's just a manipulative bastard. If he wants, he can wind anyone round his little finger. Believe me, I was one of them. I'm sure he's succeeded in persuading them butter wouldn't melt in his mouth, but that doesn't mean he's changed. It doesn't make me any safer.'

This was perhaps the longest speech Sheena had ever heard from Jude Parrish, and it largely reflected her own thoughts. Sheena was a strong believer in the possibility of rehabilitation, and she felt that the majority of prisoners were capable of redemption, given the right levels and types of support. But that required a willingness to acknowledge the reality of their past actions. She hadn't seen that in Ben Yardley. She'd seen someone who had concluded he was the real victim and who continued to bear a deep grudge towards those, including Parrish, he saw as responsible for his plight. Maybe he really had changed in prison, but Sheena suspected he'd be more interested in revenge than any kind of atonement. 'I appreciate that, Jude. And you may well be right. You know him better than anyone. But the parole board make their decisions based on expert assessments—'

'Experts? What do they know?'

'They're not always right. They're making very difficult judgements. But they do know what they're doing.'

'That doesn't help me, if they're wrong this time.'

Sheena had no ready answer to that. 'With the best will in the world, Yardley's not going to stay in prison forever, whatever happens. All we can do is take any steps we can to ensure you're kept safe.'

'Which is what?'

'The terms of Yardley's licence will prevent him from coming anywhere near you. I've spoken to the police and probation so they're primed to help if he breaches that. You need to let them know straightaway. I'll give you the relevant contact names and numbers.'

'That won't help if he's already done something to me.'

'If he contacts you at all – by phone, email, message, whatever – let them know. If he breaches the licence, he'll be straight back inside.'

'I know you're doing everything you can.' Parrish's anger seemed to have deserted her, as if she'd physically deflated. 'And I'm very grateful. But I'm scared. Not just for me. But for my daughter too. Ben was furious when I walked out on him, not just because I'd left but because I'd taken Holly with me. It was as if I'd stolen a piece of his property.'

'I can try to get you some temporary shelter at the point when he comes out. I can't make any promises but I'll see what I can do, if that would help.'

Parrish shook her head, miserably. 'I can't run forever, can I? We're settled where we are now. I don't want to disrupt Holly's life all over again. I don't see a way out of this. I'd do anything I could to keep her safe. Anything at all.'

'The protection's there, Jude. If you've any reason to be scared, contact them immediately. If at any point you feel you're not getting the support you need, just contact me. The next step is for us to prepare your submission to the parole board.'

'As if it's going to make any difference.'

'It might. At the very least, it'll mean the board are aware of your fears about Yardley's release. And I'll make sure all the relevant agencies are aware of how you're feeling too. You have a think about what you want to say. I'll make us another coffee and see if there are any biscuits in the cupboard. Then we can sit down and pull it together.'

CHAPTER THIRTY-SEVEN

'Welcome, stranger,' Annie said. 'How's it going with our friend Chris Statham?'

Zoe sat herself down by Annie's desk. 'I'm surviving. He's not so bad once you get used to his funny little ways.' She glanced over her shoulder. 'Not that I'd quite put it that way to his face.'

'He's a decent track record. Just seems to have a knack for rubbing people up the wrong way.'

'He's got his own way of doing things, let's say.'

'So I understand. Anyway, good to see you. Anything in particular, or did you just stop by for a chat? Not that I've any problem if you did. I could do with some good gossip.'

'Something in particular, actually.' Zoe looked around at the open-plan office. 'Do you mind if we go to one of the meeting rooms? I don't feel comfortable talking in here. Just a personal thing I want to talk about.'

'Sure. If we can find one free.'

Despite the familiar pressures on office space, they found a small meeting room without difficulty. Annie followed Zoe inside and sat down beside her. 'What is it?'

'I'm not quite sure where to start, actually. Well, I suppose I do. With the phone call.'

'Phone call?'

Zoe slowly explained to Annie the events that had followed Elaine Simmonds's call, concluding with the previous night's conversation with Liam Crane. 'That's where we're at. I'm just not sure quite what to do.'

'Blimey, Zo. That's quite a story. You had no idea you were adopted?'

'None at all. Even then, I didn't really believe it. It was only when we finally found the adoption certificate that I realised it was true.'

'But you don't know for sure that these people really are your natural parents?'

'Not yet. We're still waiting for the copy of the full birth certificate. Gary thinks it could all be some sort of scam.'

'It's not unheard of, I suppose. Though I'm not sure quite how it would work. But you're right to be cautious until you've got the evidence. This must be quite a shock.'

Zoe was silent for a moment. 'It's funny. But in a weird way I've been feeling better since I found out.'

'Better?'

'I'm not sure how to explain it. I feel as if I already knew something wasn't quite right, but didn't know what it was. I mean, it doesn't really change anything. I'll still think of my mum and dad in the same way. They were the people who brought me up. But it's as if – I don't know, as if a fog has lifted or a jigsaw piece has suddenly slotted into place. Does that make any sense?'

'I suppose I can see how that would work.' Annie smiled. 'To be honest, I might be pleased if I discovered I was adopted. It might mean there's less chance of turning into my mother. Presumably, your immediate concern is this Liam Crane character.'

'Very much so. It was the way his tone changed when he was talking to me on the phone. The fury was bad enough but the threat at the end was worse. There was more there than just bluster. I think he's really capable of doing damage.'

'He seems to have a track record of it. But he's not gone beyond threats yet?'

'Not yet. He stuck his foot in the door when Gary encountered him and threatened to force his way into the house. But he was still playing relatively nice at that point. Just as he was last night, until it became obvious I didn't want him in my life.'

'You reckon he'll come back?'

'I don't think he's someone to give up easily. My guess is that, if he wants something, he takes it and doesn't think about the consequences, for him or for anyone else.'

'Even if it could land him back inside?'

'Even then, I think. From what Simmonds said, that's just not the way he thinks.'

'We've all dealt with that type. I don't think you should take this lightly.'

'So what do I do?'

'It's a good question. I'm not sure there's much you can do at this stage, except make sure the control room and local response teams are alerted, in case you do need some urgent support. And take all the usual personal safety steps.' Annie shrugged. 'Sorry. That's not tremendously helpful, is it?'

'It's more or less what I'd concluded myself. I've just got to be vigilant. And make sure Gary is too. We might be worrying about nothing.'

'Let's hope so. What about Elaine Simmonds? Would you let her back into your life, assuming she's telling the truth?'

'I'm still hesitating about that. Probably no point in trying to make a decision till I've got the birth certificate. She seemed pleasant enough. I just don't know what the psychological and emotional impact might be.'

Zoe looked up at the sound of a tentative tap at the glass door. Andy Metcalfe was peering in, clearly wondering if it was appropriate for him to enter. Zoe gestured for him to come in.

'Sorry to interrupt. It's just that there's been a development on the Evans case that I thought Annie would want to hear as soon as possible.'

'Grab a seat,' Zoe said. 'We'd just about finished anyway.'

'What kind of development?' Annie said.

'I'm not entirely sure, to be honest. At first, I thought it was a real breakthrough. Now I'm not so confident.'

'Go on.'

'We've been checking through all the relevant traffic cameras in the area around Alison Evans's house to see if we could identify a SEAT León in the vicinity on the Sunday evening after her death. It took us a while but we eventually found a vehicle that seemed to match. Not clear enough for us to be entirely sure it was the right car, but the timing fitted. So we checked it out on the PNC.'

'And?' Annie couldn't quite work out where this was going. Whatever the name and address of the vehicle's keeper, it was definitely worth following up, but Andy was looking uncertain.

'That's where it gets a bit odd. When we entered the registration, we got a message saying that it's restricted.' He hesitated. 'And that the relevant authorities have been alerted. Which is a little scary, to be honest. I've no idea what that means.'

'I'm not sure either,' Annie said. 'But it sounds like you might have inadvertently opened up the proverbial can of worms. Throws a whole new light on the case, though.'

'Have I done something wrong?'

Annie shook her head. 'Not remotely. I don't know who, if anyone, is at fault here but it's definitely not you, Andy. My guess is that this means that the car is linked to one of the more sensitive agencies. So maybe Special Branch, the NCA or even the Intelligence Services.'

'Oh, shit.'

'What strikes me,' Annie said, 'is that we're in the middle of a murder inquiry, and it's possible the victim's house has been cleared by some representative of one of those agencies. In other words, one of our supposed colleagues has actively impeded the progress of our investigation. This case just gets murkier and murkier.'

'So what do we do?' Andy asked.

'The first step is for us to talk to Stuart. Before anyone else has the chance to interfere further.'

CHAPTER THIRTY-EIGHT

It all happened even more quickly than Annie had expected. She was sitting with Andy Metcalfe in Stuart Jennings's office, talking through what had happened with the PNC, when Jennings's phone rang.

He sat with the phone to his ear for several minutes, clearly listening to some diatribe from the other end of the line but offering no response, other than a grimace in Annie's direction. Finally, he said, 'Yes, of course, Archie. We'll be right there.' He replaced the receiver and, seemingly involuntarily, dropped his head into his hands. After a moment, he looked back up at Annie and Andy. 'Well, those buggers certainly work fast when it suits them.'

'Who was it?'

'Your friend and his Assistant Chief Constable, Archie McBride. He's summoned us up there, pronto.'

'Us?'

'You're coming with me, Annie. You're the one who knows this case inside out.'

'Is this about what happened with the PNC?'

'Looks like it. It seems Archie's expecting a visitor.' Jennings turned to Andy Metcalfe. 'How long ago did you enter that registration?'

Andy looked at his watch. 'I don't know exactly. Less than an hour.'

'Archie had a call about half an hour ago from someone equally senior in the NCA. Said they were sending an officer over. Made it very clear they weren't taking no for an answer.'

'When are they coming?'

'They're already on their way, which is why Archie wants a briefing. Heading down from Manchester, so we've probably got an hour or so to get our ducks in a row.'

'They're the ones who've impeded a murder inquiry, as far as I can see,' Annie said.

'Let's keep our powder dry on that one for the moment, shall we?'

'Stuart—'

'I'm not disagreeing with you, Annie. It's unforgivable. But I can pretty much guarantee it's not how they'll see it. I've dealt with them enough times to know that, somehow, it's never their fault. If we alienate them from the start, there's a danger they'll just clam up and we'll get nowhere.'

'I thought we were supposed to be on the same side.'

Jennings smiled ruefully. 'That's the idea. In fairness, I've been involved in a couple of effective joint operations with them. But they always want you to know that they're in charge and that they're dealing with bigger business than you could ever dream of. My experience is that, if you allow them to keep thinking that, they're likely to be much more co-operative.'

Annie nodded. 'I take your point. Even if it sticks in the throat.'

'Let's see how it goes. We'd better not keep Archie waiting.'

'Do you want me there?' Andy said. 'I'm the one who kicked all this off.'

Annie could see that he had no desire whatsoever to join them, but had felt obliged to volunteer. 'You're probably better off out of the firing line, Andy, unless Stuart thinks differently. All you did was enter a registration number for perfectly legit-imate reasons.'

'Annie's right. Archie didn't sound in the best of moods. I think we're better taking the flak for the moment. Okay, let's go.'

The ACC's office was in the senior officer suite on the floor above. Annie had met McBride a few times, but didn't know him well. 'Not in the best of moods, you say?' she asked Jennings as they made their way up in the lift.

'He can be a grumpy old sod, Archie, but his bark's a lot worse than his bite. I'm sure his annoyance is really with the NCA, but they're not in the immediate firing line.'

McBride's office, like those of all the chief officers, lay beyond the protective barricade that was the PAs' office. As they entered, one of the PAs glanced up uninterestedly. 'He says to go straight in. I'll bring through some coffees.' Her tone suggested that the caffeine was likely to be necessary.

The ACC – a tall slender middle-aged man who looked as if he was probably in the habit of running marathons – was already on his feet as they came into the office. He gestured for them to take a seat at the meeting table at the end of the room. 'What the hell have you buggers been up to?' The lingering trace of a Glaswegian accent made the question sound even more threatening than it might otherwise have done.

Jennings settled himself at the table, and Annie dropped into the seat beside him. 'Our jobs. But we seem to have stepped on someone's toes in the process.'

'You can say that again. I had one of their senior bods in London on the phone, reading me the riot act. Sticking our noses in where they're not needed. Risk of jeopardising their operation. All that.'

'An operation nobody's had the decency to tell us about,' Jennings pointed out. 'We're not mind readers.'

'And we are conducting a murder inquiry,' Annie added.

McBride glared at her, as if he'd almost forgotten she was present. Then his expression softened. 'Aye, I know. These buggers always think their business has to come first, though.'

'Two people are dead,' Annie said. 'Shouldn't that be a priority?' She couldn't tell from Jennings's expression whether he approved or disapproved of her intervention. He was probably just grateful she'd chosen to jump into the line of fire.

McBride finally sat himself down opposite them. 'Okay, talk me through it all. I know the headlines but I want the detail before our friend gets here.'

Annie glanced at Jennings, who nodded, and then began to talk through all the details of the Evans and Fairweather cases, pausing briefly only while McBride's PA brought in the coffees. When Annie had finished, McBride gazed at her expressionlessly, in silence. Finally, he said, 'So the guy who cleared this Evans's house was the one whose registration triggered the alert?'

Annie nodded. 'So it seems.'

'Which means either that this guy's been tagged by the NCA in connection with something else – presumably something even bigger than a double murder, at least in their eyes – or he's an NCA officer himself.'

'Why would an NCA officer clear out Evans's house?'

'Your guess is as good as mine. Maybe Evans was the one involved in whatever it is they're pursuing so they wanted to check out the evidence before we got to it.'

'Even if that hindered our attempts to find her killer?'

McBride shrugged. 'It's conceivable they already know who the killer is. Maybe that's not the priority for them.'

Annie couldn't quite believe what she was hearing. 'It became a priority for Carrie Fairweather. If they knew the killer's identity, they've enabled another death because they weren't prepared to co-operate with us.'

'I'm not arguing,' McBride said. 'I'm just telling you the way those buggers' minds work. They only co-operate when it suits them.'

'So how do you suggest we play this?' Jennings said. It was a smart question, Annie thought, throwing the problem firmly back into McBride's lap.

McBride hesitated for a moment. 'First of all, I guess we listen. They're the ones who want the meeting. Let's see what they have to say.'

'Then what?' Annie said. 'We're in the middle of a double murder inquiry. We can't just sit back and wait for them to involve us.'

McBride stared at her for a moment, and she wondered if she'd pushed him too far. 'I suggest we just play it by ear,' he said, finally. 'Yes, of course the investigation has to take priority. We'll make that clear. But ideally we need our friends onside. If they decide to take their bats home, it'll make everything even harder.'

'They've not exactly bent over backwards to help us so far.'

'Trust me, it'll be worse if they start being actively obstructive.'

Annie could see she was getting nowhere. McBride was no doubt a decent cop, but, as she knew only too well from her dealings with her mother, you didn't reach the senior ranks without being a politician as well. She nodded wearily. 'Okay,' she said. 'Let's see how it goes.'

CHAPTER THIRTY-NINE

Annie hadn't been sure what to expect of the NCA officer. She'd encountered a few over the years, but they'd mostly been former police officers and weren't noticeably dissimilar to her CID colleagues. But she knew NCA officers were a very mixed bag. The whole point of the agency had been to bring together different skills and areas of expertise – investigation, tax and revenue, forensic accounting, intelligence – which, from what she'd heard, had led to some interesting culture clashes in the early days.

On this occasion, she was imagining some smooth civil-service type, sent over to pour oil on troubled waters and placate a bunch of grumpy police officers, while ensuring that the Agency achieved its aims. The person standing behind Archie McBride's PA certainly didn't fit that stereotype. Annie would have guessed he was an academic, perhaps a brilliant mind specialising in an esoteric branch of quantum physics. He was in his early thirties, with a thick mop of unruly black hair that was beginning to recede. He was clean-shaven, though not particularly consistently so. He was dressed in a tweed sports jacket, a T-shirt sporting the name of what was presumably a band and the first pair of corduroy trousers that Annie could remember seeing in a good few years. He was clutching a blank rucksack-style laptop bag to his chest, as if afraid it might escape him.

He peered at them though a pair of large, thick spectacles, blinking as if he couldn't quite believe what he was seeing. Annie knew how he felt.

'Good afternoon,' he said after a moment. 'Quentin Soames. NCA.'

McBride had risen to greet him. 'Good to meet you, Mr Soames. I'm ACC Archie McBride. This is DCI Stuart Jennings and DI Annie Delamere.' To his credit, Annie thought, there had been only a brief hesitation before McBride recalled her name.

Soames gazed round at them all, with the air of someone examining a particularly interesting exhibit in a museum. 'Please, do call me Quentin.'

'Quentin,' McBride repeated. 'Please do take a seat. Would you like some tea or coffee?'

'Just a glass of water, if that's no trouble.'

'I'm sure we can stretch to that.' It was clear McBride was bemused by Soames's manner. Perhaps that was the intended effect. McBride gestured to the PA. 'And another round of tea and coffee, please, Mary.'

Soames had already sat himself down at the meeting table, dumping the laptop bag on the surface in front of him. After a moment's thought, he picked it up and placed it on the floor.

McBride was smiling, though it wasn't clear whether he was feeling particularly good-humoured. 'So, Quentin, I believe you wanted to talk to us?'

Soames shifted awkwardly in his seat. 'Well, not me personally, you understand. Or at least, not directly. But my superiors…' He stopped, apparently conscious he wasn't making much sense.

'Perhaps we should come to the point,' McBride said. 'As I understand it, in the course of a murder investigation, one of our officers inadvertently tried to a sensitive file, which in turn alerted you. That's all we know. Which is frankly unsatisfactory, given the urgency of our inquiry. Your people asked for this meeting, so I presume you have some explanation to offer us?' McBride's smile had widened.

Soames was looking as if he'd rather be almost anywhere else. 'The thing is,' he said, after a lengthy pause, 'that the car registration you were investigating is part of a rather important, long-running operation on our part.'

'Is that right?' McBride said. 'It also happens to be part of a rather more immediate double murder investigation. I frankly don't care how important or long-running your operation is. Two deaths have to take priority.' He leaned forward and stared at Soames, who sat back involuntarily. 'And one of those deaths occurred following a significant intervention from whoever was driving that car. Which means the person in question appears to have impeded our inquiry. Which in turn means we need some answers.'

McBride was handling this more robustly and smartly than Annie had expected. His words had clearly put Soames firmly on the back foot and he seemed to be struggling to recover. 'We've no desire to be obstructive. Or at least no more than is commensurate with protecting the integrity and security of our own operation.'

'If by that you mean you don't trust us, then your people are going to have to send over someone more senior who's prepared to explain exactly why.' McBride glared at Soames, who seemed to have shrunk into his own body.

'Trust isn't the issue,' Soames said finally. 'But on these operations we only share information on a need-to-know basis.'

'And you didn't think we needed to know why a colleague of yours stripped the house of a murder victim?'

Soames tried to straighten himself in his chair, succeeding in almost falling off it. He had the air of a whipped puppy. 'I'm sorry. It was an error of judgement on our part. We'll be sending a formal apology to your chief constable.'

Annie had been wondering why the NCA had sent over someone so patently unsuited to dealing with the likes of Archie McBride. She guessed now that the answer was embarrassment. They'd been caught out, and no one else had had the bottle to come over here and front it up. She was almost feeling sorry for Soames.

'In mitigation,' Soames said, 'at the time this happened we didn't know that Evans had been a victim of murder.'

It was a reasonable argument. Their initial assumption, even despite the reservations of the paramedic and Danny Eccles, had been that Evans's death was most likely a tragic accident. It was only after the post-mortem that they'd become more certain they were dealing with an unlawful killing. Not that it made much difference. 'You knew we were investigating an unexplained and potentially suspicious death,' she pointed out.

'A lot of our work involves making judgement calls,' Soames said. 'We always have to keep our eyes on the bigger prize. Sometimes that means turning a blind eye to more minor offences.'

'I wasn't aware murder was a minor offence,' Annie said.

McBride raised his hands with the air of a referee intervening in a boxing match. 'Annie's right. We're not talking about a speeding ticket. We understand the nature of your operations, and we do our best to co-operate with you when we can. But that depends on two things. First, we have to be aware there's a bloody operation going on to begin with. And, second, we have to be confident that you buggers won't trample your size nines all over our work without even bothering to bloody consult us. I hope I'm making myself clear, Quentin.'

'Crystal. And, yes, we should have consulted you.'

'So why didn't you?'

There was a lengthy silence before Soames responded. 'It's sensitive.'

Annie could see that McBride was struggling to contain his anger. 'I don't care how bloody sensitive it is. I don't care whose nose gets put out of joint. All I care about it that your officer waltzed off with evidence that might be pertinent to our murder inquiry. If any member of the public knowingly did that, whatever their motives, we'd be throwing the book at them. So I'm going to ask you, very gently, one more time. Why did you do this without consulting us?'

'She worked for us.'

'What?'

'She worked for us. She was an NCA officer. Part of our undercover team.'

McBride looked at Annie and Jennings, his expression one of incredulity. 'I'm assuming this isn't some kind of joke?'

Soames looked as if humour was the furthest thing from his mind. 'No, it's true. She was working on an operation for us. Obviously, her real name wasn't Alison Evans.'

Assuming Soames was telling the truth, this explained at least some aspects of Evans's character, such as her seeming lack of acquaintances and her reluctance to discuss her private life. It might also explain why her account of her own life didn't entirely hold together. The seemingly non-existent father, for example. Presumably, no one had really expected that her cover story would be investigated in any detail by those she encountered. Either that, Annie thought, or Evans had approached the job a little too casually. Which might explain why she'd ended up dead.

'What was the nature of this operation?' McBride asked.

'I'm afraid I'm not at liberty to say at the moment.'

Annie had expected that McBride might finally lose his temper. Instead, he closed his eyes and continued in a quiet, but undeniably menacing, voice. 'Then I suggest you pick up that phone, call your superiors and ask them to send over someone who is.'

'I can't—'

'Let me make myself absolutely clear, Mr Soames. We're running a double murder inquiry. It's quite possible that at least one, and perhaps both, of those deaths resulted from your organisation's failure to co-operate with us. If I don't get some immediate answers from you — and I mean immediate — I'll be escalating this to the very highest levels. If you don't make that call, I'm picking up the phone myself.'

Annie had no idea if there was any substance to McBride's threat, but it seemed to convince Soames. 'Can I make a call in private?'

'If you must. I'll get my PA to find you somewhere suitable. But I expect an immediate answer.' McBride rose and led Soames from the room. He returned by himself a few moments later and closed the office door behind him, before looking around at Annie and Jennings. 'Christ. What did you make of that?'

'It's outrageous,' Annie said. 'Even when she was killed, they didn't think to let us know who she was. Instead, they came and whipped away evidence from under our noses. I can't believe it.'

'Someone screwed up,' Jennings said. 'Most likely Evans, at least in the first place. She must have been exposed and that compromised the operation. Maybe at that point, the NCA thought they could keep a lid on things and salvage something.'

Annie thought for a moment about that. 'Surely, they'd have a good idea who killed her then? Are you suggesting they decided to protect that person rather than compromise what remained of their operation?'

'I wouldn't put it past the buggers,' McBride said. He slumped back down at the table. 'But that would've been one hell of a call for someone to make.'

'The other possibility,' Jennings went on, 'is that they weren't fully on top of what Evans was up to.'

'How do you mean?' McBride asked.

'Maybe Evans was playing her cards close to her chest. The undercover lot tend to be that way inclined. Perhaps the NCA don't know who her killer is. That would be a major source of embarrassment to them. They've lost an officer and they've got nothing to show for it.'

'So why clear her house?' Annie asked.

'Two possible reasons, which aren't mutually exclusive. One is that they hoped to find something there that might further

180

their operation or at least tell them who the killer is. The other is that they didn't want that information removed before they got to it.'

'This is all bloody speculation,' McBride said. 'Meanwhile, we're still dealing with a double murder. If I don't get some answers pronto, I'll make sure heads roll.'

He stopped speaking as the office door reopened and Soames peered inside. 'Are you okay for me to come back in now?'

'As long as you've something constructive to say,' McBride growled.

'I hope so. I've been given authority to be as candid with you as I need to be.'

'I'm hoping,' McBride said, 'that you'll be as candid as we need you to be.'

'Well, yes, quite.' Soames took a deep breath. 'Let me talk you through this from the start.'

CHAPTER FORTY

Zoe stood in the tiny backyard, looking around at the child's toys – a swing, a small trampoline, a slightly battered bicycle – that filled almost all the available space. They'd been called out to what, on the face of it, appeared to be another missing child. The Major Investigation Team had been involved because of potential links with the Lucas Pritchard case.

'Christ, this is the last thing we need. How was it even possible?' Chris Statham was pacing up and down the narrow space. 'She reckons she was watching the girl all the time?'

'Like a hawk, she says. Young Holly was playing out here, and the mother was in the kitchen, watching from the window. Never took her eyes off the child till she went to open the door to call her back inside. It must have happened in those few seconds. Parrish says it's what she's been afraid of.' Zoe peered back down the side of the house, as if she might spot some clue to the child's disappearance.

Statham's expression was, characteristically, one of scepticism. 'Even though this ex-partner of hers is still in prison. At least for the moment.'

'She's not being tremendously coherent at the moment, as you can imagine. It didn't feel like the time to subject her to a detailed grilling. But I don't think it's a rational thing. From what I can gather, the ex-partner was a physical and psychological abuser. It was a big step for her when he was sent down, but she's lived in fear of him coming back.'

'You said he was still inside for the moment, though?'

'For the moment. But he's due for release on parole. That all seems to have been a bit of a screw-up, and she wasn't informed properly.'

'That wouldn't have helped her state of mind, I'm guessing.' Statham was still walking up and down the tiny yard, as if trying to walk off his frustration.

'I'm guessing not.' Zoe hesitated for a moment, wondering whether to bring up the next topic. 'One thing.'

Statham looked up. 'What?'

'She's had support from her local MP in sorting the whole ex-partner thing. Both through the trial and, more recently, with the parole issues. In fact, she'd been to see the MP earlier today about the latter.'

'And that's interesting why?'

Zoe took a breath. 'Because her MP is Sheena Pearson.'

'Name rings a vague bell. I'm not really into politics.'

'I thought you might want to know, because Sheena is Annie's partner.'

Statham was staring at her. 'Annie Delamere?'

'Yes.'

'And when you say partner...?'

'I mean partner. Wife, I suppose, as they're married.'

Statham looked mildly astonished, though Zoe was unsure which aspect of her statement had most surprised him. He gave a low whistle. 'She's a dark horse.'

'Lots of people are married.'

'Yes, I know, but...' Zoe could see that Statham was realising he might be drifting into dangerous territory. After a moment, he went on, 'But an MP. Mixing with the elite.'

'I know Sheena a bit. There's nothing elite about her. A Labour MP from a working-class background.'

'Oh, a lefty.' Statham sounded as if this occupied an even lower position in his personal pantheon.

Zoe decided to ignore him. 'I just thought it might be worth talking to her. With Judith Parrish's permission, of course. She might be able to give us some clearer detail on the background to all this.'

'I guess so.' Statham sounded unconvinced. 'The question is whether that background's relevant.'

Zoe knew what he meant. Their first thought, when the incident had been reported, was that the ex-partner was behind the snatching. He was still inside, but he was now being held in an open prison, which meant he might have absconded. But they'd checked, and Ben Yardley was still present. He hadn't even been out on day release. So there was no possibility he'd been personally involved. Perhaps someone had been acting on his instructions, but why would anyone do that?

The other possibility was that Parrish's past had nothing to do with this. They now had two missing children within a few miles of one another. The circumstances were different, but not entirely dissimilar. In both cases, the child had apparently been snatched during a few moments' inattention.

This could turn into their worst nightmare. Most missing children cases either come to a relative quick and happy conclusion or, even when a crime has been committed, involve some family member or friend. Even when the outcome is bad, the case is usually resolved quickly, and there is no wider threat to public safety.

A random child snatcher was a far more unnerving possibility. The investigation would be far more complicated and far more dependent on luck, the nature of the threat much more unpredictable.

'We're getting the CCTV in the vicinity checked out,' Zoe said. 'We ought to be able to catch that car somewhere nearby.'

'She couldn't give you any more details?'

'No. I don't think she really took in anything in the heat of the moment. All she was able to tell us was that a car pulled out and raced away just after she came out to look for Holly. It was a dark colour, not too large, a hatchback or something like that rather than a saloon. She had no idea of the registration.'

She shrugged. 'I'm not sure you can expect someone to be a reliable witness when their child's just been kidnapped.'

'I'm guessing not.' Statham shook his head. 'I've no idea where this really leaves us. Not just with this one, but with the Lucas Pritchard case too. We've been working on the assumption that our prime suspects are either the grandfather or the father. But if these cases are connected, it throws everything wide open again.'

That's how it works, Zoe thought. Or at least that's how it should work. You have to deal with the facts as they are, and then try to find the answer that fits those facts. You don't try to bend those facts to suit the answer you've already come up with. 'We can only work with what's in front of us,' she said.

'Which at the moment is bugger all,' Statham said. 'Just two empty spaces where a child ought to be.'

CHAPTER FORTY-ONE

Quentin Soames looked uneasily around the room, as if fearing some kind of physical attack. 'First, I should say that, in some respects, all of this is my baby.'

'Your baby?' Archie McBride echoed, with a note of incredulity in his voice.

'My project, that is.'

'Brave of you to admit it,' McBride growled, 'given the shambles it's turned into.'

Soames flinched slightly at the words. 'I've had no responsibility for the operational side of it. That's not my area at all.'

'So what is your area?'

'I'm a researcher, basically. They've given me some kind of fancy job title, but what I do is research. My background's in politics and international relations.'

'What does this have to do with Alison Evans?' Annie asked.

'The main part of my job is to identify developments or trends with the potential to create substantial threats.' Soames was looking more relaxed now, as if he'd moved back into something closer to his comfort zone.

'Are we talking terrorism?' McBride sounded mildly baffled.

'Well, potentially. My involvement is at a much earlier stage, generally. An actual terrorist threat's well above my pay grade.'

'So what happens at your pay grade?'

'I liaise a lot with the Intelligence Services, here and overseas. I also have some dealings with counter-terrorism groups, but only in an advisory capacity, if they want some expert input in my field. I work a lot with academics and with some journalists.'

I should also add, given you've raised the topic of terrorism, that I don't deal with Islamist or similar groups. That's not my area of specialism at all.'

McBride was beginning to look weary. 'So what is your area of specialism, Mr Soames?'

'I deal mainly with far-right extremism of various kinds. In particular, potential trends emanating from the US.'

'I'm struggling to see what this has to do with the so-called Alison Evans, an undercover officer who was living, for reasons best known to your employers, in the wilds of Chesterfield. How does that link to far-right movements in the US?'

'I'm coming to that.' Soames seemed to have developed a new confidence. 'The point is that in recent years I've largely been focusing on developments in the manosphere.'

'The manosphere?' McBride uttered the word as if spitting out something distasteful. 'What the hell's the manosphere?'

'It's an awful term, isn't it?' Soames said. 'But then they're mostly pretty awful people. It's basically an umbrella term for the various websites, forums, blogs and suchlike that promote aspects of the men's rights movements. Everything from incels to the red pill stuff.'

'I'm not even going to ask what the red pill stuff is,' McBride said. 'But go on.'

'A lot of the men's rights movements overlap with the far-right or alt-right movements, as well as areas like white supremacy. It's all part of the same noxious melting pot. It's not easy to keep track of, because there are countless movements, many of them trivial but some influential and deeply unpleasant. My job really – well, not just mine, as there's a team of us with complementary expertise – is to try to keep on top of the various trends and identify when something might be starting to gain traction.'

'Are these groups influential in the UK?' Jennings asked.

'Much less so than in the US, obviously. But some are gaining a toehold. They present themselves as relatively uncon- troversial, sometimes as quasi-academic groupings, but we can generally link them back to some group or movement in the US which is much less pleasant. A lot of it's simple misogyny, but it appeals to people who perceive themselves as the victims in an unfair society.'

McBride's expression had cleared now that he was beginning to understand where Soames had been taking them. 'This is the kind of stuff that Alison Evans was investigating?'

'We've been looking at one particular trend which does seem to be gaining some ground here. Around the area of men's rights or fathers' rights.'

'We've long had fathers' rights groups,' Jennings pointed out.

'That's a slightly different kettle of fish. Whatever you might think of them and their views, they're mostly just campaigners. Stunts to draw attention to their issues. But there is other fertile ground in which something more unpleasant might take root.'

'And that's happened?'

'We think it's beginning to. There've been a number of US activists visiting the UK, organising meetings and rallies. There are websites and forums aimed at a UK audience, even though they're published in the US. We've found pamphlets and books being distributed with supposed "guidance" on fathers' rights, a lot of which is just frankly nonsense. This material resonates with existing far-right activists here, who are only too pleased to have another cause they can use to attract followers.'

'And you believe this potentially poses a substantial threat to public safety?' McBride asked. 'A few half-baked idiots with an axe to grind?'

'It only takes one half-baked idiot to do a lot of harm if they choose to,' Soames said. 'But there are signs of something more organised brewing. Something designed to cause larger-scale disruption.'

'In Chesterfield?' McBride asked. 'I don't mean to sound sceptical, but I've never seen it as a hotbed of radicalism.'

'Radicalism can gain a footing in some unlikely places,' Soames said. 'But not specifically Chesterfield. We're seeing signs of – well, I wouldn't call them cells, because that suggests something more organised, but clusters of activity in various places across the country. A lot of it is tapping into that sense of alienation – the people who feel left behind, if you like – that's driven a lot of political trends over the last few years.'

'So what's the story here, exactly? I mean, with Alison Evans.'

'That's what we've been trying to find out. It seems to have its roots partly in a group of individuals who met in prison. Ironically – or maybe predictably – these are largely people who were inside because of domestic abuse. The kind of people, for example, who were unlikely ever to get access to their kids. So you can see how this sort of stuff might have struck a chord with them. We've identified one or two of these individuals, and we've tried to identify who their known associates are, both inside and outside. But we've no real evidence.'

'Presumably because, as yet, they've not actually committed a crime,' Annie pointed out.

Soames smiled. 'That's part of the problem, yes.'

'It does tend to limit our ability to intervene as police officers,' McBride said.

'It's the dilemma we're often faced with, though,' Soames said. 'We can identify a potential threat but there's little we can do until someone makes the threat real. And by then it might be too late.'

'Hence the involvement of people like Alison Evans,' Annie said.

'Exactly. What we're trying to do is capture as much evidence as we can. Partly so we have as much warning as possible if some substantive action is planned. And partly so that, if we do succeed in stopping the action, we've enough to make the case stand up in court.'

'So, who was Evans looking into?'

For the first time since his return to the room, Soames's confidence seemed to desert him. 'It would be easiest for me to say that I'm not in a position to share that information, but I know you wouldn't accept that—'

'Too bloody right I wouldn't,' McBride said.

'So I'll give you the real answer, which is much more embarrassing. The truth is that we don't entirely know.'

There was silence for a long moment. Then McBride made a noise that suggested he might literally be exploding. 'You don't know?'

'Evans was a bit of a maverick and liked to do things her way. That's not unusual among the deep-cover types, to be honest. We tend to trust their judgements, at least until we've strong grounds not to. They're the ones who know the full nature of what they're dealing with.'

Annie leaned forward. 'But you presumably had a reason for placing her in this role in the first place?'

Soames nodded. 'Yes, of course. We were looking at someone we think is something of a nexus – albeit probably unwittingly – for the movement in the area.'

'A nexus?' McBride failed to keep a note of mockery out of his voice.

'Perhaps not quite the right word. But it's a solicitor in the area who specialises in handling family court and access issues from the husband's perspective. He's provided support and advice to one or two people who are – well, let's say, people of interest to us. There's no suggestion he's active in the Men First movement himself, but he seems to have become a kind of unofficial advisor to them.'

Annie was following the conversation with renewed interest. 'So what was Evans's role?'

'Her first task was to establish some kind of relationship with the solicitor. We were initially hoping we might be able to place her in the practice itself. They'd been advertising for an administrator, and we gave Evans a back-story we thought made her perfectly qualified for the role. But, for whatever reason, she didn't succeed in getting the job—'

'You lot haven't exactly covered yourselves in glory in this case, have you?' McBride snorted.

'Well, these things happen. They appointed someone who was already known to them, so there wasn't much we could do about that. It was far from ideal, but it's the kind of headache they have in those roles. It just meant she had to find another route in.'

Annie had momentarily closed her eyes while Soames was speaking, trying to take in the implications of what she was hearing. 'Don't tell me,' she said. 'Evans got to know the solicitor's wife.'

Soames blinked at the interruption. 'That's right. But how—?'

'We haven't released any details yet,' Annie said. 'But, unless I'm widely off the mark, I'm guessing that the solicitor's wife is our second murder victim.'

There was a long silence. Annie's words seemed to have struck Soames almost as a physical blow. 'Your second murder victim?'

'Assuming we're talking about Carrie Fairweather?'

Soames looked even more deflated. 'Our solicitor is Brian Fairweather, yes. But we didn't know—'

'You don't seem to know much, do you?' McBride snapped. 'But, yes, your officer – the woman we knew as Alison Evans – was murdered and so was the woman you're now telling us was Evans's route to Fairweather and this so-called men's rights movement. Does that sound like a coincidence to you?'

'Well, no...' Soames trailed off, clearly unsure what else to say.

'And you've really no clue as to who might have killed Evans?' Stuart Jennings asked.

'We'd hoped to find something among her possessions,' Soames said. 'But there was nothing.'

'What did you actually take from her house?' Annie asked.

'Not a great deal, to be honest. There wasn't much to take. Some paperwork, but that turned out mainly to be personal stuff she'd mocked up to reinforce her cover story. There was nothing in there related to her real work. She really was playing her cards very close to her chest.'

'Maybe she had reason to,' Annie said, 'given she ended up dead.'

Soames nodded. 'Our sense was that she was nervous about something. Maybe she thought someone was on to her. It may be that someone had cleared her house before we got there.'

'Sounds par for the course for you lot,' McBride said. 'If she was at risk, shouldn't you have pulled her out?'

'If she'd asked us to, we'd have done it immediately. We don't want to risk our officers' safety. But undercover officers tend to be reluctant to bail out of a mission, unless they feel they have to.'

'What about a phone or a laptop?' Jennings asked. 'We didn't find a phone on her person.'

'We'd assumed the phone must have been with her, but we found a laptop,' Soames said. 'She'd been provided with it pre-loaded with data and contacts relating to her cover. But there was very little additional information on there. Most of what was there was just related to her day-to-day life in the role.'

'What about encrypted files or messages?' Annie asked.

'There was nothing we could find. If she wanted to create any encrypted files, she was supposed to use the tools we'd provided so that, if necessary, we'd be able to access them. But there was nothing. As far as we can tell, nothing had even been deleted, though we're still checking that.'

'There was nothing else in the house?'

'Nothing of significance. We even cleared out all the rubbish, in case she'd dumped something for some reason, but again, nothing. Not even any evidence she'd shredded anything.'

'Is there any reason she should have?'

'To be honest, by that stage we were getting a bit desperate. You'd already confirmed publicly that you were treating her death as an unlawful killing—'

'So you lot realised what you had on your hands and you panicked,' McBride snorted. 'You didn't have the bottle to tell us you'd removed Evans's possessions, so you tried to come up with an answer on your own.'

'We just wanted to come up with an answer,' Soames said, miserably.

'But you still didn't think it would be a good idea to co-operate with us?' McBride said. 'Not until we inadvertently prodded you and you realised you couldn't keep a lid on this after all.'

'I'm not trying to defend it,' Soames said. 'But we are where we are. There's nothing I can do about it now.'

'Where we are,' McBride said, 'as far as I can see, is at another dead end. At least we now know who Alison Evans was, and that's answered a few of our questions, but it doesn't take us any further forward.'

'I'm not entirely sure about that,' Annie said. 'We know Evans was investigating this men's rights stuff, which provides us with a possible motive for her killing. We also know that, wittingly or unwittingly, Brian Fairweather was involved in that. It might give us another thread to pull at.'

She could see that McBride wasn't entirely happy with her for partially softening the blows he'd clearly intended to direct towards Soames and his colleagues, but after glaring at her for a moment, he said, 'I suppose that's a point. But even if that's all true, what would be the motive for Carrie Fairweather's murder? She wasn't an undercover officer.' He paused and turned back to Soames. 'Unless that's another little titbit you've failed to share with us?'

Soames shook his head vigorously. 'No. We'd no reason to think she was involved in any way. We were only aware of her because Alison proposed her as another potential route to Brian Fairweather once our first idea had failed.'

'Our first thought,' Annie said, 'before we knew about any of this was that she might have witnessed Alison Evans's murder

– or at least that the killer was worried she had some knowledge that might reveal his or her identity. That could still be the case.'

Stuart Jennings had been following the discussion in silence, but Annie could see he'd been thinking through the implications of what he'd been hearing. Now he leaned forward. 'It seems to me,' he said, 'that, whatever emotional state he might still be in, we need a rather urgent chat with Brian Fairweather. The man clearly has hidden depths, and we need to find out just what's down there.'

CHAPTER FORTY-TWO

'Nothing so far,' Zoe said. 'Not even the smell of a lead.'

Statham shook his head. 'There must be something. Kids don't just disappear without a trace.'

'At the moment we seem to have two who've somehow managed to do exactly that.'

'Which just means we're not looking hard enough. Or we're looking in the wrong places.'

Zoe nodded wearily. She couldn't disagree with Statham, but she knew the team were doing everything possible. They'd spent the rest of the afternoon searching the area around where Holly Parrish had disappeared, as well as interviewing the neighbours. This was partly in the hope that the departing car had been nothing more than a coincidence and that young Holly might have wandered into a neighbour's house or garden. Alternatively, if Holly had been abducted, as seemed most likely, one of the neighbours might have witnessed the incident or could provide more details of the car.

To no one's great surprise, this activity had proved largely fruitless. They'd found no trace of Holly in any of the adjacent houses or gardens and, on the basis of what Jude Parrish had told them, there seemed to be little point in searching further afield. Parrish had been only seconds behind her daughter and, if Holly hadn't slipped into one of the houses close by, she would still have been visible in the street.

Predictably enough, no one had witnessed anything. Many of the neighbours had been at work, which was why the interviews had extended into the evening. Those who were at home had been watching TV or in the kitchen, and had seen nothing. One neighbour thought she recalled hearing the roar of an accelerating car but had assumed it was just the usual 'young tearaways' who tended to drive down the backstreets at reckless speeds.

In parallel, they'd been checking out the traffic cameras and other immediately accessible CCTV in the area. This had been laborious and painstaking work, with little expectation it would yield anything useful, particularly given Parrish's limited recollections of the car. They'd identified a number of vehicles which potentially fitted Parrish's description, but so far none of the leads seemed promising.

'The key question,' Zoe said, 'is whether we're just dealing with an opportunistic kidnapping or whether young Holly was deliberately targeted. Jude Parrish is convinced it's the latter and that her ex is behind it.'

'She may have a point,' Statham conceded. 'If you'd just set yourself up for some random child-snatching, for whatever perverted reason, wouldn't you be more likely to hang around playgrounds or schools? If it was coincidence that the kidnapper was passing just as Holly ran out into the street, they must have moved bloody quickly. How's the mother doing?'

'We've had a family liaison officer sitting with her all evening. She's calmer than I'd have expected, to be honest. She was obviously a bundle of nerves already at the prospect of this ex-partner coming out of prison. She'd been trying to get the release delayed because they've not followed the process properly, but at best that would have really only bought her a few weeks. Apparently, she wasn't exactly reassured by her meeting with Sheena today. It mainly just confirmed how vulnerable she could be. She was already convinced that the guy was going to do something as soon as he was released, and now she's equally convinced he's behind this.'

'She could be right.'

'She could, but if the ex is looking to gain access, this is a funny way of going about it.' Zoe paused. 'Though maybe that's not what he wants. He's not likely to have much chance of getting access, given he's just served a lengthy sentence for domestic abuse. Maybe this is a revenge thing. If he can't have access to Holly, he doesn't want anyone else to either.'

'And this gives him some deniability. He's got the best possible alibi, after all.' For a second, Statham looked untypically emotional. 'Not a pleasant thought. Either way, we need to talk to him.' He looked up at the clock on the office wall. 'I'll call the prison. It would be good to do it tonight if we can.'

Zoe nodded, thinking of Gary waiting for her at home, still anxious about the possible reappearance of Liam Crane. But Statham was right. They didn't know what had happened to Holly, and there was a good possibility that, for the moment at least, she was still safe and well. The longer she remained unfound, the more likely it was that she'd come to harm. 'Okay. Let's hope we can get something out of him.'

CHAPTER FORTY-THREE

Prisons always made Zoe uneasy. She only occasionally had cause to visit one – usually, as today, to interview a potential suspect or witness – but the visits left her troubled. She'd never quite been able to pin down why. The buildings themselves were often intimidating, ranging from huge Victorian edifices to bleak-looking modern establishments with high blank walls and endless fencing. But that wasn't entirely it. And it wasn't any sense of personal danger or risk. Her visits to prison establishments were highly controlled, with no more prisoner contact than necessary.

It was an instinctive and emotional response, perhaps initiated by her awareness of the closely packed, highly constrained mass of humanity living behind the gates and doors she was almost never allowed to access.

She'd felt this unease even when visiting prisons on a bright summer's day. She felt it even more strongly on this chilly winter's night, as they wound their way up the access road to where they'd been told to park. The discomfort was intensified by the darkness, the trees lashed by the wind around them, the ghostly pale lights illuminating the road. Statham was driving and had been uncharacteristically silent on the journey over.

By daylight this would seem a relatively welcoming establishment. It was an open prison, designed to accommodate either the lowest-risk prisoners or those serving longer terms and now being readied for release. The security was comparatively minimal, and the site was designed to appear attractive and unthreatening. But in the darkness, with a strong wind and a sleety rain beginning to fall, the landscape was transformed into something more sinister.

Statham found the designated parking area, which was largely deserted at this time of night and, buffeted by the damp wind, the two of them hurried across to the Gate. The prison officer there had been briefed to expect them and processed their entry quickly, before allowing them through into a waiting area. A few moments later, a man appeared through the adjoining door and greeted them with a smile. 'DI Statham and DS Everett? Greetings. I'm Dave Greening. I'm duty governor tonight so thought I'd better come in to deal with this personally.'

Statham had risen to greet him. 'Good to meet you. Apologies for any inconvenience, but time really is of the essence on this.'

'Not at all. It's my job. Well, one of my jobs. I understand the urgency. We've got Yardley ready to meet you in one of our interview rooms. I'm assuming this isn't an interview under caution, so he doesn't need legal representation?'

'Not at this stage,' Statham said. 'We just need information from him.'

'Just making sure my own backside's covered, you understand. Presumably you think he might be involved in this kidnapping in some way?'

Greening was clearly no fool. 'We're not jumping to any conclusions at this stage,' Zoe said. 'We obviously have to look at the child's father, even if it's clear he couldn't have been directly involved.'

Greening seemed to hesitate before responding. 'Look, I don't want to prejudice your discussions with Yardley but I've got my own views about him.'

'Anything you can tell us is likely to be useful,' Statham said.

'This is just a personal view. I don't have anything substantive to back it up. But I've been doing this job for more than twenty years. You develop an instinct. Gaol craft, they sometimes call it.

The ability to read people, get a sense of what they're thinking, how they might behave in certain circumstances. It can be invaluable if something starts kicking off. I imagine there are similar skills in your line of work.'

'Copper's gut,' Statham confirmed. 'So what about Yardley?'

'The long and short of it is I don't trust him. He's very smart – a lot smarter than most of the people we get in here – even if he's not quite as smart as he thinks he is. But he's basically a manipulative bugger. He can wrap people round his little finger. I wouldn't trust him an inch.'

'So why is he being released on parole?' Zoe asked.

'Because it's not my call. He's managed to secure the support of the people who do make that decision.' He shrugged. 'But I'm just a lowly governor, and they're all experts in their field.'

'Do you think there's a risk in him being released?'

'That's where I run into a brick wall. I honestly don't know. His record inside has been exemplary. Kept his head down. Focused himself mainly on improving his education. Stayed on the right side of the really bad guys. Built relationships with prisoners like himself. Nothing to fault.'

'But?'

'Look, I've only picked up on the tail end of this. Since he's been in here. Even then, as a governor, I don't have a great deal of personal contact with prisoners. I usually only get called in where there's a problem. I only became involved with Yardley's case because of the cock-up about his parole hearing.'

Zoe had spoken briefly to Sheena Pearson before they'd set off, so now had a more coherent and objective version of what Jude Parrish had previously told her. 'This was about Yardley's ex-partner not being informed about the hearing?'

'A screw-up somewhere along the line, though no one's been prepared to take responsibility for it. These things happen, but I initially wasn't sure what the implications might be. In particular, whether there was any risk that the parole decision might be reversed. So that sent me back to have another look at Yardley's file.'

'And?' Statham asked.

'Mostly it just confirmed what I've told you. But there were a couple of things that gave me a moment's pause. He'd spent part of his time inside working towards an Open University degree in politics. He'd specialised in US politics, and had spent some time looking at far-right and alt-right movements. Notably, stuff around men's rights.'

'That didn't ring any warning bells with anyone?' Zoe asked.

'There was no particular reason it should. It was a piece of academic work, and what he produced was apparently suitably balanced and objective. It just caught my attention because of the reason why Yardley was inside in the first place. His line was that the educational stuff was part of his rehabilitation. He recognised now the seriousness of what he'd done, and he wanted to understand more about the political and social context that generates that kind of misogyny.'

'In my experience, what generates that kind of misogyny,' Statham said, 'is usually that the individual involved is a vicious bastard.'

'I'm just telling you what the file said.' Greening smiled. 'Not that I'm disagreeing with you. But this stuff did worry me. Not least because Yardley's been quite an influential figure among some of his fellow prisoners.'

'Influential in what way?'

'People like Yardley – by which I mean people who are inside for some form of domestic abuse – tend to be low status in here. Prisoners create these hierarchies to help some of them feel better about themselves and their own offences. Someone like Yardley is typically a few notches above sex offenders and paedophiles, but in a similar ballpark. Yardley's largely risen above all that, mainly because he's that bit brighter than most of the others. He's helped them out with various issues. Nothing major. Just things like minor domestic issues or dealing with admin stuff. So some of them listen to what he has to say.'

'And what does he have to say?'

'He's talked a lot about this men's rights stuff. Not in a rabble-rousing way, as far as I'm aware, but more in terms of supposedly encouraging others to think about the rights they have or should have in domestic relationships and suchlike.'

Zoe snorted. 'Won't somebody think of the real victims?'

Greening shrugged. 'Yardley's the barrack-room lawyer type. He's advised other prisoners on their rights while they've been going through discipline adjudications and suchlike. He's become a quietly influential figure among the other prisoners.'

'We'd better get on and see whether he can influence us, then,' Statham said. 'We don't want to take up any more of your time than we need to.'

'Just wanted to give you a heads-up. Everyone thinks the sun shines out of his backside. Even a lot of the officers. But I just look back at the reason he's in here in the first place. Like you say, it strikes me he was a vicious bastard, and in my experience once a vicious bastard, always a vicious bastard. But he's also a slippery bugger.' Greening shook his head. 'Anyway, see what you make of him.'

CHAPTER FORTY-FOUR

Zoe was likely to be working late this evening, so Gary had delayed as long as possible at work. He knew he was being a coward, but he felt uneasy about being in the house without her. He imagined Crane might be less likely to resort to violence if Zoe was present.

Zoe had phoned him just after seven to let him know that she was likely to be even later than she'd feared. Something about having to travel to Sudbury Prison to interview a potential witness. As always, Gary hadn't pursued the matter any further, but his heart had sunk. At the same time, he was beginning to resent his own anxiety. Who the hell was Liam Crane to make him afraid even to be in his own home?

After another five minutes, he finally packed up, with the intention of heading home. By now, this part of the building was largely deserted, except for the cleaning team making their way gradually through the rooms. He stepped out of the office and walked down the silent corridor to the lifts. As he pressed the call button, a voice whispered close to his ear. 'Do you enjoy working here then?'

Gary twisted around to stare at the figure behind him. Liam Crane, leaning calmly against the wall, smiling.

'What the hell are you doing here?'

'Thought I'd pay you a visit. See you in your own environment.' Crane gestured around him, as if taking in the entire building. 'Not really my sort of place.'

'How the hell did you get in here?'

'It's not difficult if you're the friendly type like me. Got chatting to the security guy on the desk downstairs. I reckon he's an ex-con himself. Don't know how he managed to swing a job like that. Some people just have the gift of the gab.' The smile had broadened.

'He shouldn't have let you in the building.'

'You'll have to tell him that. He didn't raise any objections, not once we'd been chatting. I guess he trusted me. I told him I was meeting you for a beer. Asked him if he had any idea how long you'd be, because I thought you'd be down by now.' Crane shrugged. 'He offered to phone you up, but I said I might as well come up and surprise you.'

'You've done that.' Gary was trying his hardest to sound calm, but his heart was beating furiously. 'What is it you want?'

Crane pushed himself away from the wall and moved towards Gary, who involuntarily backed away. 'I just want you to know I'm serious. I'm not pissing about. Zoe is mine. My daughter. I want her back.'

'That's her decision. She's not your property, no matter how you're related to her.'

'I want both of you to know what the consequences will be if I don't get my way. I don't take kindly to being crossed.'

'You can't compel someone to allow you back into their life.'

Crane was inches away from him now. 'Don't you reckon I'd make a good father-in-law, Gary? After all, we like to go for a beer together, don't we?'

'That's what you told the guy on the desk? That I am your son-in-law?'

'It's true, isn't it?'

'I don't know if it's true. Even if it is, it changes nothing. It's still got to be Zoe's decision.'

'In that case, you'd better tell her to make the right one.'

'It's not up to me.'

Crane laughed, close enough that Gary could smell the stale beer on his breath. 'Not much of a man, are you, Gary? *It's not up to me.'* The last words were spoken in a mockery of Gary's voice. 'You let her walk all over you. I'm not going to do that. And neither should you, if you've any sense.' He leaned forward, his face almost pressed against Gary's. 'Just tell her to make the right decision. Otherwise, you'll both regret it.'

'If that's a threat, I'm calling the police.'

Crane laughed. 'I'm not threatening. I'm stating a fact. Bear it in mind.' He reached past Gary and pressed the call button on the lift. 'We can leave together, if you like. Your security guy can see how fond we are of each other.'

'I don't want to be anywhere near you.'

'But, as you say, it's not your choice, is it?'

Before Gary could offer a response, the lift door had opened and Crane stepped inside. He gestured mockingly for Gary to follow, but Gary stepped back, feeling as if he was about to vomit.

He waited till the lift doors had closed, before returning to his office. He could only hope Crane would leave immediately and not hang about waiting for Gary's departure. That didn't seem like Crane's style. He made his point and left you dangling. He'd wait for Gary and Zoe to dwell on what he'd said, before he made any further move.

Even so, Gary wasn't inclined to rush out into the darkness. He sat down at his desk and killed time for another half hour, experiencing the same sick feeling in his stomach. He'd wanted to phone Zoe and warn her about what had happened, but if she was making a prison visit, she'd have had to surrender her phone. There'd be plenty of time for them to talk later.

Finally, when his nerves had calmed slightly, he made his way downstairs. In the entrance lobby he paused at the reception desk. The security guard, who'd been engrossed in a copy of the *Daily Mirror*, looked up with an expression of curiosity and mild disapproval. 'Father-in-law managed to track you down then? He reckoned you were too busy to go for a beer.'

Gary took a breath. 'He's not my father-in-law. I assume he's left the building?'

The guard frowned. 'Yes, but he said—'

'I know what he said. It's a lie. You shouldn't have let him into the building.'

'But—'

'If you'd called me, I'd have come down and dealt with him. But I don't want him in here again.'

'Sorry, guv, but I thought—'

'I know what you thought, and I know how persuasive he can be, so I'm not going to say anything. But if he reappears while you're on duty, don't let him past. And if he causes any trouble, call the police.'

'Whatever you say, guv. I didn't realise—'

'Forget it,' Gary said. 'But remember what I've just told you. Night.'

Without waiting for a response, Gary continued to the main doors and stepped outside into the cold night. He looked around him anxiously. It was going to be a very long walk to where his car was parked.

CHAPTER FORTY-FIVE

Brian Fairweather's car was parked in the drive, and there was a light showing through the curtains of the living room. 'Looks like he's in,' Annie said to Stuart Jennings.

It was a few minutes before Fairweather opened the door. He peered at them bewilderedly. If their aim had been to surprise him, they seemed to have succeeded.

'Do you mind if we come in, Mr Fairweather?' Annie asked. 'We'd just like to ask you a few additional questions?' Fairweather had already given a statement about the circumstances of his wife's death, which had simply confirmed what Annie had witnessed and what they'd learned about his movements earlier in the day.

'Yes, of course, but I thought—'

'It shouldn't take long, Mr Fairweather. We just want to check on some background details.'

'No, that's fine. Please come in.'

They followed Fairweather into the living room. The TV was playing at low volume in the corner, and he reached for the remote control to turn it off. 'How can I help you?'

Fairweather didn't exactly look a mess, but he certainly didn't look like the rather dapper individual Annie had first met. He was wearing an old threadbare jumper and a pair of jeans that looked too large for him. A glass of what Annie took to be whisky stood on the low table by his armchair.

'It's just a few questions, Mr Fairweather.' Jennings lowered himself on to the sofa. 'Are you aware of the men's rights movement?'

Fairweather blinked. Whatever he'd been expecting, it clearly wasn't this. 'Men's rights? You mean things like Fathers 4 Justice?'

'Along those lines, yes. It's a movement that's been growing in the US and is increasingly gaining ground here. Some of it's less innocent than Fathers 4 Justice.'

'I'm aware of the idea. But I don't see what this has to do with me.'

'You specialise in divorce and custody cases, I believe?'

'So do a lot of solicitors.'

'We had a look at your website,' Annie said. 'It implies that you provide services primarily for men in those circumstances.'

Fairweather shifted uncomfortably in his seat. 'That's really just to carve out a business niche. We're happy to provide services to anyone, of course.'

'But that must attract a few male clients who see themselves as disadvantaged in the process?' Jennings asked.

'The law's generally a lot fairer and more balanced than people realise. We try to help all our clients to make a realistic assessment of the likely result of a divorce or a custody challenge.' Fairweather sounded as if he was reciting a prepared marketing spiel, something he'd said a dozen times before.

Jennings nodded, as if giving appropriate consideration to what Fairweather was saying. 'The reason I'm asking these questions, Mr Fairweather, is that we have reason to believe a number of your clients have been active participants in the men's rights movement.'

Annie could see that Fairweather was trying to process what Jennings had just said. He hesitated momentarily before responding. 'I've really no idea. I'm just there to provide legal services. I've no interest in what they get up to otherwise.'

'The information we have,' Jennings continued, 'is that, for whatever reason, your practice has become something of a focus for people who are active in the men's rights movement in this part of the world.'

'Can I ask where you're getting this from? I'd prefer to keep my clients' affairs private, unless I'm given reason to believe client information is pertinent to your inquiry. For the life of me, I can't begin to see how this is relevant to my late wife's murder.'

'You haven't provided any advice or support directly to any men's rights organisations?'

There was another brief hesitation, which, at least to Annie, seemed more telling. Jennings might have struck a nerve. Eventually, Fairweather said, 'I provide support and advice to many individuals and organisations, as long as what they're asking for is legal and ethical.'

That sounded very much like a yes. 'Can you provide us with details of the men's rights organisations you've advised?' Jennings asked.

'I don't see what relevance this has to your investigation,' Fairweather said. 'You're surely not suggesting my wife's death had anything to do with these kinds of organisations?' Fairweather's expression was unreadable now, as if he were trying hard not to react to anything Jennings was asking. Annie was increasingly certain Fairweather had something to hide.

'At present we don't know what lies behind your wife's death. We just want to fill in as much of the background as possible. Some of these groups have been on our radar for various reasons, so we can't discount a connection. We need you to tell us anything you can.'

Fairweather picked up his whisky glass. He took a sip and then sat for a moment before responding. It wasn't clear whether he was seeking moral support from the alcohol or buying himself a moment to think. 'There's not much to tell you. As I said, I've tried to position myself as a specialist in supporting men through these kinds of legal battles. Not because of any personal preference or bias, but just because I thought it might help distinguish us from some of the local competition. It's certainly brought us in some business. Mostly, it's relatively well-off men who want to make sure they hang on to as much as possible when they go through a divorce. Sometimes it's about custody or access battles. Most of it's routine and, to be honest, in most cases we don't do anything that any other solicitor wouldn't. But over the years we've gained knowledge and experience which can help our clients to present their cases to best effect. We've had a few successes against the odds, and word gets around. So we've attracted some clients, particularly in custody or access cases, where the barriers to success are higher. Typically, where there are issues which might persuade the family court not to grant access.'

'You help unsuitable fathers gain access to their children?' Jennings asked bluntly.

'The court makes the decision. All we do is help the client present the case as persuasively as possible. But we're realistic with them about the chances of success, and we're very clear that they need to tell the truth.'

'These are presumably individual cases. What about men's rights organisations?'

'I was approached a while ago by one of my clients, who asked if I'd be willing to speak to a small group of his friends and associates about these issues and take any questions they might have. I told him I couldn't offer my services for free, although I'd be happy to have an initial complimentary chat with any individual who might be considering legal advice. He said the group in question was part of a larger organisation who'd be prepared to pay me for my time. In the end, that's what happened. I was paid to give a talk to about a dozen or so men, and to answer any questions they might have. In fact, I've now done it on a couple of occasions. I've no problem with it. The fee's reasonable for the time I put in, and I've gained one or two clients from it.'

'Can I ask the name of this group?' Jennings said.

'It's a group called Men First. I believe, as you said, that they're an offshoot of an American organisation. That's where some of their funding comes from. I certainly wasn't aware there was anything illegal or clandestine about them.'

'What sort of issues did they raise?'

Fairweather was looking uncomfortable again. 'To be honest, they were rather a mixed group. Most of them were just regular husbands or fathers undergoing the stress of a break-up. There were a few who seemed more problematic.'

'Problematic?' Annie echoed.

'I'm not sure exactly how to describe it without sounding snobbish. Some were people who'd had domestic problems. It wasn't a discussion I wanted to get into, but there were a few, at both sessions, who I thought might have been abusive to their wives or children. There was a – I don't know – a slightly thuggish air to them.'

'Not all abusers are working class,' Annie pointed out.

'I wasn't intending to imply otherwise,' Fairweather said. 'It was more about their attitude, the kinds of questions they asked. It made me feel uncomfortable.'

'But you went back a second time?' Annie asked.

'My job was to explain the law to them, not to make moral judgements about their behaviours or characters.' He hesitated, clearly wondering whether to continue. 'Having said that, I'm not sure I'd accept a further invitation. Some of them did concern me, and there was something about the overall tone of the discussion...'

'In what way?' Jennings prompted.

'It was their approach to the whole topic. A sense of victim-hood, I suppose. An assumption that the law was designed to disadvantage them. I pointed out that the primary purpose of the process is to ensure fairness and to protect the interests of children in particular. But some of them didn't buy that. They felt the whole system was skewed against them. I've sometimes seen that attitude in individual clients. All you can do is tell them to avoid using those arguments in court. But it was more unnerving to encounter it en masse, as it were.'

'Did you get any sense that these people had any kind of criminal intent?' Annie asked.

There was another hesitation. 'I'm not sure I'd put it as strongly as that. Some talked darkly about taking action to put things right. But it sounded like hot air to me. A way of expressing their frustration. I didn't think they'd be capable of organising anything serious.'

'It's sometimes surprising what people are capable of,' Jennings observed. 'And they don't always let the fact that they're incompetent stop them from trying.'

'Did they seem willing to talk openly?' Annie asked. 'I mean, were the discussions in the meeting supposed to be treated as confidential?'

'Certainly nothing as formal as asking me to sign a confidentiality agreement. I'd have refused to do that anyway. But there was an implication that what was being said should stay in that room.'

'You didn't talk to anyone about it?'

This time there was a noticeable hesitation. 'Not in any detail, no.'

'Can I ask about your relationship with Alison Evans?' Annie had intended this as a routine question. She'd initially been told Evans was primarily a friend of Carrie Fairweather rather than her husband, but she knew now that Evans's real target had been Brian Fairweather. Annie was wondering how far Evans had succeeded in her mission, and whether she'd found any opportunity to talk with Fairweather about his experiences with the Men First group.

Fairweather's response startled her. The colour seemed to have drained from his face, and his posture, which had increasingly relaxed as they'd talked, stiffened sharply. 'How do you mean?'

'I'm just wondering how well you knew her?'

'I – well, she'd been a friend of my wife's initially, as you know...' He trailed off, as if unsure how to proceed.

'Is there something you're not telling us, Mr Fairweather?'

Fairweather was silent for so long that Annie thought he might not respond at all. Finally, he said, 'You know, don't you?'

Annie glanced at Jennings, who nodded for her to continue.

'I don't know if we know everything,' she said. 'But I think you'd better tell us.'

CHAPTER FORTY-SIX

Zoe had been briefed by both Jude Parrish and Sheena Pearson about Ben Yardley, so she wasn't surprised by the figure sitting in front of her. He was relatively short, fairly good-looking, and was looking back at them with what appeared to be an amused expression. Even in his prison garb, he managed somehow to look almost elegant.

'I'm honoured,' he said, as Statham and Zoe took their seats on the opposite side of the table from him. Greening, who'd led them into the room, silently took a seat in the corner. 'A detective inspector and a detective sergeant. Though I've no idea what you want from me.'

'I'm afraid we come bearing bad news, Mr Yardley.' He hadn't yet formally been told about the kidnapping of his daughter and it hadn't yet been reported in the media. Statham had been keen to see how Yardley responded.

'Bad news?' The amused smile had disappeared and Yardley was regarding them with suspicion.

'About your daughter. Holly. She's missing. It seems possible she's been kidnapped. I'm sorry.'

Yardley's face revealed nothing. 'Kidnapped?'

'She was snatched from outside her mother's house earlier today. As yet, that's more or less all we know. We're trying to trace a car that was seen driving away from the scene.'

'Where was her mother while this was happening?' Yardley's expression still gave nothing away.

It was an interesting first response, Zoe thought. Not an expression of shock or even anger, but a question about Jude

Parrish's culpability. 'Holly apparently slipped out of the back garden. It was a matter of moments.' Statham glanced at her, and Zoe realised that Yardley had already provoked her into defending Jude Parrish. She was allowing him to dictate the direction of the discussion.

'If I may say so,' Statham intervened, 'you don't seem unduly shocked by the news.'

'How am I supposed to react?' Yardley said. 'Break down in tears? That's not really my thing. But of course I'm shocked. Who wouldn't be if this had happened to their daughter? Of course I'm worried about what might have happened to her. People who take children – well, there's only one word for them, isn't there?'

'What sort of people do take children, Mr Yardley?'

'I'd have assumed they're mostly paedos.'

'Not parents who've been refused access to their children?'

If Statham had been attempting his own brand of provocation, he was unsuccessful. The amused smile returned to Yardley's face. 'Is that why you're here? Because you think I might have had a hand in this?'

'We thought you might have some thoughts about what's behind this.'

'Like I said, a paedo. Some evil bastard snatching a kid at random.'

'We've reason to believe this wasn't random,' Zoe said.

'That right? You just said you didn't know anything, except that she'd been taken. Sounds like you know more than you're saying.'

Zoe didn't allow herself to be deflected. 'If Holly wasn't taken at random, can you think of any reason she'd have been chosen?'

'I haven't a clue how that kind of evil nonce thinks.' The smile had almost transformed into a smirk now.

Zoe wasn't sure how much pontificating she could take from someone still serving time for domestic abuse. 'I'm surprised you say that.' She kept her tone sweet. 'Given you were convicted of abusing Holly as well as her mother.'

For the first time she detected a glint of anger in Yardley's eyes, though his manner remained unruffled. 'Physical abuse, yes. Never anything sexual.'

'Abuse nonetheless.' Zoe felt she was finally succeeding in pushing Yardley's buttons. She didn't risk looking at Statham to check whether he approved of her line of questioning, but he'd made no attempt to intervene.

'I regret it every day. I was a different person then. I had no idea how to behave. I've made my contrition clear. If there was anything I could do to change things or to make it up to Jude and Holly, I'd do it in a moment.' It sounded like a line he'd used many times before, including probably at the parole hearing. Zoe was all in favour of rehabilitation, but she didn't believe the man in front of her meant a word of what he was saying.

That was interesting in itself. Everything she'd heard about Yardley suggested he was a man more than capable of playing whatever role suited him. If the parole board wanted evidence of repentance and contrition, he'd give it to them by the bucket-load and convince them he was sincere. With her and Statham, he barely seemed to be trying. It was as if he was laughing at them, allowing them to see how the trick was performed. The only sign of emotion he'd shown was when he thought he was being accused of sexual abuse, but that apparent spark of anger had quickly been extinguished.

'You still seem oddly unconcerned about Holly's fate,' Statham observed.

'You don't know what I'm thinking or feeling. Just because I'm not emotionally incontinent, it doesn't mean I don't care.'

'And you deny having anything to do with your daughter's disappearance?'

'I'm in prison, man, in case you hadn't noticed?'

'In an open prison. In the last weeks of your sentence.'

'You think I'd risk getting sent straight back inside by breaching the terms of my licence?'

'As you said,' Statham observed, 'I don't know what you're thinking or feeling. I'll try once more with a different question. Do you know anything about your daughter's disappearance? Can you tell us anything that might help locate her?'

'Why would I know anything? You think I'd kidnap my own daughter?'

'I don't know, Mr Yardley. I know you're never likely to gain legal access to her. I know you've been capable of harming both her and her mother in the past. But if you do know anything, we're giving you an opportunity to tell us before anything happens to Holly.'

'You don't know that I'll never gain legal access to her. I can be very persuasive.'

'Is that right? All I do know is that, if you have any involvement in this, you've definitely destroyed any chance you might have had.'

Yardley shook his head slowly. 'We're wasting each other's time. I've nothing to tell you. But feel free to keep asking. I'm going nowhere. Not for a few weeks anyway.'

Zoe could tell that Statham was barely keeping his temper under control. There was something about Yardley's responses calculated to get under Statham's skin. That was part of Yardley's skill. He knew how to read people. If he'd wanted something from her or Statham, he'd have made the effort to win them over. As it was, he was needling Statham to the point where the DI would either do something he'd regret or be forced to terminate the interview. Zoe didn't want the former, so she decided to take the initiative. 'I think you're right,' she said. 'You're not going to tell us anything unless you want to, whatever you might know. But if you do know something, this interview will be on the record. Whatever happens to Holly will be on your conscience. Let's call it a night, Chris.'

Statham glared at her, and for a moment she thought he was going to resist. 'Yeah, okay. We'll leave you to your own thoughts, Yardley. Whatever those might be.' He rose and they followed Dave Greening into the adjoining room.

'I did warn you,' Greening said. 'I knew you'd get nothing from him.'

'We might have if we'd continued.' Statham was still glaring at Zoe.

'It wouldn't have helped anything if you'd punched him, Chris.'

'Oh, for Christ's sake, I wasn't going to punch anyone.'

'No, but you wanted to, didn't you?'

'I'd have happily done something to wipe that smirk off his face, yes. But I'm not an idiot. I could see it was what he wanted. But I suppose you're right. He wasn't going to give us anything. Though he was lying through his teeth.'

'That was my sense. But we've no leverage to get anything from him. If he really is involved in this, he'll have made sure he's very hands-off.'

'The rules in here are much looser than in a higher-category establishment,' Greening said, 'but we still keep tabs on prisoners' contacts with the outside world. We're not aware of anything unusual in Yardley's behaviour over the last few weeks.'

'That doesn't necessarily prove much,' Zoe said, 'if he's trusted someone else to do this. Might not need a lot to trigger it.'

'But why wait till now?' Statham asked. 'If this is about revenge, why not do it earlier in his sentence?'

'Could be various reasons,' Zoe said. 'We know Jude Parrish spent her days worrying about this. Maybe he enjoyed toying with her. Keep her on edge all that time and then take her by surprise when she's focused on the prospect of him coming out.'

'That's exactly the kind of thing that bastard would enjoy,' Greening said.

Zoe was still thinking. 'Or maybe he couldn't do it until the right person was available.'

'How do you mean?' Statham asked.

'Maybe the person who snatched Holly is someone Yardley met inside. Maybe they couldn't do this until that person was released.'

'It's possible, I suppose. But why would anyone be prepared to do something like this on Yardley's behalf?'

'I've no idea. But, as Yardley said himself, he can be very persuasive.'

'So I keep hearing.' Statham turned to Greening. 'Sounds as if we're going to have to do more digging into Yardley's prison career. His file might be a good place to start, if we can have access to it?'

Greening shrugged. 'Don't know how useful it'll be.'

'Let's give it a go while we're here. It's better than nothing.'

Zoe nodded, thinking about Gary still stuck on his own at home. She assumed nothing would have happened to him, but at present he was more anxious than she'd ever known him to be. The business with Liam Crane had rattled him. On the other hand, she knew Statham was right. If there was any chance of preventing Holly coming to harm, every second was likely to count. 'Yes,' she said. 'It's worth a try. Let's see what we can find.'

CHAPTER FORTY-SEVEN

Brian Fairweather sat in silence for what felt to Annie like an eternity. He'd obviously realised too late that they knew no more than what he had already revealed to them. He also knew it was too late to bite back his words. Annie could tell that he was desperately trying to calculate whether it would be possible somehow to bluff his way out of this.

She and Jennings remained silent, allowing the pressure to build. Fairweather's nervousness was obvious, and she sensed that, more than anything, he wanted to reveal whatever he'd withheld. Finally, he dropped his head into his hands. For a second, Annie thought he was crying, but when he looked up again, his eyes were dry. 'You didn't know, did you? You didn't know anything at all.'

'But now we do,' Stuart Jennings said quietly. 'We know there's something you haven't been telling us. It's time you told us the truth.'

'I was having an affair with Alison Evans.'

'Go on.'

'I know I should have told you straightaway. But I was afraid it would just put me firmly in the frame for her death. Or even worse, Carrie.'

'You didn't kill her?' The question had to be asked, even if only to ensure they had Fairweather's denial on the record.

'Of course not.'

'And you don't think your wife killed Alison Evans?'

'I'm sure she didn't.' Fairweather fell silent again, and Annie could tell he had more to say. 'Look, the truth is that she'd found out about the affair and she was angry about it. That was why Carrie turned up the night Alison died.'

'This isn't what you told us before,' Annie pointed out.

'No, well, Carrie and I concocted the story about us taking her to dinner. We thought it would sound less incriminating. I'd arranged to take Alison for dinner. I'm not even sure why. Mainly because I wanted to see whether our relationship could be anything more than a sordid sex in the afternoon thing, I suppose. I'd told Carrie I was attending a business dinner, but she'd obviously guessed the truth. She must have followed me, because she turned up out of the blue to issue an ultimatum. Either Alison and I ended our affair or Carrie would divorce me and take every penny she could.'

'Isn't that your job?' Jennings asked. 'Helping men to prevent that happening?'

'That was the problem. Carrie had been a lawyer herself, and I'd talked to her extensively about my work. She knew all the tricks and mechanisms I use to help my male clients. And she knew how to avoid them.' He shrugged. 'I don't know whether she'd have succeeded or not, but it was a battle I'd have preferred not to have.'

'But despite her anger, you don't believe she killed Alison Evans?'

'Carrie wasn't that sort of person. She could have a temper but she wasn't capable of hurting anyone. And I didn't want to leave her, or for her to leave me. If I was being presented with a choice between her and Alison, I was always going to choose Carrie. She knew that.'

'Even if she didn't kill her deliberately,' Annie asked, 'isn't it possible they got into some argument that night? It wouldn't have taken much, just a push or shove, to make Evans slip off that hillside.'

'Of course it's conceivable. But I don't see how. She didn't go outside when Alison did. We only went out afterwards to try to find her.'

'Tell us about the affair,' Jennings said. 'How long had it been going on?'

'Just a couple of months.' Fairweather shook his head. 'I was already regretting becoming involved with her.' He offered a thin smile. 'I'm not that sort of person.'

No, Annie thought, men never think they are. 'So why did you do it?'

'It was Alison who made the running. I was – well, just too weak to resist, I guess.'

Annie would normally treat that sort of response with the scepticism it deserved. But in this case, she could probably believe it. Evans had wanted to get close to Fairweather and this would have been the quickest way to do it. As long as you weren't too bothered by the ethical niceties. That would also explain why Evans was so uncommunicative with her contacts in the NCA. Presumably, her tactics would never have been officially sanctioned. 'You met through your wife?'

'Yes, she got to know Carrie through the wildlife group. I don't think Carrie was even that keen on her, but Alison had a knack of inveigling her way into relationships, so she became part of Carrie's circle of friends.' He paused. 'Then one day she turned up at the office.'

'Your office?'

'Yes. She asked if I could spare her a few minutes. I wasn't too busy, so I was happy to do it. We sat in my office and chatted for a while, and she told me she'd applied for a job with us and been disappointed to get turned down. To be honest, I hadn't made the connection till that point. We get a lot of applications for any admin job we advertise. From what I remember, she'd been fairly well qualified for the role, but we'd decided to go with someone we already knew. She said she'd been disappointed because she was keen to get into legal work. She asked if she could pick my brains about how to improve her chances of getting a job.'

'Pick your brains?' Jennings made it sound like an innuendo.

'To be honest, I didn't think there was much I could tell her. But she said she was happy to buy me lunch in return so I thought, why not. We met for lunch a couple of days later. Nothing fancy, just one of the local pubs.' He laughed, though without any obvious mirth. 'I even ended up paying. But I didn't mind. By that stage, she'd made it clear her interest was really in me rather than in obtaining a job. She'd met me briefly once or twice when she'd visited Carrie, and she said she was keen to get to know me better.'

I bet she was, Annie thought. She could easily imagine how Brian Fairweather – approaching middle-age, balding, slightly overweight – would have been flattered by the attentions of an attractive, relatively young woman like Alison Evans. It wouldn't have taken much to sucker him in.

'So that's how it happened,' Fairweather said. 'I'm not proud of it. I started to regret it as soon as it started.'

'So why didn't you bring it to an end?' Jennings asked.

'It's not that easy, is it? I didn't want to hurt Carrie, but I didn't want to hurt Alison either. I mean, I liked her, even if I regretted getting involved with her. To be honest, I'm not sure how balanced she was. She struck me as a bit neurotic. I was afraid that if I called it off, she'd go and tell Carrie. I felt stuck between a rock and a hard place.'

'So what brought things to a head?'

'Carrie found out. My own stupid fault. Looking back, I wonder if I subconsciously wanted her to. Apparently, I'd accidentally sent a text intended for Alison to Carrie. I didn't realise I'd done it, but it even had Alison's name in it. Turned out that Carrie had already been suspicious that something was going on. I'd been doing the clichéd stuff. Pretending to work late at the office. Supposedly meeting clients after work. It had all seemed odd to Carrie, because it wasn't how I usually was. So the text confirmed what she was already suspecting.'

'And it was after that that she gave you the ultimatum?'

'Like I said, she just turned up. She said she wanted to see me and Alison together. She wanted me to make a choice.'

'And what actually happened?' Annie was thinking back to that evening in the snowbound pub.

Fairweather offered a rueful smile. 'The snow had its own ideas, didn't it? We'd just got stuck into this increasingly painful conversation when the landlord made the announcement about the snow. The last thing we wanted was for us all to get stuck up there together. So Carrie told us she'd made clear what she wanted and she'd leave us to think about it, but she expected an answer quickly. She'd be taking her car home, leaving me to travel back to Alison's. Not that either of us was exactly in a romantic mood.'

'But you got stranded anyway?' Jennings said. 'That must have been awkward.'

'Very. We'd carried on arguing for too long, and we were among the last to leave. Alison and I went first. I shouldn't have let her drive — I'd driven us up there and she'd had a couple of drinks — but she was angry and I couldn't persuade her not to. We were halfway down the road when she lost control, skidded and ended up with her front wheels in the ditch, blocking the road. We tried to move the car but there was no traction, so we had no choice but to return to the pub. Carrie almost refused to go back up with us, saying she'd find a way through somehow. But there was clearly no possibility of that. So in the end we all traipsed back up. As you say, awkward.'

'And your account of the rest of that night?' Annie said. 'Was that accurate?'

'I think so. We'd all positioned ourselves in different parts of the room on the camp beds the landlord had provided. To be honest, it felt too difficult for us to do anything but keep our distance from each other. I'd already decided that my future lay with Carrie — assuming she was prepared to allow me back — rather than with Alison. But I wanted to have that conversation with Alison in private. For the moment, we just wanted to avoid each other.'

'So, talk us again through what happened?'

'You really do think I killed her, don't you?'

Jennings leaned forward. 'Mr Fairweather. You lied to us in a murder inquiry. You lied to us in an investigation into your own wife's death. I'm hoping you're telling us the truth now, but you'll forgive us for any scepticism.'

'Everything else I've told you is true. There's not much else to say. We all retired for the night. I don't know if it was because we'd had a few drinks – to be honest, we'd needed them to make the situation bearable – or just the stress, but I felt exhausted. Even so, I thought I'd end up lying awake, worrying about what to do. But I didn't. I fell asleep almost straightaway. I didn't wake up till that alarm went off.'

'Then what happened?'

'I was very groggy at first. And of course the lights were still off, so I didn't have much of a clue about what was going on. Then I realised the room was cold and the main doors were open. Then we saw Alison was missing. We went outside to search for her and – well, you know what we found.'

Annie had checked Fairweather's statement before they'd set off here. He and his wife had presumably kept quiet about the affair because they'd been afraid it would seem to implicate them in the killing. But everything else seemed consistent with what they had explained at the time. That didn't necessarily mean it was true, but it was still difficult to see how Fairweather would have had sufficient time to kill Evans and then return to the pub in the moments after the alarm had been triggered.

'Tell us about your relationship with Alison Evans,' Jennings said. 'I don't want the gory details, but tell us what sort of person she was. Sounds like you must have got closer to her than anyone else seems to have.'

The real question, Annie thought, was what information Fairweather had divulged to Evans, and she guessed that this was what lay behind Jennings's question.

'What can I tell you?' Fairweather said. 'Like I said, she made all the running initially, though I can't pretend I was an unwilling participant. I thought at first she was just flirting, flattering me so I'd give her the benefit of my experience. But it quickly became clear that she was serious about wanting a relationship with me. I couldn't believe it at first. I was afraid I was misreading the signals, but they became fairly unambiguous. One afternoon she invited me to come over to her house after work and – well, you can guess the rest.'

'What sort of person was she?' Annie asked.

'You said I got closer to her than anyone else,' Fairweather said. 'That might be true, but I didn't feel I got very close to her. She was a very private person. She mentioned about her father and this supposed former boyfriend, but apart from that she hardly mentioned family or friends. She talked about her job, but she didn't feel the work was interesting, so there wasn't a lot to say about that. She never talked about her past. Looking back, it feels a bit weird, but I was too caught up in it to stop to think. I probably did most of the talking, to be honest.'

I bet you did, Annie thought. No doubt Evans had been expert at extracting information from those she dealt with. The ethics of embarking on a sexual relationship to achieve that were questionable to say the least, but Annie could envisage the post-coital pillow talk would have been highly conducive to achieving Evans's aims. 'What did you talk about?'

'She genuinely did seem fascinated by my work. I didn't particularly want to talk shop but that was what she seemed most interested in.'

'Did you discuss individual clients?'

Fairweather shook his head vehemently. 'Not by name, obviously. But we talked about the cases I dealt with and I gave her examples. She focused most on the divorce stuff. At the time, I wondered if it might be because she was thinking about me and Carrie, but she just wanted to know how it all worked from a legal perspective.'

'Did you talk to her about any of the Men First stuff?'

'She seemed particularly interested in that. Alison had been struck by the fact that we specialise in helping men through divorces. She asked quite a lot about that. I can't remember exactly what I said, but I did talk about the Men First sessions. She was fascinated by some of the more extreme characters, but I told her that, as far as I could see, it was all hot air.'

Annie wondered how much Fairweather had actually told Evans. Much more than he realised and perhaps more than he was admitting, she guessed. They knew she hadn't fed that back to her handlers in the NCA. Presumably because she knew that, if they discovered exactly how she'd obtained this information, she'd have been taken out of the field, perhaps permanently. It was possible she'd been keeping the information to herself until she'd finished with Fairweather. If that was the case, then what had happened to it?

'Okay, Mr Fairweather. I'm conscious it's late. That's probably enough for tonight, but we will need to talk to you again.'

Fairweather stared into his empty whisky glass as if hoping it might somehow replenish itself. Annie guessed that the bottle would take a hammering after their departure. 'Will I get into any trouble for lying to you?'

'Obstructing the police is a serious matter, Mr Fairweather. Especially in a murder inquiry. At this stage, I can't guarantee you won't. It'll go much better for you if you co-operate fully with us from now on. And by co-operate I mean tell us the truth, the whole truth and nothing but. If I find you haven't, I'll make damned sure we throw the book at you.'

'Of course.'

'Think about it, and make sure you've told us anything that might be pertinent.' Jennings climbed to his feet. 'Enjoy your Scotch, Mr Fairweather. We'll see ourselves out.'

CHAPTER FORTY-EIGHT

There'd been a brief flurry of snow in the night, and Margaret Delamere woke to see a thin coating of it on the skylight above her bed. The skylight had a blind but she never bothered to close it. Her sleep was disturbed by many things, but daylight was rarely one of them, even in the height of summer. At this time of the year, the question was irrelevant.

She sat up and peered at the clock. Seven thirty. One of her better nights, though her sleep had been troubled by a series of anxiety dreams she could no longer recall. All she remembered was having to complete a basic task which, for some unfathomable reason, was beyond her abilities. Which, she acknowledged, was more or less how her life felt at the moment.

But what her life mostly felt was empty. She was barely even existing. She spent the days trying to read or watch some nonsense on the TV, but she didn't have the concentration to take anything in. She forced herself to eat to a regular schedule because she knew that otherwise she wouldn't bother. Sometimes – and she was always grateful when it happened, even though she knew it would affect her sleep the following night – she dozed off in her chair and woke to find that hours had passed. She'd never done that previously, but now there was nothing to keep awake for.

As she entered the kitchen, she avoided looking at the boxes of painkillers and the bottle of whisky. They were developing an almost hypnotic attraction. She ought to put them away – or even throw them away – but couldn't bring herself to. She did manage to avoid looking back as she filled the kettle and made herself a coffee.

She'd also been plagued through the night by memories of Liam Crane, inspired by her reading of the online article the previous day. She was disturbed by the story mainly because she knew what an unpleasant figure Crane was. At the time, she'd thought about tipping off her daughter about Crane's apparently influential position in the Men First movement. But now the idea felt slightly absurd. Even if she could bring herself to call Annie, what would she say? As far as she was aware, Crane was doing nothing illegal. It occurred to Margaret that she was simply seeking an excuse to talk to her daughter, but what would be the purpose of that?

Even so, the memory of Crane continued to nag at Margaret. She carried her coffee through to the living room and, as she did every morning, booted up her tablet. While she waited, she walked over to the window and looked down on the streets below. The snow was still there, whitening the pavements and grassed areas, but it was only a thin sprinkling. The traffic into the city seemed to be running normally and the main roads looked clear.

She returned to the sofa and picked up the tablet. She gave the news headlines a cursory look then carried out a search on Crane's name. There wasn't a great deal. A couple of articles mentioning him in the context of the Men First group, which added little to the piece she'd already read. Then, in a selected archive from one of the local papers, she found a report on the court case that had followed the investigation Margaret had been involved in all those years before. The report was very short – the edition had been archived because it had carried a much more prominent story about one of the local football teams – and told Margaret nothing she hadn't known already, other than to remind her of the names of Crane's two accomplices.

Margaret re-read the report and frowned. The two names had been long lost to her memory, but one of them now seemed oddly familiar. She'd seen it somewhere recently, though she couldn't immediately recall where. A more recent news story but in some completely different context. The name had presumably stuck in her mind because she'd recognised it, if only subconsciously.

After a moment, she tapped the name into the search engine in the hope she might identify the article she'd been reading. There were a couple of recent news reports which included the name, the second of which was the one she'd read previously. She re-read it now, intrigued by the apparent coincidence.

If that was what it was. Unlike her daughter, Margaret had never had an instinctive feel for an investigation, but something about this didn't feel right. She ought to speak to someone about this, at least draw attention to the background of the individual in question. But Margaret was a pariah in the force among the few people who remembered her. She could call anonymously, but no one would pay any attention. It wasn't as if she really had much to tell them. Just that one of the people involved might have been part of an investigation years before. The individual had been charged with no crime, and she had no knowledge of what they'd been doing in the intervening period.

The only person she could tell about this was Annie. Annie might well be involved in the investigation. If not, she'd at least know whether Margaret's information was likely to be of any value. For all the tensions between them, she'd at least take Margaret seriously.

That seemed to be the only available channel to tell the authorities what she knew. But it would involve speaking to Annie, and that was still the last thing Margaret wanted at the moment.

She looked again at the two news reports that mentioned the name, trying to persuade herself she had nothing that was likely to be of value to the police. But the thought kept nagging at her. It was probably not important. It would probably go nowhere.

It might be nothing more than a coincidence. But it was just conceivable it might be significant.

Margaret picked up her phone from the table, cradling it in her hand, trying to decide what to do.

CHAPTER FORTY-NINE

Zoe dropped her bag heavily by her desk and then slumped on to the chair behind it. 'I'm knackered already.'

Annie looked up from the file she'd been reading. 'Bad night?'

'Pretty bad. Though for once I wasn't the cause.'

It was clear she wanted to talk. The open-plan office was largely empty and Annie was happy to listen. 'What's the problem?'

'Gary. Well, not Gary. But this Liam Crane character.'

'Don't tell me he's reappeared already?'

'Not only that. He turned up at Gary's work.'

'Oh Christ. You've got to do something about this, Zo. Have a chat with our uniformed colleagues.'

'Told the guy on security he was Gary's father-in-law and supposed to be meeting him for a beer. The security guy was stupid enough to let him into the building, so he took Gary by surprise.'

'Sounds to me like he's doing just enough to keep you both intimidated without crossing the line into actual threats.'

'That's certainly what it feels like.'

'I'm assuming you've already checked his record?'

'Yeah, and everything she'd told me about that is true. But he's been out for a while now.'

'How are you feeling about it? You could do without this additional stress after all you've been through.'

'Funnily enough, in that respect, I feel better than I have in a long while. Before this, I'd been feeling a kind of unfocused anxiety, as if there was something troubling me that I couldn't even understand, let alone do anything about. This at least feels like a practical problem, even if there's no easy solution.'

Annie was about to offer some response when her phone buzzed on the desk. She picked it up and glanced at the screen. 'Speaking of parental challenges, Margaret. I'd better take this in private. Maybe she's heard about the CPS's decision.' She took the call. 'Mum. Just bear with me a sec. I'll go and find somewhere quiet to talk to you.'

With a wave to Zoe, she left the office and walked down the corridor till she found an unoccupied meeting room. 'Okay, Mum, what can I do for you?'

She was half-expecting Margaret to respond with one of her usual sarcastic jibes. But instead, in a meeker tone than Annie had heard from her before, she said, 'I'm sorry to have disturbed you at work. I wouldn't normally.'

'You can call me whenever you want, Mum.'

'Well, you're busy. I haven't wanted to intrude.' Any statement of this kind from Margaret would normally have been uttered with a passive-aggressive undertone, but Annie didn't pick up any sense of that. Margaret sounded almost sincere. 'I've some information that I thought might possibly be of value to you or your colleagues.'

'Work-related information, you mean?' In all her years in the force, Annie couldn't recall Margaret ever offering any information connected to Annie's work. Most of Margaret's comments about Annie's job had been disdainful, typically implying that Annie's career hadn't progressed fast enough or comparing Annie's time in the job adversely to her own.

'It may be nothing. Just a coincidence. But I know that the most trivial piece of information can sometimes be valuable.'

'Anything can help,' Annie agreed. 'Go on, Mum.'

She listened while Margaret told her what she'd spotted. Margaret finished apologetically, 'That's all it is, really. It seems even less now I've told you. I don't want to waste your time.'

Annie had never heard her mother talk like this. In some respects, it was a welcome change from the old abrasive Margaret. But it also worried her. Her mother sounded defeated, almost literally beaten. 'It might be really useful information, Mum. It's certainly an interesting coincidence.'

'Well, I've told you. It's probably nothing.'

'No, really. This might be valuable. Mum—' She was about ask if she could visit Margaret, start to rebuild some bridges, but her mother had already ended the call, not even pausing to say goodbye. Annie stared at her phone for a moment, wondering whether she should call Margaret back. She suspected that her mother would simply let the call ring out.

Perhaps she should visit Margaret. Turn up at her flat without warning. But again, she'd probably get no further than the entrance lobby. Even so, the call had left her concerned. Not by the content, though that was interesting enough. But by her mother's manner.

Annie felt she needed a chat with Sheena to help her think what to do. But that would have to wait until later. For the moment the priority was the investigation into the two still unexplained murders. And what she'd just heard might conceivably offer a new and unexpected lead.

CHAPTER FIFTY

'Looks as if we might finally be getting somewhere,' Statham said. 'Though I'm not entirely sure where.'

The previous evening, Dave Greening had allowed them to examine Ben Yardley's prison file. The content itself had been largely unilluminating, not least because of Yardley's unblemished record during his time in prison. He'd been subject to no adjudications or disciplinary action, and the file notes were largely a bland recognition of his good behaviour. Zoe could see now why, despite the reasons for Yardley's conviction, the parole board would have struggled to find any justification to delay his release on licence. There were a few mentions of Yardley's work on men's rights issues, but they were approving references to his academic efforts and achievements.

Nevertheless, the file did contain details of all the prisons in which Yardley had been accommodated during his time inside. He'd been luckier than some prisoners and had only been moved twice prior to his most recent move to the open prison. The next task had been to identify prisoners Yardley might have come into contact with and who'd subsequently been released.

That information had proved harder to obtain, because the relevant data wasn't held locally within the prison. Statham had decided to restrict their initial search to prisoners, released in the previous twelve months, who'd spent any part of their sentence in the establishments where Yardley had been held.

For the moment, the two missing children cases were being handled as a single inquiry. The physical search for Lucas

Pritchard had been suspended, and the first round of local house-to-house enquiries was complete. The team was now systematically pursuing any credible leads emerging from Amy Pritchard's TV appeal, but so far with no success. Zoe had sensed that, as time passed with no breakthrough, the energy had begun to ebb from the inquiry. Although the snatching of Holly Parrish was horrific in itself, it had at least re-energised the team, prompting the hope that this new development might generate new avenues of investigation.

The missing children were being treated as the major priority, and further resources were being drafted in to support the inquiry. Andy Metcalfe had been temporarily taken off the Alison Evans case and entrusted with the task of trying to find out more about Ben Yardley's contacts during his time in prison. After several abortive calls, he had eventually been directed to someone in Prison Service HQ who, at least in theory, should have been able to help.

After some backside-covering consultations with more senior managers, a list of names had been provided, along with the dates when each individual had been in the relevant establishment. No analysis had yet been carried out on which of these individuals had actually overlapped with Yardley, but Statham had felt it would be quicker and more reliable to analyse the data themselves. The task had been allocated to Andy Metcalfe, working with one of the analysts on the team. Statham had asked Zoe and a few other team members to join them as they talked through the findings.

'Andy's done most of the hard work here and understands the detail, so probably best if he explains it,' Statham said.

Andy cleared his throat nervously and said, 'It's all pretty straightforward, really. We were able to eliminate quite a lot of the original names simply because they hadn't been at the relevant establishments at the same time as Yardley. It's unlikely he would have encountered them. That still gives us a fairly long list because Yardley didn't move much during his sentence.

Here's the detail.' Andy handed out a copy of the list to each of the people round the table. 'I've organised the list by establishment in chronological order of the time Yardley was there. I've also included the dates when each of the other individuals was also there. There are a few where the overlap was very brief so contact may have been limited or non-existent. Conversely, there are some where the overlap was considerable – and a couple that overlapped with Yardley in more than one establishment – so contact would have been more likely. I've put an asterisk next to those ones, as we should probably treat them as the priority.'

'We're going to have to look into each one of these names,' Statham said. 'First, check out their police record, find anything that looks like a red flag. We don't yet have information on why these people were inside, so first priority should be to see if we have any paedophiles, sex offenders and the like.'

'We might be wasting our time,' one of the team pointed out. 'We don't even know if Yardley's actually involved.'

Statham glared at the speaker. 'So far we've hit a dead end with the Pritchard kid. This is just one line of inquiry but it's more promising than most.' He didn't need to add the words, 'So shut it, sunshine,' Zoe thought, but it was clearly what he was thinking.

'I'll divvy these up in a second,' Statham went on. 'Before we start digging, though, does anyone recognise any of these names?'

Zoe ran her eye down the column of names. Then her breath caught in her throat. For a second she could hardly bring herself to speak. Finally, she broke the silence. 'I recognise at least one.'

Statham nodded encouragingly. 'Great. Which one?'

The name was partway down the first page and had been asterisked. Zoe tried to keep her voice steady. 'Liam Allan Crane.'

'Where did you come across him?'

Zoe looked around the room, conscious all eyes were on her. She couldn't bring herself to answer Statham's question with all these people listening in. 'Not in a work context. It's a long story. Look, Chris, I'd rather discuss this in private first of all. It has some personal implications.'

Statham looked at her with undisguised curiosity. 'Okay, let's have a chat. The rest of you continue going through the list and see if you spot any other familiar names.' He turned to Andy Metcalfe. 'I don't imagine we'll be long, but if you finish before we get back, divvy up the names among the team here as you think best. Save some for me and Zoe to deal with. We need to get on with this as quickly as we can. Okay, Zoe, let's find somewhere quiet where you can tell me about Liam Allan Crane.'

CHAPTER FIFTY-ONE

'Still some snow up here,' Stuart Jennings observed. Annie was driving and he was in the passenger seat, gazing out at the rugged landscape. The black hillside rose above them, stark against the morning sky.

'Some of that'll be from last night,' Annie said. 'Though it does linger up here, in the shadier corners.'

She'd turned off the main road, heading uphill towards their destination. 'I hope I'm not wasting our time with this. You didn't need to come.'

'What, and let you claim all the credit if there does turn out to be something in it? No chance.' He laughed to signal that he was joking, though Annie wasn't sure he entirely was.

'Well, your choice. We'll see what he has to say.'

'You think there might be any significance to this?'

'I've no idea, but it's an interesting coincidence. It's not as if we're overwhelmed with other leads.'

'True enough. And as we all know, lesson one in the invest-igatory rule book is never to trust coincidences. How did you come across this nugget anyway?'

When Annie had shared the information with Jennings, she'd been vague about its provenance, but she'd known Jennings wouldn't be satisfied with that. 'Would you believe from my mother?'

Jennings looked at her in surprise. 'The blessed Margaret? I thought you were *persona non grata* with her.'

'So did I. She phoned me out of the blue just to share this titbit of information. It was something she'd spotted in the local media. I was as surprised as you are. To be honest, the whole thing left me a bit worried. About her, I mean. She didn't seem her usual self, if you get my drift.'

'She's got a lot on her plate,' Jennings commented.

'No word yet from the CPS presumably?'

'Not that I'm aware of. Must be hell, waiting like that.'

'I want to help her, but I'm not sure she wants my support.'

'Has to be her choice, I guess.'

Annie took another left and the road grew steeper. 'Nearly there.'

'There was nothing on record about this?'

'Nothing. I checked back in case we'd missed something, but there's no police record. But that's not surprising. No charges were brought. I imagine there's relevant material on this Liam Crane's file, but we had no reason to look at that until my mum provided this information.'

'And Crane's interesting because he's involved in this Men First stuff?'

Annie still hadn't told Jennings about Crane's apparent link with Zoe Everett. Zoe had divulged that information to Annie in confidence, and as yet Annie had no reason to break it. She'd hoped to be able to speak to Zoe before they'd left, but Zoe had been tied up in a meeting with Chris Statham. Even so, it was another odd layer of coincidence to overlay on what was already feeling like a convoluted and baffling picture.

'I tracked down one of the articles my mum was referring to. It was in one of the national tabloids, not some local paper. Seems as if Crane's been appointed – or more likely appointed himself – as a kind of leader or spokesman for this group. The article is largely just him mouthing off but, from what my mum said about his character, there are a few comments that might give us cause for concern.'

'Sounds as if the next step is for us to track down this Liam Crane then?'

'I've got someone working on that. He should be easily traceable. Just thought the link here was worth checking out.

Feels like the first time we've had an opportunity to join any dots, even if it is a bit of a long shot. Here we are.'

The entrance to the pub car park was a sharp right from the road. The place felt very different from her previous visit. Then it had been closed, the car park largely deserted. Now, on a late weekday morning shortly before Christmas, there were welcoming decorations across the front of the building and the car park was already filling up. The previous night's snow flurries were long gone, and the day was clear and bright. Annie parked as near to the entrance as she could, and they made their way inside.

It was still some time until the start of the lunchtime service, and the interior was far from busy, except for an elderly man at the bar and a couple of small groups enjoying pre-lunch drinks. In the next hour or so the place would become busy. Some tables were already laid out for groups – presumably the first of the office or similar parties. There were a couple of staff behind the bar, including Ellie Brompton who'd been present on the night of Alison Evans's death. Robbie Crowther, the landlord, was patrolling the room, checking the settings on the reserved tables. He looked up as they entered, and Annie thought she caught a look of surprise on his face, quickly replaced with a welcoming smile. 'DI Delamere.'

'Good morning,' Annie said. 'This is my colleague, DCI Jennings. We wondered if you might be able to spare us a few minutes.'

'To be honest, it's not an ideal time. We're going to be rushed off our feet this lunchtime. It's that time of year.'

Jennings looked pointedly at his watch. 'We do appreciate that, Mr Crowther. It shouldn't take us very long. Just a couple of points we want to check out.'

Crowther hesitated, clearly wanting to say no. 'I suppose I can spare a few minutes.'

'That's very good of you. Is there somewhere we can talk in private?'

'We can use the office at the back.' He led them past the bar and though a door opening on to a corridor. To the left, they could hear the noises from the kitchen. Crowther took them through a door on the right into the small administrative office. 'My wife's running the kitchen. I need to let her know I'll be tied up for a little while. Can I get you a coffee or anything while I'm in the kitchen?'

Jennings shook his head. 'Don't trouble yourself. We won't keep you any longer than necessary.'

While they waited for Crowther to return, Jennings idly walked around the office, peering at the papers on the desk. 'Not exactly orderly.'

'He's a publican, not an accountant. Seems to be doing all right with this place, though.'

'Bucking the trend, then. A lot of pubs struggling these days. He must have a decent dining offering to bring people out here.'

'That's my impression. There are a few locals at the bar, but it's mainly people coming to eat.'

'I'd be interested to see the books—' Jennings began, then cut himself off abruptly as Crowther re-entered the door. He sat himself at the desk, facing them, and gestured for them to take the remaining two chairs. It was a room furnished for practicality rather than comfort. 'So what can I do for you?'

Annie decided to jump straight in. 'Does the name Liam Crane mean anything to you?'

She could see that the question had startled Crowther. His face showed no obvious reaction, but there was something in his eyes that suggested she'd caught him by surprise.

'That's a name from the past.'

'So we understand. Perhaps you can tell us how you knew Crane?'

Crowther's eyes narrowed in suspicion. 'I'm assuming you know. Otherwise you wouldn't be here asking. Though I don't understand what it has to do with anything.'

'I'd be grateful if you could just humour us for a few moments, Mr Crowther,' Jennings said.

'Okay, he was a mate. Someone I hung around with years ago.'

'When are we talking about?' Annie asked.

'Twenty years ago or so.'

The timescale fitted Crane's time inside. He'd been sentenced to fifteen years for the manslaughter and, partly because of his behaviour inside and partly because of his extensive previous record of violence, he'd been refused parole on several occasions. Annie estimated Crowther was in his early forties, which meant he'd known Crane in his early twenties.

'When did you last see him?'

Crowther looked from Annie to Jennings and then back again. 'You obviously know he's been inside since then.'

'We also know you were with him shortly before he committed the crime that put him there.'

There was silence for a moment before Crowther responded. 'I'd been with him earlier, along with another mate, but he'd left us when he ran into this guy he had the problem with. I didn't know anything about it until the police took me in. But Crane himself confirmed he acted alone.'

He was talking too quickly and saying too much, Annie thought. He was lying, and he was worried they knew he was lying. He didn't know what they knew. 'You initially provided an alibi for him?'

'Only because it wasn't a good idea to cross Liam Crane. In retrospect, I was stupid. Should have told the truth from the beginning. I was lucky to get away with it, but I learned my lesson.'

'You were a witness at Crane's trial?' Jennings asked.

'All I could do was tell the court what I saw, which wasn't much. And the defence wanted me to provide something of a character statement about Crane.'

'And you did that?' From what she'd read about Crane, she imagined it would be quite a challenge.

Crowther shrugged. 'As best I could. It was mainly a matter of saying I'd never really seen the violent side of him. Which was true. I'd seen him lose his temper once or twice, but I'd never seen any real evidence of physical violence.'

'Are you aware he's out of prison now?'

Another silence. Annie had the sense that Crowther was choosing his words very carefully. 'I imagined he must be.'

'He's not been in touch with you?'

Crowther was looking very uncomfortable now, and Annie had little doubt he wasn't telling the whole truth. She could see him glancing uneasily at Jennings, as if he thought some surprise was about to be sprung. 'Not directly.'

'Not directly?'

'I've... I've come across him.'

Jennings leaned forward. 'What does that mean, Mr Crowther?'

'We still have some common associates. I was aware he was out.'

'You said you imagined he must be. Now you're saying you actually knew.'

Crowther was looking confused. 'That's what I meant. I didn't know exactly when he was due for release but I heard he was out.'

'Would you expect him to get in touch?'

'I wouldn't know how he feels about me now.'

'Are you aware of the Men First movement?' Annie asked.

She immediately knew her question had struck home. She could see from Crowther's expression that this was exactly what he'd been worried about. He was afraid they knew more than they did. It took him several seconds to come up with a response. 'I've come across it.'

Annie nodded encouragingly. 'In what context?'

This time, the silence was longer. He was trying to decide whether to lie to them. She glanced at Jennings, both of them allowing the silence to extend. Finally, Crowther took a breath. 'Steph's my first wife but I had a couple of kids with another woman, years ago. Truth is, I was a mess when I first met Steph.

Drinking too much, doing some drugs. That was when I fell in with Liam Crane, which in retrospect was a big mistake. I'd walked out on my former partner and our kids. Probably for the best, because I hadn't been good to them. It's not a period I'm proud of.' He stopped, as if unsure where to take the narrative next.

'Go on.' Annie wasn't sure whether Crowther was really telling the truth, but he seemed to want to unburden himself.

'Crane going inside was a turning point. Not that I realised it at the time. I'd thought for a while that I'd end up inside myself. If Crane had tried to implicate us in what he'd done, that might have happened. I met Steph not long after that, working behind the bar in a pub I went to. We got together and, well, she helped me see how lucky I'd been and she pretty much dragged me back on to the straight and narrow.'

'Where does Men First fit into this?'

'Only in the last year or so. I've cleaned up my act now, and I'm doing all right with this place. I decided to try to get some access to my children. Their mother refused point-blank. From her perspective, that's understandable. She still thinks of me as the person I was back then. I've had no contact with the kids since, and I've never paid any maintenance, mainly because she's never asked for it. So she's not happy for me just to waltz back into her life, especially as she's now married and the children are teenagers who think of her husband as their father.'

'But you felt you had the right to?' Jennings asked.

'It wasn't really like that. Steph can't have kids. It's not been a big deal for us, but I just felt I'd missed something. And, yes, I know that was my own fault. I just wanted to find out what might be possible. I tried consulting a solicitor, but they weren't much help. Then someone – someone who'd known both me and Liam in the past – mentioned this Men First movement. Said it was about promoting men's rights. To be honest, I'm not really interested in all that political campaigning stuff. But he also mentioned they'd been talking to some solicitor who was a specialist in supporting men through divorce proceedings and family-court type stuff. He thought it might be worth me sitting in on one of their sessions to hear what the solicitor had to say. I might be able to grab a few moments with him afterwards and see if it would be worth setting up an individual session with him.'

'And the name of this solicitor is?' Annie wanted to see if Crowther would try to lie to them.

Crowther closed his eyes for a moment, as if he was realising he'd talked himself into a corner. 'Brian Fairweather.'

'So you already knew Fairweather?' Annie said. 'That wasn't the impression you gave me when I spoke to you after Alison Evans's death.'

'I know. I'm sorry. I just wanted to distance myself from all that. I mean, I didn't really know Fairweather. I'd been to one meeting where he was a speaker and I'd chatted to him for a few minutes afterwards. I was still trying to decide whether it would be worth paying for a formal session with him. I recognised him when he walked into the pub and I think he recognised me – he gave me a friendly nod – but I don't think either of us wanted to risk embarrassing the other by acknowledging how we'd met. I didn't think it was worth mentioning when you spoke to me, and presumably he thought the same.'

'It's a pity you didn't tell us this at the time,' Annie said. 'We don't take lightly to people withholding information in a murder inquiry.'

'I didn't think it was important,' Crowther said. 'I'm sorry.'

'And did you encounter Liam Crane at this meeting?' Jennings asked.

'No. To be honest, at that point, I wasn't even aware he was involved. The guy who'd told me about the group hadn't mentioned him. I might have had second thoughts about going if I'd known. I didn't know how Liam felt about me. It was only when I got there that I discovered he was supposed to be at the meeting. He couldn't make it on the night for some reason. I wasn't entirely sorry.'

There was something about Crowther's account – or perhaps his manner of recounting it – that didn't quite ring true to Annie. He was speaking fluently enough, but he wasn't telling them everything. 'Have you had any contact with Crane since?'

This time the pause was telling, and Annie knew that Jennings had spotted it as well. Finally, Crowther said, 'No. Nothing at all.'

'You're absolutely certain about that?'

'Of course I'm certain. Look, I really do need to be getting back to the restaurant.' He looked down at his wrist watch, as if checking the time, but Annie suspected he was simply trying to keep his expression concealed from them.

'What would you say if I told you we have evidence that you have been in contact with Crane?' Jennings was clearly just chancing his arm, his question carefully worded.

Crowther still had his head down, but Annie could partly see his startled face. 'I – I'd say you must have got it wrong. I don't know what kind of evidence you could have. I've had no contact with Crane.'

Annie noticed that, despite Crowther's words, his reaction had given Jennings the information he needed. She was expecting Jennings to press Crowther harder, but instead he glanced over at Annie. 'Well, thanks for that, Mr Crowther. I appreciate this isn't the most convenient time to be talking to you, so we'll leave it there for the moment. Thank you for your time.'

Crowther looked up, surprised. 'That's it?'

'We may want to talk to you again. But we'll leave you to get on.' He didn't wait for any response from Crowther and rose to usher Annie out into the corridor. Neither of them spoke till they were outside, standing in the chilly sunshine.

'I thought you were going to push him harder at the end there.'

Jennings shrugged. 'I couldn't see any point. We don't have any proof yet that he has been in contact with Crane. If we'd continued, I might have been forced to admit that. As it is, he still doesn't know what we know.'

'He's lying, though.' It was a statement, not a question.

'Through his teeth. Which is why it's better to let him stew. And our next step is to track down this Crane character.'

CHAPTER FIFTY-TWO

'He's claiming to be your father?' Statham's jaw hadn't quite literally dropped, but his expression suggested it still might.

Zoe nodded. 'Although Elaine Simmonds tells me it's almost certainly untrue.'

'You should have raised this formally before now, Zoe.'

'Why? Until a few minutes ago, this had nothing to do with work. It still may not have. All we know is that at some point Crane was in the same prison establishment as Ben Yardley.'

It was clear that Statham had no answer to that. 'So what do we know about this Liam Crane?'

'He is – or at least was – a pretty unpleasant character. He's a lengthy record, culminating in a manslaughter conviction. He may have turned over a new leaf but I'm inclined to doubt it.'

'How was he when he saw your husband?'

'Gary found him threatening. He was very insistent about wanting to see me and Gary was equally insistent that could only be my choice. When I spoke to him on the phone, he was pushy and clearly not happy I didn't just agree to what he was asking. I had the impression of a man who doesn't like being told no.'

'But he's not actively tried to do anything? Tried to force his way into your house or anything like that?'

'Nothing yet, other than inveigling his way into Gary's workplace. When Gary stood up to him, on both occasions, he eventually just turned and walked away. The question is what might happen if his patience runs out.'

'And the other more urgent question is whether he's the sort of man who might snatch young Holly Parrish on behalf of Yardley.'

'It's hard to say. There's no doubt in my mind that Crane has a proprietorial approach to children. I can imagine he might feel that even more strongly about young children, so I'd guess he'd at least be sympathetic to Yardley's position. But it's a big step from being sympathetic to actually snatching a child. We know Yardley can be persuasive, but it would take a hell of a lot of charm to talk someone into doing that.'

'Unless Yardley has some other hold over him.'

'It's possible, I suppose.'

'We'd better head back to the main meeting. See if anyone's spotted any other interesting names in that list. Thanks for telling me about all this, Zoe. I wish you'd felt able to share it with me before, if it was causing you concern.'

'Like I said, I didn't think it was anything to do with work.'

'I bet you told Annie, though.'

'Annie's a friend as well as a colleague. With all due respect, Chris, you and I haven't quite reached that stage yet.'

'Maybe one day, eh?'

'Let's get back, shall we? Look, I'd prefer it if you didn't share this with the rest of the team, unless you really feel we need to. I'd rather get to the bottom of this for certain before I start spreading the news.'

'I don't see it's relevant at the moment. I'll just say you've come across Crane outside of work so you were concerned about a possible conflict of interest. We can also say we've checked out Crane and there are good reasons to investigate him more formally.'

'Thanks, Chris. Appreciated.'

'There you go. Maybe that friendship might be closer than you thought.'

When they re-entered the main meeting room, the discussion was ongoing. Statham sat down and looked round the room. 'You buggers all look bloody smug. What's going on?'

'We were just starting to divvy up the names,' Andy said. 'But there are a few on there that are familiar to people.'

'Any likely child snatchers?'

'Not sure. A couple who were apparently inside for sex offences, but nothing involving children as far as we're aware.'

'Still, it's a start. Treat them as a priority.'

'There's one other name on there that's also particularly interesting,' Andy said.

'Okay, then, spit it out. I can see you're dying to.'

'Tom Kenning.'

'Kenning? Lucas Pritchard's father?'

'One and the same. Thomas Simon Kenning. We've checked while you were out. No question it's the same guy. He only served a short sentence, but he overlapped with Yardley for a couple of months.'

'Well, well. We knew Kenning had served time, but there was nothing that directly put him in the frame for child snatching. Most likely a coincidence, but we're finding a few of those now. Kenning has no solid alibi for the time of Lucas Prichard's disappearance. This definitely puts him back on the list. Let's bring him in for another chat. Meanwhile, we need to work through the rest of the names to see what else we turn up. Zoe and I will follow up on this Liam Crane.'

Zoe could see that one or two of the team were regarding her with curiosity so she added, 'I've come across him in a personal capacity. Nothing important, but I wanted to avoid any potential conflict of interest.'

Statham nodded. 'I'm good with that for the moment, but if it looks like it might be a problem, you can step back.'

That hadn't done much to satisfy the curiosity, Zoe knew, but it was all they were going to get for the moment. Most of the team were happy they finally seemed to be making some progress. The last thing anyone wanted was to think too closely about what might have happened, or was happening, to Holly Parrish or Lucas Pritchard. All they wanted was to find them.

They left the rest of the team sorting through the list of names, and Zoe followed Statham back through to the office.

'First thing is to track down this Liam Crane,' he said.

'That should be easy enough,' Zoe said. 'We can presumably get his address through probation.'

'You said he'd given you his mobile number? That would be a quicker way of contacting him than wading through the bureaucracy.'

'I'd feel uncomfortable acting as some kind of decoy, unless we're absolutely certain he's involved.'

'At this stage, all we want to do is talk to him. If he is involved…'

'I know.'

'Look, Zoe, all we need's an address.'

'Okay, but let me play it my way. If he's not involved in this, I still don't want him in my life. I don't want to lead him on until I really know the truth.'

'I don't care how you play it, as long as you get the address.'

She'd almost thrown away the number that Crane had left with Gary. She'd entered it into her phone only so she could block the number. Now, feeling unaccountably nervous, she found the number and dialled. She felt almost relieved when, after ringing for a few seconds, the call went to voicemail. She glanced at Statham, then said, 'Mr Crane. This is Zoe Everett. I want to speak to you. Can you call me back on this number? Thanks.' She tried to keep her voice steady and toneless, not wanting to leave Crane with any clue as to her reasons for phoning.

She ended the call and said, 'Voicemail. If he's as keen to hear from me as he claims, it shouldn't take him long to call me back.'

It took even less time than Zoe had expected. Crane was obviously a man who screened his callers. She nodded to Statham and took the call.

'Zoe. You got my message through that husband of yours, presumably. I'd be delighted to talk.'

She took a breath. 'I don't want you to jump to any conclusions. I still don't really know who you are or if you're telling the truth. Even if you are, I don't know that I want you in my life.'

'Zoe—'

'We've already been through this. I don't owe you anything. You've never been part of my life and you've done nothing for me. You have no rights at all.'

'So why are you calling me?'

'I'm calling you because if you are who you claim to be, I want to know more about you before I make any decisions. I'm prepared to talk to you. But for the moment that's all I'm prepared to do.'

There was a moment's silence, presumably as Crane absorbed what she'd said. 'So what do you want to do?'

'I'm willing to meet you. Just to talk.'

'Fine. Where do you want to meet? Your place?'

'I've thought about that. Definitely not there. I don't want Gary involved any more than he needs to be. Not at this stage. So I thought about meeting somewhere neutral.' She paused, wondering whether she could make her next words sound convincing. 'Then I thought, no, that's not what I want. I want to meet you wherever it is you're living. See you in your own environment.'

'It's not exactly—'

'I don't care what it's like. If I'm going to make a decision about this, I need to know who you really are. I need to get a sense of you. We either meet and talk this way, the way I want, or we don't meet at all.'

'You're not worried about meeting me alone in my own flat?'

253

'I'm not afraid of you, if that's what you mean. Should I be?'

'No, of course not. It's just—'

'It's the only offer on the table. Take it or leave it.'

'Okay, I'll take it. When do you want to do this?'

'I can't do it for another few days. I'm up to my ears at work and just haven't the time. But as soon as we can.'

They agreed a time the following week and Crane finally divulged his address. She recognised from the postcode that it must be somewhere in the vicinity of Buxton. 'I'll see you then,' she said.

'I'm looking forward to it.' After a pause, Crane added, 'Thanks.'

As she ended the call, Statham put his palms together in a gesture of mock applause. 'Well done.'

'I don't feel good about it. If he's not involved in taking Holly Parrish, I'm taking advantage of him. And when he receives an immediate visit from the police, it won't be hard for him to guess who tipped them off.'

'I know, and I know this is a long shot. But we've got to follow up any possible lead. Our priority has to be finding the children. We may be too late with Lucas, but there's still a chance with Holly. You've done the right thing.'

'I know. And I know you're right. It doesn't stop me feeling bad about it.'

'Trust me, you'll feel a whole lot better if this helps us get to Holly in time.'

'And if we don't?'

'I don't even want to think about that, Zoe. Not yet.'

CHAPTER FIFTY-THREE

Annie arrived back at the office to find Zoe at her desk, her eyes glued to the computer screen. There was no sign of Chris Statham.

'Can you spare me a couple of minutes, Zo? I've something I want to talk to you about. Somewhere private?'

'That seems to have been my day so far,' Zoe said. 'A series of clandestine chats. But, yes, sure. The meeting room across the corridor should still be free. That's where I was for the last one. Clandestine chat, I mean.'

'Perils of the open-plan office, isn't it?'

Annie led Zoe out to the meeting room, not speaking till she'd closed the door firmly behind her. 'It's about Liam Crane.'

'I had a funny feeling it might be,' Zoe said. 'He seems to be the centre of everyone's attention at the moment.'

'How do you mean?'

'He's being looked at in connection with the Holly Parrish kidnapping.'

'Really? On what grounds?'

'Pretty tenuous ones, to be honest. Just the possibility that, during his time inside, he might have had dealings with Ben Yardley, Holly's father. We're looking at the possibility that someone might be acting on Yardley's behalf, given he's still inside. Crane's one of the names in the frame. I had to tell Chris about my link to Crane, though he's promised to keep it in confidence. He knows you know.'

'I'd like to have seen Chris's expression when you told him,' Annie said. 'But that's interesting. Because he's just come up on our radar too.'

'In what context?'

'Similarly tenuous, really. Long story, but it relates to Crane's conviction for manslaughter. He had two mates who were supposedly with him at the time and who initially provided him with an alibi. Under pressure, they eventually cracked and admitted Crane had done what he was accused of. They both claimed they weren't involved in the attack and had tried to dissuade him from going ahead. Crane was charged and convicted. The other two weren't.'

Zoe nodded. 'I remember Elaine Simmonds mentioned that when she was telling me why Crane was inside. She said it was Crane and a couple of cronies. Surprised the other two walked away.'

'Interestingly, Crane supported their account. Said they weren't involved. There was no other evidence to prove their involvement. The police weren't too bothered about trying to convict them. They were both small fry, no previous convictions.'

'So what's brought Crane on to your radar now?'

'It's the identity of one of Crane's mates. Turns out he was Robbie Crowther, landlord of the pub where Alison Evans was killed.'

Zoe frowned. 'That's an interesting coincidence. But I don't see why Crane's of interest to you in the first place.'

'This is where it gets convoluted. Crane's of interest because he's involved in a men's rights group called Men First. As is, in a slightly different way, Brian Fairweather, husband of the late murdered Carrie Fairweather, as well as Crowther himself. And it's turned out that the so-called Alison Evans was actually an undercover NCA officer investigating the activities of the men's rights movement in the UK.'

'That's quite a set of links,' Zoe said. 'But I might be able to add to them.'

'Go on.'

'Funnily enough, this Men First outfit's come up in the kidnapping case too. Ben Yardley carried out research into men's rights movements as part of an Open University degree while inside. He's apparently been proselytising about it, as well as providing informal legal advice and general support to other prisoners.'

'Nobody minded that?'

'He was seen as a model prisoner. Studious. Well-regarded. Wouldn't surprise me if he was providing advice to prison officers too. You know the type. That's partly why we think he might be behind Holly's kidnapping. We've also found another potential link. There's a possibility Yardley might have known Tom Kenning, Lucas Pritchard's father. Again, they were inside together for a time during Yardley's sentence.'

Annie gave a low whistle. 'So the two investigations may be linked?'

'I think it's possible. We've a hell of a lot of coincidences here.'

'We need to talk to Stuart and Chris. If these two cases really are one, we must get our ducks in a row. The last thing we need is for us to be tripping over each other.'

'We may need to move quickly then. We're bringing Tom Kenning in again, and Chris is sending someone out to talk to Crane.'

They found Statham in his office, barking angrily into his phone. He looked irritated as he gestured for them to take a seat, and then continued haranguing whoever was on the other end of the line. Annie watched impatiently, feeling sympathy for the poor bugger in question. Statham finished, 'We need to get a warrant then. Or arrest him.' It wasn't clear whether this was a direct instruction, but he ended the call anyway. 'Christ.'

'Problem?' Zoe asked.

'Liam Crane.'

'What's happened?'

'We sent a couple of the team out to talk to him. I told them to play it low-key. Just get in there, try to find out if he does know Ben Yardley or Tom Kenning. Anyway, they tried to do that – at least I bloody well hope they did – but Crane wouldn't play ball. Told them he wouldn't talk to them unless they arrested him and he wouldn't let them into his house unless they came back with a warrant. Basically told them to bugger off. Didn't help that one of our guys lost his rag slightly, so it turned into a slanging match. So much for low-key.'

'It might be worse than you think,' Annie said.

Statham looked at her. 'Have you just come in here to brighten my day?'

'Something like that. Look, can we track down Stuart and get him in here too? I think there's some stuff you both need to hear.'

'We're trying to track down a missing child. We haven't got time—'

'That's the point. You need to hear this before we go any further. Your investigation, our investigation. They may be one. In which case, you may be dealing with someone who's already cold-bloodedly killed two people. We need to be sure about what we're dealing with.'

Statham sighed. 'Okay, let's get Stuart in. Like I said, Annie, you really know how to cheer a person up.'

CHAPTER FIFTY-FOUR

Gary pulled into the driveway and sat for a moment, the engine still running. He hadn't been as open with Zoe as he perhaps should have been. He'd told her what had happened with Liam Crane at the office, but he hadn't told her how it had left him feeling. That was partly because he hadn't been able to articulate it fully, even to himself. He'd been shaken, certainly. He'd been taken aback by Crane's unexpected appearance, and he'd felt intimidated by his words and manner.

But it was only when he'd finally returned home that evening that he'd realised how unnerved he really was. He felt oddly exposed and vulnerable, as if there was nowhere that would provide him with safety or security any more. Crane had seemingly walked into his workplace without any real difficulty. He hadn't as yet actually entered the house, but Gary had little doubt he could, if he wished.

He hadn't told Zoe any of this. Not explicitly, anyway. Partly because at that point he still hadn't quite worked out what he was feeling. Partly because he didn't want her to be worrying in the same way. And partly, he knew, because he hadn't wanted to acknowledge what he inevitably saw as his own weakness.

He told himself he was feeling exactly how Crane wanted him to feel. That was the point of Crane's behaviour: to unsettle Gary, leaving him unsure what he might do next. Soften Gary up, in short, so that he'd go along with what Crane was asking simply to put an end to the tension. But Crane wouldn't hurt him. If he did, he'd be straight back inside.

Gary opened the car door and climbed out into the cold winter evening. The neighbours had their Christmas decorations showing. The most ostentatious ones had strewn their houses liberally with glittering coloured lights, but almost all the houses had brightly illuminated Christmas trees visible through their windows. So far, Zoe and Gary had done nothing, both lacking any enthusiasm for celebrating the season while their current issues remained unresolved.

He fumbled for his house keys, his attention focused on getting the door unlocked. He wanted to be inside, with the door locked behind him. He didn't want to be standing out here. It took him a moment to identify the right key, and then he slid it into the lock.

At that instant, a voice spoke close to his ear. 'Evening, Gary.'

Gary started and then turned. Liam Crane was standing close behind him, smiling gently. Gary couldn't imagine how Crane had approached so silently. He forced himself to respond calmly. 'What do you want?' He gestured towards the dark house. 'You can see Zoe's not here. You're wasting your time.'

'It's not Zoe I want.'

'What do you mean?' Gary took an involuntary step back, trying to work out if he could open the door and enter the house without Crane following.

'I'm disappointed, Gary. I thought we were mates.'

'We're not—'

'You've let me down, Gary. I've just had the police turn up on my doorstep. The only person who could have given them my address was Zoe. But she wouldn't have done that by herself. You must have told her to do it.'

'I don't know what you're talking about.'

'You want rid of me, don't you, Gary? You want me out of your life, even if Zoe doesn't. You set me up.'

'I'd happily never see you again. I won't pretend otherwise. But I didn't set you up.'

Crane shook his head. 'It doesn't much matter what you do, Gary. I'm calling the shots.'

'You can't—'

The blow seemed to come from nowhere, catching Gary on the side of the head. He staggered sideways, crashing against the edge of the porch. The second blow struck him against the back of the head. This time it was sharper, more painful, as if Crane had been holding some heavy object. Gary fell to the ground, rolling on to his back. For a moment, Crane's silhouette loomed over him, and then consciousness slipped away.

CHAPTER FIFTY-FIVE

Stuart Jennings rubbed his temples with the air of someone trying to persuade his brain to start working. 'So you're saying this may have been one case all along?'

'We can't be sure of that. Not yet,' Annie said. 'But there are some strange connections. And Liam Crane seems to be at the heart of it.'

'So we need to talk to this Crane character?'

'That bird's already flown,' Chris Statham said morosely. 'When we sent our guys back out there, there was no sign of him. We've a couple of guys keeping watch on the place but I'm not hopeful. My guess is that he put two and two together, and realised that Zoe must have given us his address.'

'Not the most difficult calculation,' Zoe added. 'But the fact that he responded as he did suggests he's something to hide.'

Zoe was looking troubled, Annie thought. She was no doubt torturing herself about whether she'd done the right thing in extracting Crane's address from him. If it turned out that Crane really was linked to the killings and the child snatchings, the answer was undoubtedly yes. If not, the question might be more problematic.

'We're applying for a warrant to search Crane's flat, but I don't know if we'll succeed,' Statham said. 'We don't have a lot to work with. At the moment it's all circumstantial. We don't even know whether Crane, Yardley and Kenning actually knew each other. We do know that Crane knew Robbie Crowther, but we can't be sure they've actually been in contact since Crane came out of prison.'

'I'm pretty sure Crowther was concealing something from us,' Annie said.

'But we don't know what or how what or how significant it might be,' Jennings added. 'And meanwhile we still have two children missing. So let's think about what we need to do. First thing is to track down this Liam Crane. Does he have a vehicle?'

'Seems likely,' Zoe said. 'He's turned up at our place and at Gary's offices. You could get to both on public transport, but it's not straightforward.'

'Okay, let's get someone on to trying to get the registration,' Jennings said. He turned to Statham. 'You're bringing Tom Kenning in?'

'May even be here by now.'

'Okay, I think we should bring Crowther in too now.' He paused. 'And Brian Fairweather. Put these buggers under some pressure. See if anyone cracks. My guess is that Fairweather in particular won't be accustomed to a serious grilling. We can try Ben Yardley again, but he's too cool a customer to give away anything, unless we've got something more substantive to throw at him. Any other thoughts?'

Annie could see Zoe hesitating before she responded. 'It's just a thought, but what about Elaine Simmonds?'

'The woman who's claiming to be your mother?'

'She told me Crane had just called her out of the blue. Gary was suspicious that she and Crane might be working some kind of scam together. It's a long shot, but she might be another route to tracking him down.'

'Do you have contact details for her?' Jennings asked.

'Only a mobile number. No address. She gave me the impression she lived somewhere fairly remote, but she didn't say where.'

Jennings sighed. 'Okay, if she is working with Crane, there's no point in you calling her. We could try some kind of subterfuge – call her and pretend to be a delivery driver or something – but, if Crane's already alerted her, that might give her a heads-up we're trying to find her. So let's try all the usual routes to find her address first.' He stopped, shaking his head. 'We might be wasting our time anyway.'

'I'm all out of other bright ideas,' Statham said. 'But let's bring Fairweather in and give him a tough time. If he's involved in this, he's likely to be the weakest link.'

As he spoke, there was a knock at the meeting room door and Andy Metcalfe stuck his head inside. 'We've got Tom Kenning here now. In one of the interview rooms. He's ready for you as soon as you've finished.'

Statham glanced at Jennings. 'I know every second's precious, but my instinct's to let him stew for the moment. Might be useful if we can have Crowther and Fairweather here, so we're talking to them at the same time.'

Jennings nodded. 'Let's do these under caution. We've some grounds now for treating them as potential suspects. That'll put some pressure on Kenning. And if he has the option of getting legal advice, it'll buy us a bit of time till the solicitor gets here. We can do the same with Crowther and Fairweather.'

'Sounds good to me,' Statham said. 'I'll enjoy breaking the news to him.' He looked around the table. 'Okay, folks, let's decide who's doing what and then we can get on with it. The priority is still to track down Crane. Given the way he's flown the coop, he's the bastard I really want on the other side of the interview table.'

CHAPTER FIFTY-SIX

Elaine Simmonds turned down the volume on the TV set, and sat in silence for a few moments, straining her ears for any sound. She'd thought she'd heard something a moment before, but hadn't been sure of the source. That was the problem, she told herself. She had to be constantly vigilant, and that meant she was permanently on edge, tensed for a threat that might never become real.

The baby monitor she kept on the table beside her was silent, except for the gentle rhythmic sound of breathing, as soft as the wash of waves on an untroubled beach. Still sleeping, then, as she'd hoped.

She rose from the sofa and walked over to the window. There was a cold wind blowing up the valley, and the location of the cottage left it exposed to the elements. Perhaps that was it. Perhaps the wind had blown something over outside.

From here, she could see down the hillside to where, in the daylight, the curves of the river glittered in the midwinter sun. She wondered now whether she should have moved out of here, at least temporarily. The place was exposed in more ways than one.

Initially, she'd thought it better to stay, telling herself that the very isolation of the place offered protection in itself. There were no close neighbours to wonder what might be happening inside the cottage, no one she had to explain herself to. She could see for miles in all directions, including from the rear of the house down the track that provided the only access to the place. In the daytime at least, she'd hoped it would be difficult for anyone to get up here without her being aware. She could hide herself away here, for as long as it took, without anyone knowing.

She wondered now whether she'd been deluding herself. She'd always been a very private person and there were very few people – just those directly involved in this and a few others she really trusted – who knew her address. That hadn't been a conscious tactic. It was just the way she was. But when she'd embarked on this, she'd hoped that it would offer her sufficient protection. It was no doubt possible for someone to find her, but it would be difficult and it would take time.

But she should have been warned when Liam Crane had phoned her out the blue. She'd tried to tell herself it was just a coincidence. He'd said nothing about Men First or about any of the information Carrie Fairweather had passed on to her. He'd seemed interested only in Zoe, the woman he still insisted was his daughter. Now he was out of prison, he wanted to make an attempt to contact her. Despite what she'd told Zoe, Elaine had long ago identified her daughter and obtained her address. She'd told Zoe the truth when she'd said she'd been in two minds about whether to get in touch. What she hadn't told her was that she'd eventually decided it would be better not to intrude into Zoe's life.

It was only after Crane had reappeared that she'd changed her mind, wanting at least to take the opportunity to alert Zoe. She'd contacted her only with the intention of warning her about Crane, but the moment Elaine had heard Zoe's voice over the phone, she'd become conscious of maternal feelings she hadn't known she possessed. Now Elaine felt that if Zoe was willing to let her back into her life, she'd be happy to take up the offer.

But that might never happen. This had been a hare-brained plan from the start, she thought now, even if their intentions had been good. They hadn't thought through the consequences of what they were doing, or considered how this might end.

They'd just acted in panic on that awful Sunday after Alison Evans's death, and it had all escalated, seemingly unstoppably, from there.

Carrie Fairweather had known for some time that Brian was having an affair with Alison Evans. She'd been suspicious of Evans from the first time she'd met her, sensing that the woman wasn't telling the truth about her background. Carrie had also felt that Evans had an interest in her husband which was more than mere interest in his work, and probably more than an unlikely sexual attraction. Carrie knew that Evans had visited Brian's workplace on a couple of occasions – Brian had clearly felt it too risky not to mention that to Carrie, in case she'd subsequently learned about it from a different source.

From the little Brian had told Carrie, Evans had claimed to be interested in a job in the legal profession. But she'd also seemed to be aware of Brian's involvement in the Men First group and had spent some time discussing that, showing a particular interest in Liam Crane. Elaine and Carrie had wondered how Evans knew about him, and had even considered whether she might be a potential ally in their efforts to deal with him and his plans. That possibility had evaporated once Carrie had learned about the affair.

Even so, when Carrie had called her in the early hours of that Sunday morning to break the news that Alison Evans had died in potentially suspicious circumstances, Elaine's immediate thought was that Crane might be responsible. If he'd seen Evans as a threat, for whatever reason, Elaine knew he'd have had no hesitation in dealing with her.

She'd been planning to talk to Carrie Fairweather and the others about what they should do next. They'd originally agreed there was no point in taking their story to the police. It would sound far-fetched and they had no substantive evidence, other than what Carrie had gleaned from Brian. Their claims might not even be true. This might all be nothing more than Crane shooting his mouth off, although Elaine knew him well enough to know that, once he'd mouthed off, he usually felt obliged to put his money where his mouth had been.

With Evans's death, she'd felt that the danger had suddenly become real and immediate. That Sunday morning, they'd acted in panic, simply wanting to ensure that Crane would be unable to take the action he'd been planning. Afterwards, Elaine had finally forced herself to call Zoe. She'd almost blurted out everything there and then, but she'd felt too confused to work out the likely consequences if she'd told her the full story. By the time she met Zoe, a day or two later, she and the others had agreed it was safer for the moment to continue with their plan, at least until they had a clearer idea of Crane's real intentions.

Then Carrie herself had been murdered.

In retrospect, at that point, the sensible thing would still have been to approach the police. In the face of two unlawful killings, the police would surely not have been able to dismiss their story.

But it hadn't felt like that. She and the others were in too deep to extricate themselves, and the spotlight would have been on them rather than the real threat. That was how they'd seen it, anyway. Their only priority had been to stop Crane. So they'd decided they had no option but to proceed with the plan, half-baked as it was.

Now it felt as if there was no way out. They were dealing with a psychopath – Elaine had little doubt of that – and all they could do was try to prevent him getting what he wanted. But she couldn't help thinking about how Crane had got hold of her mobile number. Of course, more people had that than had her address, but she wouldn't have expected any of those people to pass it on to Crane. But Crane, of all people, would have the ability to track her down if he wanted to. A few threats and dogged persistence usually did the job for him. If he'd obtained her number, he'd be capable of obtaining her address.

She'd been standing at the window, staring into the darkness, as she'd been thinking all this. For those few moments, she'd allowed her attention to wander. But now something had drawn her back into the moment. Another sound. Not something in this room, not something from the baby monitor. But from somewhere close by. The hallway, immediately adjacent to the living room she was standing in. Probably just the wind again. This was a draughty old place.

Then she heard it again, and this time she was in no doubt. Perhaps she never had been. Perhaps she'd just been trying to deceive herself, persuade herself nothing was wrong.

But something was, and now she was sure about it. What she'd heard had been a footstep, the sound of one of the old, slightly warped floorboards creaking under someone's weight.

Someone in the next room.

CHAPTER FIFTY-SEVEN

They'd made no real progress with Tom Kenning. Zoe hadn't really expected that they would. She'd not met Kenning face to face previously, but she recognised the type as soon as she saw him. Would-be tough guy who wasn't likely to be fazed by much they could throw at him, short of actual substantive evidence. And, for the moment, that was precisely what they didn't have. He didn't seem disconcerted by the news that they were also in the process of interviewing Robbie Crowther and Brian Fairweather.

'Who the hell's Robbie Crowther?' he said, not unreasonably. 'Never met the guy.'

'He's an old associate of Liam Crane,' Statham said. 'You have met Crane?' Statham's tone made it barely a question.

Kenning glanced at his solicitor, who remained stony-faced. 'I've come across him,' Kenning said finally.

'You met him while you were inside?'

'Originally. He was seen as the Mr Big among the prisoners. The one you didn't cross. So I kept on the right side of him. I thought he was okay. He knew I was a newbie, and he looked after me. I've not kept in touch, but I went along to one of these Men First sessions to see if they could help with my custody issues, and I ran into him there. I didn't know he was involved, but we chatted and I thought he had some interesting ideas about how to raise awareness of men's rights issues.'

'What sort of ideas?'

'Campaigning. Ways of getting people to see what's going on. Not really my thing, to be honest. I'm not the political type. Just want to get what I'm entitled to. But Crane seemed more passionate about it. That's about all I can tell you.'

'What about Brian Fairweather?'

This time there was no hesitation. 'Solicitor, isn't he? Spoke at a couple of those sessions. Had a chat with him after the first one. Just about my situation. He was quite helpful, though I'm not sure there was much he could really suggest.' Kenning shrugged. 'That's all I know about him.'

'You know his wife was murdered?'

Another glance to the solicitor, who again offered no reaction. 'Didn't know anything about that. Recently?'

'Very recently. You don't watch the news?'

'As I said, not my thing.'

So it went on. Kenning very effectively playing a straight bat to pretty much whatever they threw at him. His police record was mostly relative minor stuff, but Zoe had the impression he'd been through plenty of these kinds of interviews. Unless they had something more solid to put to him, they weren't likely to get very far.

'Okay,' Statham said. 'We've not finished yet, but let's have an adjournment. We'll organise you some refreshments.'

'With respect,' the solicitor said, 'this feels like not much more than a fishing expedition. You seem to be wasting my client's time.'

'With respect,' Statham echoed, 'we're doing our job. Which is investigating two murders and two child kidnappings.' He didn't wait for a response but rose and left the room, Zoe following close behind.

She waited until they were far enough from the interview room before speaking to ensure there was no risk of being overheard. 'We're wasting our time with Kenning. He's like Yardley. Not going to give an inch unless we have some genuine leverage.'

Statham nodded. 'Let's just hope they're doing better with Crowther.'

Annie and Stuart Jennings were interviewing Crowther. They'd decided to leave Fairweather till last, on the basis that his anxiety would increase if he were left to wait. Annie had also registered that Fairweather had called on the services of one of the most experienced and effective local criminal solicitors, a woman called Margot Revell. Presumably, particularly through his late wife's contacts, Fairweather knew the profession well enough to identify the best. Revell would do her utmost to protect her client's interests, so they wanted to be as well armed as possible before they interviewed him.

Crowther was looking uncomfortable, Annie thought. He'd opted to proceed with the interview without legal representation, telling them he had nothing to hide. To Annie's ears, it had sounded like bravado when he'd first said it, and that seemed even more true now. The room wasn't particularly warm, but there was a bead of sweat on Crowther's brow and he shifted repeatedly in his seat.

'When we spoke to you previously, Mr Crowther, we asked you whether you'd encountered Liam Crane recently,' Annie asked. 'Perhaps we can begin by asking you again. Have you encountered Crane again since his release from prison?'

Crowther was silent for a moment, and then finally said, 'Yes. Yes, I suppose I have.'

'You *suppose* you have?' Annie placed a gentle emphasis on the second word.

'It's not straightforward.'

'It seems a straightforward enough question.'

Crowther sighed but offered no immediate response. Jennings leaned forward. 'Mr Crowther, some years ago your association with Liam Crane almost resulted in you going to prison. You were fortunate to escape that fate, even though everyone knew full well you'd been involved. In the intervening years, you've built up a successful business and you're doing well for yourself. It would be unfortunate if you threw that away because of a further association with Crane.'

Crowther closed his eyes for a moment, as if hoping he could somehow wish himself out of the room. 'I don't know what you mean.'

'We're investigating a series of very serious crimes,' Jennings said. 'We believe Crane may be involved. Withholding inform- ation may be a very serious matter.' He finally sat back, his eyes still fixed on Crowther.

'I haven't—'

'You told us you hadn't been in contact with Crane since his release. Now you seem to be telling us something different.'

'Crane protected you when he went to prison,' Annie said. 'You may think you owe him something. But believe me, Crane only ever does things for his own reasons. He'd have known he was going down anyway. He might have thought it better to leave you in his debt. Is that it?'

Crowther was silent for so long, Annie became convinced that he wasn't going to answer. But finally he said, 'Something like that.'

'Go on.'

'Look, I've done nothing wrong. I don't know...'

'Just tell us, Mr Crowther.'

'I ran into him by accident. I didn't even know he was out. But someone had told me about this Men First group, and how they were organising sessions with a solicitor to discuss custody issues and suchlike. I thought it was worth going along to see if they could give me any advice. Anyway, it turned out that Liam was running the session.'

'That's not what you told us before.'

Crowther shifted uncomfortably on his seat. 'He wasn't an acquaintance I was particularly keen to renew, to be honest, but I couldn't really avoid him. Anyway, we chatted for a bit and I told him what I was up to. He seemed interested and a week or so later he just turned up in the bar. Popped in for a beer and, as he put it, see what we had to offer. Again, I can't say I was exactly pleased to see him, but I couldn't just turn him away. He came back a couple of times after that.'

'So why didn't you tell us about this?'

'That's not quite the end of it. After those first couple of visits, he turned up at the pub one afternoon. I reckon he picked his moment. A Tuesday when we were quiet, so I didn't have an excuse not to talk to him.'

'What did he want?'

'To be honest, I was a bit baffled by it. He reckoned that Brian Fairweather — the solicitor — was going to book in for dinner on Saturday night in a couple of weeks. Liam said he'd recommended the place to Fairweather for a discreet dinner. I thought at first that Liam was just going to ask me to look after him, make sure he had a good night, something like that. But it was odder than that. He told me that Fairweather had been having an affair but wanted to bring it to an end. He was expecting the woman to take it badly, and Fairweather was worried about how she'd react.'

'Why would Crane care?'

'That's what I wondered. But Liam reckoned Fairweather had done him a few legal favours and he owed him one. Anyway, he thought the woman might kick off so he wanted to be on hand, in case Fairweather needed any moral support.'

'Moral support?'

'My words, not his. He said he thought Fairweather might need looking after. He wanted to be there to step in if things turned nasty.'

'You went along with this?'

'To be honest, I wasn't even sure at first why he was asking me. I'd have taken the dinner reservation anyway, and Liam could have turned up to watch from the sidelines, without asking me. I thought maybe he was just giving me a heads-up in case anything did kick off. But then he asked if he could hide himself away somewhere on the night. He reckoned the woman knew who he was and about his connections with Fairweather, so he didn't want to be spotted until Fairweather had said his piece. He'd only intervene if it was needed. All he asked of me was to keep shtum about the whole thing, no matter what happened.'

'And you agreed to that?'

'Reluctantly. The whole story stank to me. But – well, the truth is I was scared of him. You don't say no to Liam Crane. I agreed he could hide himself away in the office at the back and I'd give him a shout if things showed any sign of getting nasty.'

Annie frowned. 'So what happened?'

'Well, the first bit went to plan. Fairweather and this woman – the woman who turned out to be Alison Evans – arrived and ordered. Then it all went pear-shaped. First, as soon as they'd sat down, Fairweather's wife turns up. Obviously not expected. I don't know if she'd followed him or just discovered that they were going to be there. I thought it might blow up then, but she drags a seat up to their table and they sit there having one of those very British quiet rows. It might have been funny in other circumstances. But that was only the start of it.'

'The snow?'

'Nobody had expected that. Once I made the announcement, everyone cleared out pretty quickly. But Evans and the Fairweathers were the last to go. They were still in the middle of having the world's quietest blazing row. That was how they ended up getting stranded.'

'What about Crane?'

'He was stuck up there as well. There's no way out of the office without going through the pub, and he still didn't want the woman to see him. So I told him to stay put till they'd gone. I thought he'd be okay to leave after that, but of course the road was already closed. He didn't seem too fussed when I broke the news to him. Said he'd just stay in the office till the road cleared and then make his way out when the weather improved. I told him it wasn't showing much sign of improving but he didn't seem bothered.'

'What did your wife think about all this?' Annie asked.

'Steph knew nothing about it. She never goes into the office when we're open – too busy in the kitchen. She hadn't a clue Liam was there, and to be honest I thought it better she didn't.' Crowther stopped and sat in silence for a few moments. 'I need to tell you everything, don't I?'

'Mr Crowther, you've already misled us about your contact with Crane and about what happened that evening. That's a serious matter as it is. You might just drag yourself out of the mire if you're completely open with us now.'

Crowther nodded. 'Okay, it was like this. I'd told Liam I'd leave the alarm off for the moment because I didn't want him setting it off when he left. He said that was fine, but he asked me to tell the others it was on before they went to sleep. He came up with some guff about not wanting anyone to run into him if they tried to leave before he'd got away. But if I'm honest, I didn't think he was telling me the real reason.'

'But you did it anyway?'

'Like I said, you don't argue with Liam Crane. And, whatever his real motives, I couldn't see what harm could come of it.'

'What happened after that?'

'After that, it's what I've told you before. I made the announcement about the alarm. We all went to bed. And the next I knew, I was wakened by the alarm going off.'

'But you hadn't set it?'

'No.'

'So what do you think happened?'

Crowther's head had dropped. He was staring at the tabletop. It took Annie a moment to realise he was crying. 'There's only one possibility, isn't there?'

'Go on.' Annie wanted to hear him say it.

'When I got up, Liam had gone. My guess is that he'd already been outside once, then he'd come back in, primed the alarm – it's simple enough and you don't need the code to turn it on – and then left through the main doors, setting it off.'

Jennings was looking baffled, but Annie was ahead of him. 'Why would he do that?'

'There's only one reason, isn't there? He'd left his car parked in the village somewhere, so that there was no chance of Fairweather spotting it in the car park. Once he'd opened the doors and triggered the alarm, he could easily have left the car park and be well on his way into the village before any of us could follow him. I'm guessing he sheltered in his car for the rest of the night, and then slipped away as soon as the police had the road cleared in the morning.'

Annie could see that Jennings was finally beginning to catch up. 'So the reason he set off the alarm...'

Crowther finished the sentence. 'Was to suggest that Alison Evans's death must have happened within a very short window – the time between the alarm going off and the rest of us going out to find her. Which threw the suspicion firmly on to the few people in the pub – particularly Brian and Carrie Fairweather.'

Jennings nodded, 'Whereas in reality...'

'He'd already killed her.'

CHAPTER FIFTY-EIGHT

She wasn't going to give Crane the satisfaction of opening the door. She stood by the window and waited.

She'd half-expected that he'd throw the door open in some dramatic manner intended to intimidate her, but it opened slowly. Even so, she had no doubt as to who would be standing on the other side.

He was smiling. 'You didn't really expect to get away with this, Elaine? Even by your standards, it's idiotic.'

She straightened her back, trying her utmost not to look frightened. 'I thought I might. For long enough, anyway.'

'That was your trouble, Elaine. You always looked on the bright side, even when everything was going to shit.'

'Which was most of the time I was with you.'

Crane laughed. 'Never boring, though.'

'Never that, no. But that's because you're a psychopath. A sadistic psychopath. I didn't realise that at the time. But it's obvious now.'

'I do what I want. Doesn't everybody?'

'Not the way you do. And you manipulate people so they don't even realise what you're doing.'

Crane was looking bored with the conversation. 'Where are they?'

'Where are who?'

He took a step forward and struck her hard across the cheek. 'Don't play games, Elaine. I'm not an idiot. Tell me where they are. If you don't, I'll tear the place apart till I find them.'

'Feel free.' She had no real plan other than to play for time, hope she might find some opportunity to seek help. She'd foolishly left her phone on the low table by the sofa. She should have done more to prepare for this eventuality. She should have known it was likely to happen. Crane was right about that, at least. She was always too optimistic, expecting that somehow she'd muddle through. Usually she'd managed it, but now her luck had run out. If you had any dealings with Liam Crane, that tended to happen in the end.

She considered other possibilities. There were no nearby neighbours to hear any calls for help. She could try to get past Crane and out to her car, but she knew the likelihood of success was small. There were no other options she could think of. The phone was her best chance, if only she could gain access to it without alerting Crane.

'Are you going to tell me?' Crane raised his hand to strike her again.

'I don't know what you're talking about.'

Crane gestured towards the baby monitor on the sofa. 'Just doing some babysitting for the neighbours, are you? Oh, I forgot. You don't have any neighbours, do you?' He hit her again, even harder this time. She fell against the wall, barely keeping to her feet. 'Oh, for fuck's sake. Stop wasting my time.'

He strode back towards the hallway. Before she could do anything to try to stop him, he began systematically kicking open all the doors, the crashes echoing through the house. From beyond the furthest door, she heard a scream of terror. Crane walked over and peered through the door, then turned and smiled. 'You don't know what I'm talking about? Christ, you're going to pay for this, Elaine. And these poor little bastards will suffer even more. Suffer the little children, eh?'

She'd taken the opportunity of his momentary distraction to pick up the phone, holding it behind her. 'You can't hurt them. Surely that was never the plan? Even you couldn't have intended that. I thought this was just some kind of publicity stunt.'

'I've never really cared. Their fathers were sold the idea it was a protest, a way of asserting their rights. Drawing attention to their cause. They believed me when I presented it that way. I've always been more interested in revenge. Making the mothers suffer. It worked out better than I could have hoped, because I'll be making you suffer too. Not to mention that bloody daughter of mine.'

'Christ, Liam. How many times have I told you she's not your daughter?'

'Countless times. I still don't believe you. But I'm not here to listen to you talk crap.' He turned back towards the bedroom.

She could hear the terrified sounds from behind him, more whimpering than screaming now. Her instinct was to run forward to stop him, but she forced herself to take the opportunity to use the phone while his back was turned. She had given some thought to this and knew she had only a few seconds to send a very short text. She tapped in the words and pressed send.

'What the hell are you doing?' Crane strode back across the hall towards her. He snatched the phone, dropped it on to the floor and crushed it under his heel, twisting his foot until it was clear the phone was no longer functional.

'You really are a stupid bitch, aren't you?'

She took a step back, staring at him defiantly. 'If you harm them or me, you'll be back inside for life.'

'You think I care about that? There's nothing for me out here.'

She wanted to argue with him, keep him distracted, but it was clear he'd lost interest. She was still considering what else she could do, when he hit her again, much harder this time. She fell back through the living room door, and he hit her again. After that, she was aware of nothing else.

CHAPTER FIFTY-NINE

'As far as I can see, what you've just said implies that this...' Margot Revell paused and made a play of consulting her notes. 'This Liam Crane is now your prime suspect in this case. I really don't understand why you're interviewing my client.'

'We want a full picture of what happened on that night,' Stuart Jennings said patiently.

'In which case, why are you interviewing my client under caution? Are you still treating him as a suspect?'

'We haven't ruled out the possibility,' Jennings said. 'Mr Fairweather made the decision to take Alison Evans for dinner that evening. Crane knew he was going to do that. I'm asking your client how Crane could have known.'

Brian Fairweather looked across at Revell, as if hoping for some kind of intervention. But it was clearly a reasonable question. 'I told you – I just wanted to take Alison for dinner, see whether there could be more to the relationship than just sex. I wanted to go somewhere discreet where there was no possibility I'd be recognised. Crane recommended that place. Far enough away from Chesterfield. He said it was run by an old friend of his who'd look after us.'

'So Crane was aware of your relationship with Alison Evans?'

Fairweather blinked and glanced across at Margot Revell. She offered no response, except for a slight nod. 'I told you she'd been interested in the Men First stuff. She seemed keen to meet Crane for some reason, so I took her along when I met him to plan one of the Men First sessions. To be honest, I mainly just wanted to show her off,' he added miserably. 'I didn't say anything, but it must have been obvious there was something between us. Crane seemed okay with her. Asked her a lot of questions about her background. Afterwards, he joked about me being a dark horse, said he'd give me some tips about playing away from home. Well, you can imagine.'

'I'm not sure where you're going with this line of questioning,' Revell said.

Jennings leaned back in his chair. 'Where we're going, Ms Revell, is to suggest that Crane knew that your client and Alison Evans would be there that night because they'd set it up together.' He directed his attention back to Fairweather. 'Were you aware that Crane was present that night? In one of the back rooms of the pub?'

'I—' Fairweather looked again to Revell, who made no effort to intervene. 'No, I'd no idea. I don't know why he'd have been there.'

'He'd told the landlord you were planning to break up with Alison Evans that night. He'd offered to be there to help if things turned nasty.'

'I don't understand. I wasn't planning to break up with Alison. Not that night, anyway. It was the opposite, really. A last-ditch attempt to see if we could make it work. I don't know why Crane would have done that.'

'Can I ask quite what you're implying?' Revell addressed Jennings. It was clear she wanted him to set out his accusations explicitly rather than allowing Fairweather to talk himself into a corner.

'I'm implying nothing,' Jennings said. 'I'm simply trying to make sense of the conflicting accounts we've been given about that night. Either Crane lied about his reasons for being there, or you're lying to us now.'

'Why would I lie about this?' Fairweather said.

'One possibility is because you were complicit with Crane in planning Alison Evans's murder. That you'd cooked up an excuse to take her somewhere remote, feed her a few drinks and then, between you, perhaps engineer a convenient accident.'

'This is preposterous,' Revell said. 'What motive would my client – or indeed Mr Crane – have for wanting Alison Evans killed?'

This was a tricky moment. As yet, they hadn't revealed that Evans had been an undercover NCA officer. The truth was likely to emerge at some point, even if the Agency did have some expertise in suppressing that kind of revelation, but Jennings had wanted the opportunity to consult at more senior levels before making anything public. 'We know your client wanted to bring his relationship with Evans to an end. He told us he'd been regretting getting involved.'

'Even if that were the case, he could have done that just by ending the affair. Conspiring to have her murdered would seem a rather extreme response.'

Jennings nodded to Fairweather. 'You told us you thought Evans was unbalanced. You were desperate your wife shouldn't find out about the affair, though as it turned out, she already had. My guess is that you were worried that, if you simply split up with her, she'd get her revenge by letting your wife know what had been happening.'

'These are no more than wild suppositions,' Revell said. 'Unless you're prepared to charge my client, I suggest we bring this interview to an end.'

Jennings ignored her. 'Then there's the question of your wife's murder, Mr Fairweather. Can I ask what your relationship with her was like after Evans's death?'

'I'm afraid I don't see what—'

Jennings cut Revell off. 'It must have been strained to say the least, Mr Fairweather.'

Revell was poised to intervene but Fairweather held up his hand. 'Yes, of course. And Alison's death had been a shock to us both. I was trying to persuade her it had been a one-off, that Alison had meant nothing to me. I told Carrie I still loved her and wanted to be with her.'

'Is that right?' Jennings's response was infused with cynicism. 'And was she buying this?'

'I think she was beginning to realise I was sincere, if that's what you mean. She hadn't moved out, though we were sleeping in separate rooms. I think she was coming round and then – well, that.' There were tears in his eyes now. 'You can't believe I was involved in her death?'

'That's what we're trying to find out, Mr Fairweather. We have two murders, and you're the most obvious link between the two of them. There are aspects of your involvement in Alison Evans's death that you've been unable to explain satisfactorily. Tell me why we shouldn't treat you as a suspect – even if only as an accessory – in both murders.'

Annie took her cue, as they'd planned before the interview. 'We're in the process of tracking down Liam Crane, Mr Fairweather. We know from his track record that Crane's a ruthless operator. If we charge him with Alison Evans's murder, he won't hesitate to throw you under the bus if it'll help save his own skin. It might be better if you were to tell us the whole truth before he has a chance to do that.'

She could see that Fairweather was on the point of responding, but this time Revell managed to get in first. 'I think it might be better if I had the chance for a discussion with my client before we proceed. Could we adjourn the meeting to allow that?'

Jennings glanced at Annie. 'Of course. Take as long as you need. We'll be waiting.'

CHAPTER SIXTY

Annie and Jennings returned to the main office, where Zoe and Statham were waiting. Statham looked up as they entered. 'How's it going?'

Jennings dragged up chairs for himself and Annie. 'I think we're getting there. Revell knows her stuff, but that might be an asset in the end. She'll tell Fairweather the score.'

'You think he was involved in Evans's death?' Statham asked.

'I don't know, to be honest. He's bloody naive. He might just be an innocent patsy in all this. But it looks as if Crane had sussed that there was something suspicious about Evans and had set up that night as a convenient opportunity to deal with her – and I don't see how he was originally planning to do that without Fairweather's co-operation. The unexpected snow presumably scuppered Crane's original plan, so after that he just improvised and didn't need to involve Fairweather. He just needed to make sure neither Fairweather nor Crowther spilled the beans about his presence, but my guess is that he knew that both were too scared to risk crossing him.'

'Assuming we're right,' Annie said, 'why did Crane kill Evans anyway? If they'd discovered who she was, they could have strung her along.'

'Maybe it was too late for that,' Jennings said. 'Maybe she'd already found out something significant from Brian Fair-weather.'

'Such as what?' Annie could see that Jennings was playing along with her, as she tested out the hypothesis that they still hadn't fully clarified in their own minds.

'If we're right about Crane's involvement in these child snatchings, it could be that.' Jennings paused. 'To be honest, I'm clinging to the hope that these kidnappings are some sort of gesture, some sort of protest on behalf of these Men First fuckwits, and that the kids are unharmed somewhere.'

'Let's hope,' Annie said. 'And let's hope that the fact that Crane knows he's being pursued doesn't change that.' She looked across to the adjacent desk where Zoe had been making a series of phone calls. 'You okay, Zo?'

Zoe looked up. 'Just a bit baffled. I've been trying to call Gary to let him know we're going to be running very late here. But there's no response. Not on his mobile or his office number or the home landline. It's not like him.'

'Maybe he's driving?' Zoe said.

'I've been trying him for half an hour. He'd be home by now.'

'In a meeting?' Statham suggested.

'Gary's not like us,' Zoe said. 'He does a sensible job. They wouldn't be having a meeting at this time. Most likely he's put his phone down somewhere or has it on silent. But it's not like Gary.'

There was the ping of a text arriving on a phone, and Zoe looked down, clearly expecting it would be a message from Gary. She looked up, frowning.

'Gary?' Annie asked.

'No.' Zoe was silent for a moment. 'It's from Elaine Simmonds. I gave her my mobile number because I thought it was better than her calling on the landline.'

'What's she saying?'

'That's what I don't understand. It's just three random words. Look...' She rose and brought her phone over to the others.

Jennings looked at the screen. 'Maybe it's a mistake. Auto-correct or something.'

'But for what?'

Annie was looking thoughtful. 'Can I have a look?'

286

'Sure.' Zoe handed her the phone. 'Mean anything to you?'

'Not in itself, but I wonder…' She picked up her own phone and spent a moment searching on the internet. 'Here we are. Let me just try those words.' She was silent for a moment, then said, 'It's a location up in the hills between Bakewell and Buxton.'

'What is?' Jennings said.

'The spot indicated by those three words. Have you come across the what3words application?'

Jennings nodded. 'I've heard about it. A way of identifying very precise locations.'

'Exactly. People use it for various things, but one use is for identifying locations without a regular address or where, say, the postcode isn't sufficient.'

'So why has Simmonds sent that to Zoe?'

'I don't know. Maybe try calling her back, Zo?'

Zoe nodded and dialled the number. She shook her head. 'Nothing. Just cutting straight to voicemail as if the phone's turned off.'

'It can't just be a coincidence, given the location,' Jennings said. 'So why send a message with a location, but no explanation, and then turn off your phone?'

'It might be cutting to voicemail because she's on the line to someone else,' Annie pointed out. 'But that doesn't explain the text.'

'So what would?'

'She knows Zoe's a police officer.' Annie paused, still thinking. 'Maybe I'm being melodramatic, but I think this may well be a call for help.'

CHAPTER SIXTY-ONE

'This could be a waste of everyone's time.' Statham stared morosely out of the car window, as if he could see into the darkness.

Annie glanced across at Zoe, who was sitting beside her in the rear seat. In other circumstances, she might have found Statham's change of mood amusing. He'd been all in favour of taking whatever rapid action might be needed to find Lucas Pritchard and Holly Parrish before it was too late. But as soon as they'd made the decision to follow up what was admittedly little more than a hunch, he'd looked increasingly uncomfortable. Annie wasn't sure if this was because the hunch had come from someone else, or if it was because they were now committing substantial resources to an idea that might well go nowhere. Possibly a little of both, although she suspected that Statham would try to shift responsibility on to Stuart Jennings if anything went wrong, and quite possibly Jennings would try to shift it on to her. Welcome to the wonderful world of policing.

For the moment, Jennings looked positively energised. He was behind the wheel, his eyes fixed firmly on the road revealed by the full-beam lights, driving as fast as possible without taking risks. She knew how he felt. The lack of progress in the two investigations had been frustrating everybody and, until the last few hours, there'd been no sense of any of the details resolving themselves into any coherent picture. Now, suddenly, they had an objective, a purpose. It might be a dead end, but at least for the moment they had a focus.

They'd certainly pulled out all the stops on this one, to an extent that was even beginning to make Annie nervous. They had a backup team of uniformed officers behind them, and an armed response unit on the way. They'd also called out one of the trained negotiators.

The truth was they had no idea what they might be dealing with. It might be nothing at all – Annie was haunted by the possibility that Elaine Simmonds could have just accidentally texted three random words – but it might also be the stuff of their worst nightmares. They had to be prepared for the worst.

'Right,' Jennings said. 'I think this is where we turn off.'

They'd checked out the location indicated by the three words on a detailed Ordnance Survey map, and discovered that it lay in a small isolated building high up on the moors, presumably some kind of cottage. It would be a tricky place to find even in broad daylight, much harder at this time in the evening. Jennings slowed and looked for the expected turning. He located it and took the left turn. Statham called to the cars behind them and told them where to follow.

The first question was how close they could get to the cottage. It was impossible to be sure without having some opportunity to reconnoitre the surrounding landscape. It was quite possible that their headlights had already revealed their presence to anyone in the cottage, although they'd hoped that the contours of the landscape would conceal them for as long as possible. Jennings had, as planned, switched down to the sidelights and was driving more cautiously now.

Finally, they saw the lights of a building ahead of them. Jennings slowed still further, then found a place to park just off the narrow single-track road. They would be joined in due course by the armed team and the negotiator, but by that the point the element of surprise might be less important.

Jennings turned off the engine, and turned to look round at the others in the car. 'Well, here we are, folks. Wherever here might be.' He pushed open his door and leaned out into the night. There was a strong wind from down the valley, and some first flakes of snow were beginning to fall. 'Great,' Jennings added. 'All we need.'

Ahead of them, set back away from the road, there was a small, single-storey cottage. It looked like an old farm building which had been renovated to make it inhabitable. There were lights showing in several windows, though all looked to be curtained.

'First thing is for us to check out the lay of the land,' Jennings said. 'See what we might be dealing with before we go wading in.'

There was no fencing round the cottage, and, other than some terracotta pots, no effort had been made to create a garden. Jennings circled round to check out the rear of the building, gesturing for the others to remain where they were. By now, the team of uniformed officers had joined them, and they clustered together. The snow was beginning to fall more heavily.

'Similar set-up at the rear,' Jennings said. 'No fencing, so effectively the cottage backs on to open moorland. There are two cars parked at the side of the building. I've jotted the registrations down if someone can get the ownership checked out. There's a back door, so if anything kicks off we'll need to keep that covered.' He looked up as another car pulled up behind those already parked. 'Looks like we have some reinforcements.' He waited as a further two uniformed officers climbed out of the car and walked over to join them. The armed response unit.

'Not the easiest place to find,' one of them said.

'We like to set a challenge.' Jennings smiled. 'But you seem to have risen to it.'

'We do our best. And you really don't know what's going on in there?'

'Haven't a clue. Could just all be nothing, and we'll just find there's a solitary person watching TV. Or it could be something much more serious. But we can't ignore it when we've got two missing children.'

'Fair enough. What do you want from us?'

'Ideally, nothing, if you won't take that the wrong way.'

'We're much happier when we don't have to do anything.'

'I'm not sure we've any option but to play it low-key in the first instance. If there really is nothing going on in there, we can call it a night and get back home. But there's also a possibility that there's someone dangerous in there. Not to mention the possibility that there might be two young children.'

As if in response to his words, Zoe signalled to him. She'd moved away from the group and had been talking on her phone. 'I've had the cars checked out. One belongs to Elaine Simmonds. The other's registered to Liam Crane.'

'So either they're working together or Simmonds has an unwelcome visitor. Most likely the latter, given she sent that text.' He turned back to the armed officer. 'Either way, it's not just one innocent person sitting watching TV.'

'Okay. At least that gives us some idea where we stand. We'll be ready if we're needed.'

Jennings turned to the others. 'We'll still start low-key. I'm reluctant to kick off before the negotiator gets here, but if there's a possibility that Crane is in there, I'm not sure we can afford to wait.' He looked up. 'The snow's getting heavier too.'

Statham had been staring at the cottage. 'What do you suggest?'

'I'm thinking I should go and ring the doorbell.'

'Ring the doorbell? And let him know we're here?'

'Let him know someone's here. I'd suggest the rest of you keep out of sight till we've a better idea of what we're dealing with. There's a chance we might be able to stop this escalating. Do you have any better suggestions?'

Statham was silent for a moment. 'Not really, to be honest. We can't go busting in there until we've some idea what we're walking in on.'

'Exactly.'

'Do you want one of us to come with you?' Annie asked. 'We don't know whether Crane's armed.'

Jennings shrugged. 'If he is armed, that'll just mean he's got twice as many sitting ducks to shoot at. I'm going alone.'

Statham showed no signs of wanting to challenge Jennings's decision. 'Good luck.'

Jennings smiled wryly. 'Thanks. If there's any shooting, you'll find out how quickly I can run.' He gestured for the others to step back, then walked across the rough moorland towards the front door. He pressed the bell and stepped back, watching the lit windows across the front of the house.

There was no movement at first. Then a curtain was pulled back in one of the windows and the silhouette of a head was briefly visible. Jennings stepped forward and pressed the bell again. The curtain dropped back into place, but there was no other response. Annie could feel herself tensing as she waited for something to happen.

Zoe's mobile phone buzzed in her hand. Statham gestured for her to take the call. She thumbed the phone and spoke, keeping her voice low. 'Yes.'

'You out there, Zoe?'

'Out where?'

'Don't play games, Zoe. I've had enough of that today. You're brighter than that. I'm assuming that's one of your colleagues standing on the doorstep. I don't know how he's found me up here, but I'm guessing he's not risked coming up alone.'

There seemed no point in bluffing further. 'Yes, I'm up here too.' She switched to speakerphone so the others could hear the exchange.

'You and how many more?'

She glanced up at Statham, who nodded to her. 'Plenty,' she said. 'It's time to come out, Liam, so you can tell us what's going on.'

'I think your mate on the doorstep should know that if he stays there much longer, I'll be tempted to take a pot-shot at him.'

'You're armed?'

'I'm not talking a bloody catapult.'

Statham was gesturing for Jennings to move away from the door. After a minute, Jennings did so and made his way back towards them, taking a circuitous route so that Crane wouldn't easily be able to see where they were gathered. 'What is it?'

Statham pointed to where Zoe was holding the phone to her lips. 'Crane,' he mouthed. 'Inside. Reckons he has a gun. Could be bluffing.'

Jennings nodded, then pulled a notepad from his pocket. He scribbled on it and then held it up in front of Zoe. 'Keep him talking. Find out what you can.'

She nodded. 'What's this about, Liam?'

There was silence for a moment, and Zoe wondered if he'd ended the call. 'It's about nothing, Zoe. Nothing but my shit life.'

'This isn't going to make it any better.'

'You don't get it, do you? I don't want to make it better. I've tried that and I just get more shit. I'm at the end now. I just want to make sure I wreck a few lives along with my own.'

'What will that achieve?'

'Nothing. I don't care. This isn't about achieving anything. It's about revenge.'

'On who?'

'On the whole fucking world, Zoe. The whole fucking universe. I'm going nowhere, except back inside. If it doesn't happen now, it'll happen soon. There's nothing else. You don't want me. I never thought you would, but it seemed worth a chance. But I know I was just deluding myself.'

'Look, Liam—'

'Don't soft-soap me, Zoe. Nothing you can say is going to change my mind. The only question is how many people I take with me.'

'Who's in there with you?'

'Well, let's see. There's Elaine. There's the two wee kiddies—'

'They don't deserve this, Liam.'

293

'Don't they? Maybe I'm doing this for their own good. Stop them having a life like mine.'

Jennings and Statham had moved away and were conferring with the armed officers. After a moment, Jennings gestured for Annie to join them. 'From Crane's tone, I don't think we can waste any more time. We're going to try to get in from the back, take him by surprise.'

'It's risky if there are children in there,' Annie said.

'Tell me about it. But I'm not sure we've any other option. Crane sounds like he's ready to blow, whatever happens.'

'He could be bluffing.'

'He doesn't sound to me like a man who's bluffing,' Jennings said.

Annie couldn't disagree with him. There was something in Crane's tone – a deadness, a lack of emotion – that sent a chill down her spine. She thought he was being entirely sincere.

'Tell Zoe to try to keep him talking,' Jennings said. 'And you stay with her. She'll need the moral support.'

She was tempted to argue with him, but she knew he wasn't just trying to protect her. He was right about Zoe. Her exchange with Crane would be challenging in any circumstances, but much more disturbing to be talking like that with a man who was claiming to be your own father. 'Okay. Good luck.'

She returned to join Zoe, who was saying, 'I don't understand this, Liam. This can't have been the plan. This can't be what their fathers wanted.'

Crane laughed. 'I don't imagine so. They just wanted a gesture. Something to generate headlines for their so-called cause. But I really just wanted to make an impact. I think I knew it was always going to end up like this, once we'd kicked it off. They did their best to stymie us – Elaine, Fairweather and those bloody mothers – but we got here in the end.'

'And where does Men First fit into this?'

'For me, it was mainly a convenient vehicle. I mean, it struck a chord. Men like me are always the victims.' Zoe looked up and raised an eyebrow. Annie nodded. Crane had made many others into victims, but he'd never been one himself, except in his own head. 'But it was mainly just a way of creating some sort of momentum, getting others to buy into my vision. Even Ben Yardley. *Especially* Ben Yardley. He thought he was the great intellectual, bending others to his will. But I had him just where I wanted him. He gave me the polished words, that's all. Same with Fairweather. He gave us the legal input, but I'd dragged him in far enough that he knew I could have wrecked his career if I'd wanted to.'

'So why'd you snatch the children?'

'That's the hilarious thing. We didn't. I mean, we'd planned to. As far as Yardley and Kenning were concerned, it was just a gesture, a protest. A way of putting their grievances on the map. They knew there was little chance of them ever getting access to their kids, so they just wanted to raise awareness of it. They thought if I was the one who actually did the deed, they might avoid retribution. Fat chance. Brian Fairweather knew what we were up to but was too scared to go to the police. Persuaded himself the kids wouldn't come to any harm.'

'But you said you didn't kidnap them. So who did?'

'Carrie Fairweather somehow got suspicious of what we were up to. I don't know if her husband actually told her, but it's possible she just put two and two together from things he'd said. She was a smart lady. Too smart for her own good. The only thing she got wrong was assuming at first that Alison Evans was working with us. She thought that was how we'd suckered Brian into taking part. She knew about me because her firm had represented me back in the day.'

'Where does Elaine Simmonds fit into this?'

'Carrie Fairweather had first come across her when her firm were dealing with me. She got to know her later because, long after she'd left me, Elaine somehow dragged herself up by her bootstraps, got herself a law degree and became a criminal solicitor. She managed to get herself a job in Carrie Fairweather's old practice, with a bit of help from Fairweather herself. You see what I mean about my shit life? I'm guessing Fairweather approached Elaine because she was the only one who knew me well enough to believe I'd be capable of doing something like this. And Elaine would have jumped at the chance to screw me over. They didn't think the police would take them seriously so they came up with their own hare-brained scheme to remove the children before we could get to them.'

'Were the children's mothers aware of this?'

'They were part of the plan. Elaine persuaded them it was the only certain way of keeping the kids safe. From what Elaine's told me, they'd intended it only as a last-ditch option, but they panicked when Evans was killed. The Pritchard kid's mother just wanted to keep the kid safe at all costs. Like I said, hare-brained.'

Zoe was silent for a moment. 'Where do I fit into all this?'

'Where you always did. You're Elaine's daughter. And mine. I told her I was intending to contact you. She'd been intending to keep out of your life, but that changed her mind. She called you to bad-mouth me. She didn't want you involved with me. But she also thought it might intrigue you enough to start you delving into my life and what I was up to. She'd hoped to get me back inside, one way or another, before I did any more damage. If she could do that quickly, they could come clean about what had happened to the children.'

The whole thing sounded insane to Annie, but she had little doubt that, abnormally calm as he sounded, the most insane participant was the man speaking to Zoe. He frightened or intimidated all those in contact with him to lose their minds also. She looked over at the house, wondering what was happening at the rear. The snow was swirling more thickly now, obscuring the outline of the building.

'So what—?' Zoe began.

Crane cut her off. 'I've just heard a noise. I hope your mates aren't about to do something stupid. Jesus, they'll regret it if they do. So will you, Zoe.'

'What do you mean?'

'I didn't finish telling you. There's one other person in here.' There was silence for a second. 'Your husband.'

Then he cut the call.

CHAPTER SIXTY-TWO

'Christ, Zoe.'

Zoe was staring at her phone, as if expecting Crane to call back. 'We've got to get in there, Annie. I can't just stay out here if Gary's in danger.'

Annie knew better than to argue. 'Let's head round to the back. See what's going on.'

Keeping to the shadows, they made their way to the rear of the house. Light was streaming out of an open doorway, catching the flakes of drifting snow. The door had been battered open with an Enforcer, presumably the noise that Crane had heard. The question was whether the police had been able to move quickly enough to prevent further harm.

The door led into the cottage's kitchen. Through a further doorway, they could see a hallway. Annie had been expecting noise and movement, but the interior was eerily quiet. Somewhere she could hear voices.

They passed through the kitchen and looked into the hallway. The team who'd entered the building were scattered between the various rooms opening off the hallway – as far as Annie could see, a living room, a bedroom and a bathroom – checking they were empty. But attention was focused on the bedroom at the end of the hall. Jennings was standing in the doorway with one of the armed officers. Beyond them, Annie could see Crane holding a terrified-looking child in front of him. He was holding a revolver.

Crane was speaking, his voice as dead and toneless as it had been through the speaker of Zoe's phone. 'It doesn't matter what you do. I'm going to kill this one, and then I'll try to kill the other. I'll kill as many people as I can before you stop me. I probably won't get far, but at least one of these children is going to die.'

'Put the gun down, Liam,' Jennings said gently. 'You don't need to do this. There are other ways.'

Crane shook his head. 'I've seen the cop shows. I know how this is supposed to pan out. You talk me down, and eventually I drop the gun and hand myself over to you. But life isn't like that. Or at least my shit life isn't like that. There's nothing to stop me doing this. I've no future, whatever happens.'

'That isn't true.'

'It is. It's probably true for you too, but you just don't know it yet. We're all fucked. It's as simple as that.'

'You don't have to kill a child, Liam.'

'Why not? There's nothing for him to live for anyway, poor little bastard.'

As far as Annie could see, the only positive was that Crane was still talking. He sounded disengaged, emotionless, but he was still conversing with Jennings. He could have done what he was threatening before now. Which didn't mean he still wouldn't.

'You don't have the right to make that decision, Liam.'

'If I don't, who does?'

'No one does.'

'Someone's got to. Someone's got to do the honest thing. Reveal the truth about this shitty life.'

'Even if you don't want to live, Liam, you've no right to make that decision for anyone else. Just put the gun down.'

Annie shifted slightly so she could see further into the room. There was another small child in the corner, looking even more scared than the first. There was a woman lying unconscious on the bed, presumably Elaine Simmonds. Beyond the bed, she could see another figure on the floor. Was that Gary?

She looked around to see that Zoe had joined her. She knew Zoe wanted to intervene, to do something, but there was no intervention that wouldn't make everything worse. They had to trust Jennings.

'I've told you. That's not how this story ends. It's my ending. It's the one bit of power I've got left.' He raised the gun and pointed it at the child whimpering at his feet. She could see the armed officer tense. 'So let's go.'

Then there was nothing but confusion. The child in the corner screamed and ran forward. For a second, Annie thought the child was going to throw herself in front of the gun, but instead she headed towards the bedroom door. The moment of uncertainty was enough. Zoe pushed past Jennings and threw herself at Crane, forcing his arm away from the child. Jennings, only momentarily taken aback, followed her into the room and grabbed Crane's flailing arm. They fell backwards beside the bed.

Unsure what else to do, Annie scooped up the child, handing him to one of the uniformed officers in the hall. Then she turned back to where Zoe and Jennings were wrestling with Crane. Jennings was hammering Crane's wrist against the floor, trying to force him to release the gun.

It was a moment before Annie realised that the figure on the floor on the far side of the bed was moving. She watched as Gary stumbled to his feet and took in the sight in front of him. He moved quickly around the bed and, still wearing his work shoes, stamped hard on Crane's wrist. Hard enough to break it, Annie thought.

Crane screamed and twisted, still gripped firmly by Zoe and Jennings. And then there was a deafening noise as, finally, the gun was fired.

CHAPTER SIXTY-THREE

'Christ, Mum. Why?'

Annie stood at the foot of the bed. Margaret was lying on her back, festooned with tubes and monitors. She'd briefly been in intensive care, although primarily as a precaution. Her condition had improved and stabilised through the night, and now she was considered to be out of danger. Annie had assumed Margaret was sleeping, but her eyes had opened at Annie's question. 'I suppose it seemed a good idea at the time.'

'You should have called me.'

'Would you have answered?'

It was a better question than her mother realised. At the moment when all this had happened, Annie had been in the middle of the incident with Liam Crane. If Margaret had called her just then, there was every chance she wouldn't have taken the call. At least not immediately. 'I didn't realise, Mum.'

'Neither did I. Or at least I didn't take it seriously. I didn't take myself seriously, I suppose. I didn't realise how low I'd become.'

Annie had received the call from the hospital early that morning. Late the previous evening, her mother had apparently made an attempt on her own life, consuming an unholy cocktail of pills and whisky.

The question – which Annie was going to make no attempt to answer – was how serious the attempt had been. Margaret had called 999 in the minutes immediately afterwards and told the call handler what she'd done. Fortunately, a combination of police and paramedics had managed to arrive and gain access to the flat relatively quickly, and Margaret had received rapid treatment. Annie had spoken to one of the nurses, when she'd arrived on the ward, who'd told her they'd treated Margaret's case with extreme caution because no one, including Margaret herself, could initially be sure how much she'd actually consumed. The conclusion now was that she hadn't taken enough to pose a serious threat to her life, though it wasn't clear whether or not that had been a deliberate decision. Quite probably, Margaret herself didn't know.

'But why do it, Mum?'

'It just felt like the only thing in that moment. The thought's been nagging at me for a while. I couldn't see any real reason to continue. I've no real friends; I've no career now. I still don't know if I'm going to be prosecuted. What's the point? I've even lost you.'

'Mum—'

'Don't pretend otherwise. Were you intending to invite me over for Christmas?'

The question took Annie by surprise, but it was another pertinent one. She'd discussed it vaguely with Sheena some weeks before and both had been unsure about the idea, even assuming Margaret would be willing to come. In recent weeks thoughts of Christmas had been low on Annie's list of priorities. If she was honest, she'd probably have been glad not to think about it, unsure how best to approach Margaret on the topic. Now she said, 'We'd be delighted to have you over for Christmas. Would you come?' She was aware – and she knew Margaret would be aware – that she hadn't fully answered the question.

Margaret closed her eyes. 'Well, let's see. I know you're busy.'

'Not as much as I was. Everything came to a head on the current investigations last night. There'll be no shortage of fallout, but it's not so frantic now.'

Her mother reopened her eyes. 'On both investigations?'

'It's a long story. But it turns out there was really only one investigation after all.' A thought struck her as she was talking. 'Actually, it was your information that really broke it.'

'You're joking. What I told you was nothing.'

'Like I told you at the time, Mum, it was exactly the kind of seemingly trivial bit of intelligence that gives us a thread to pull on. That's what happened here. What you told me was the first real link we had between the two cases.' She wasn't sure whether she ought to be talking to her mother about an investigation that was, no doubt, about to enter the endless protracted legal process, but she wanted to keep talking, recreate some connection with her mother. She recounted the events that had led to the previous night's incident.

'So you think Crane killed this Alison Evans and Carrie Fairweather?'

'We need to check whether there are any forensic links to Crane from the scene of Fairweather's murder, but we're working on that assumption. Crane was suspicious that Evans was an undercover officer and wanted to make sure he'd removed any evidence. We're searching Crane's flat, but we think he'd managed to search and strip her house even before her NCA colleague got there. Carrie Fairweather was working with Elaine Simmonds on the information she'd managed to get from her husband about Crane's plans.'

'So he had the motive.'

It struck Annie that, despite her condition, Margaret sounded more alert and engaged than she had for months. 'Exactly. The outstanding question is whether Robbie Crowther and Brain Fairweather were accessories to the killings. Both of them initially withheld critical evidence, but they can claim that was simply because they were scared of Crane. Crowther can offer an innocent explanation for what he did that night, and he's probably tough enough to style it out, especially as Crane's no longer here to contradict him. Fair-weather's a different matter. He was already partly implicated in what Crane was up to, and he potentially had his own reasons for wanting rid of his wife. If he was involved, he'll crack under pressure. We'll see.'

'And the two children are okay?'

'Fortunately, yes. Physically at least. We got them out of the room, and they were far enough away not to see anything that happened after that. Just hope they're young enough to come through it relatively unscathed.'

'What about this Elaine Simmonds and the mothers? Will they be prosecuted?'

'It's too early to say, but my guess is not. The children were taken with their mothers' permission, so the only real crime would be wasting police time. Given the way things panned out, I'm not sure we'd really make that stick. It probably wasn't the smartest plan but they were all terrified of what Crane and his cronies might be capable of. And I suppose it at least made sure the police had to do something.'

As she spoke, Annie thought back to something Quentin Soames, the NCA officer, had said when they'd been discussing Alison Evans's work: 'We can identify a potential threat but there's little we can do until someone makes the threat real. And by then it might be too late.' Maybe that was how the two mothers had seen it. They'd identified the threat, but they'd known the police wouldn't do anything until it became real.

'The truth is they panicked after Evans's killing,' Annie went on. 'Jude Parrish resisted at first. She'd been talking to Sheena about her case – though without mentioning her additional worries about Crane's involvement – but in the end that just confirmed her view that there was no other way to protect young Holly.' She paused. 'Lucas Pritchard's grandfather's the one I feel most sorry for. He wasn't in on the plan – Amy Pritchard knew he wouldn't have supported it – so he genuinely thought he'd been negligent. Might take a while to rebuild that bridge.'

'And is Simmonds really Zoe's mother?'

'We still need to check that out, but it looks as if it might well be true. The bigger question is whether Liam Crane was her father. He was convinced he was, but Simmonds insists otherwise.'

'You can do a DNA test?'

'If Zoe wants it. That has to be her choice. With Crane dead, she may prefer not to pursue it.'

'At least you're not left with the need to prosecute Crane.'

'No, though we'll be investigating the roles played by Ben Yardley, Tom Kenning and a number of Crane's other Men First associates. And there'll be an inquiry into the circumstances of Crane's death. In the confusion, no one seemed sure what happened. Maybe it was an accident. My guess is that, as he'd been threatening, he managed to turn the gun on himself right at the end.'

'A bit more successful than my effort,' Margaret said wryly. There was a humour in her tone that Annie hadn't heard for a long while.

'Thank goodness.'

Margaret offered no response. 'How's Zoe taking it?'

'Surprisingly well, actually. I spoke to her afterwards, and she said that, somehow, all of this had lifted a weight from her. There may be other factors at play, but my guess is that something about her background had been nagging at her for a long time, probably not even consciously. She just knew something wasn't right, and it had sat there like a shadow in her past. I wonder if, at least subconsciously, she even had some lingering childhood memories of the days before she was adopted.'

'Is that possible?'

'I'm no psychiatrist. I don't really know how early those kinds of childhood traumas can happen. But maybe even small babies take in more of the surrounding atmosphere than we realise. All I know is that Zoe seems more relaxed than she has for a good while. She seems to have accepted that Elaine Simmonds is her mother, even though we don't know for sure yet. If she's genuine, Zoe's more than happy to let her back into her life.' Annie was about to conclude that everything had ended well, when she recalled that her own mother was lying before her, having made an attempt on her own life. 'What about you, Mum? How are you now?'

Margaret was silent for a moment. 'I think I'm okay, funnily enough. I don't know what I intended to do last night, but somehow it feels as if it's reset things. I'd lost any sense of perspective. I mean, I still don't know what's going to happen with the prosecution, but I'm not sure I care much any more. I just need to get on with whatever life throws at me.'

'I'm still here for you, Mum. I know it's not always been easy between us, but I'm here to help.'

Margaret had never been one to reveal her feelings, but Annie could see that her eyes were damp. 'Thanks. I'll probably need it.'

It was perhaps the first time that Annie had ever heard Margaret acknowledge that she was anything other than entirely self-sufficient. It wasn't a lot, but it felt like a start. 'And, yes, we'd love you to join us for Christmas.'

Margaret closed her eyes again, perhaps in an attempt to avoid any further show of emotion. 'Thanks,' she said. 'I'd like that.'

Acknowledgements

As always, many people contributed to this book, some of them without even knowing it. But sincere thanks as always to everyone who offered views and suggestions on the early drafts, and particular thanks to my agent, Peter Buckman, and to my excellent editor at Canelo Crime, Siân Heap, both of whom were invaluable in helping me to shape and tighten the narrative.

Above all, thanks to Helen, always my first and best critic, who not only displays infinite patience when I'm wrestling with narrative knots and plot-holes but then invariably comes up with some simple and elegant means of resolving them.

Do you love crime fiction and are always on the lookout for brilliant authors?

Canelo Crime is home to some of the most exciting novels around. Thousands of readers are already enjoying our compulsive stories. Are you ready to find your new favourite writer?

Find out more and sign up to our newsletter at canelocrime.com